"LURIE'S RICH AND DELICATELY TEX-
TURED NOVELS ARE DEEPENING IN COM-
PLEXITY AND FORCE. . . The child's world
has never seemed saner than in this keenly ob-
served, lovely countryside—and rarely have grown-
ups' perplexities seemed more touching."

—*The Kirkus Reviews*

"RIPE WITH HUMOR. LURIE HARVESTS
PLENTY OF IRONIC INSIGHTS AND FUN-
NY MISPERCEPTIONS FROM THE LITTLE
GIRLS' ACTIVITIES . . . Lurie's gentlest, most
sympathetic satire."

—*Atlantic Monthly*

"Lurie is a genius at human relationships . . . after
winter we all need a summer weekend with starry
nights, picnics and twilit bedrooms. The mood may
be nostalgic, but the landscape of love is very
familiar."

—*The Chicago Sun-Times*

ONLY CHILDREN

Alison Lurie

FAWCETT POPULAR LIBRARY ● NEW YORK

ONLY CHILDREN

This book contains the complete text of the original hardcover edition.

Published by Fawcett Popular Library, a unit of CBS Publications, the Consumer Publishing Division of CBS Inc., by arrangement with Random House, Inc.

ISBN: 0-445-04557-4

Printed in the United States of America

First Fawcett Popular Library printing: May 1980

10 9 8 7 6 5 4 3 2 1

For John, Jeremy, and Joshua Bishop

ONLY CHILDREN

July 3

—Once upon a time, Mary Ann tells herself, there was a beautiful princess named Miranda who had a wish-box. It was black with shiny gold dots and a long thin hole in the top like a piggybank for the wishes to come out of, one each day. She got it from her fairy godmother for a present, and every day after breakfast she took it out and made a wish very carefully.

—First she wished for a big red horse with wings like on gas stations that could fly up in the clouds and take her anywhere in the world she felt like going. And next day a stable for him to live in, with lots of oats and hay.

—Then the day after that she wished for a castle, with a swimming pool and a Jungle Gym in its backyard. And a tree house exactly like the one the Newbury boys down the street won't let girls into. Only bigger. And she wished that the boys' tree house would fall down into little bitty pieces next time they were in it and they would get bumped and scratched and all their arms and legs would be broken especially Buddy's.

—Then Princess Miranda wished for a free candy store full of every kind of candy there is. And a hundred new story books she hasn't read yet. And the much-too-expensive chemistry set from F. A. O. Schwarz, and a Southern mansion dollhouse with real electric lights like Lolly Zimmern has.

—And then she wished for a magic mirror, the kind in "Beauty and the Beast" that shows you anybody anyplace in the world so you can see what they are doing and if you want to go there.

—And another castle next door for Lolly, and a flying horse for her, a nice quiet blue one. And then Princess Miranda wished for the Depression to end and everybody in America to have a job and enough to eat. No. Kind Princess Miranda wished that sooner, right after the flying horse. And his stable, because otherwise he would be cold and hungry.

—She wished for it never to rain except on school days, or at night if it wanted, and

"Look at that," Mary Ann's mother's voice says from the front seat of The Franklin. "Mary Ann's gone right off to sleep, with her arms round her Teddy."

"Mm," Mary Ann's father's voice says.

Teddy's real name that nobody but Mary Ann knows is Theodore Ilgenfritz. He is named after a boy in fourth grade who can stand on his head. Teddy can stand on his head, too, and at night when everybody else is asleep he wakes up and turns into his real size eight-and-a-half feet tall, and he walks around the house on big furry feet. In the daytime he doesn't do much or say much but he always feels nice and is a good listener.

"Seems to me," Mary Ann's father's voice goes on, "she's getting kind of big to be carrying a toy bear around everywhere. After all, she'll be nine in September."

"Ah think she looks real sweet."

Mary Ann keeps her eyes shut and tries not to look sweet which she isn't and doesn't want to be. Sweet is dumb and sappy and Yes please and No thank you and never losing your temper. It isn't any use except once in a while when company comes with a box of candy, but not always even then, and not everybody is fooled. Mary Ann's mother isn't fooled mostly. "You're no Shirley Temple," she says sometimes after the company has gone. "So what?" Mary Ann says, because she hates Shirley Temple and Shirley Temple hair and dolls and dresses and coloring books. At the movies she always wished everything would turn out wrong for Shirley and she would have to stay in the orphanage. But of course it never did.

"It's a mercy she can sleep at all, in this awful heat and mean old traffic," Mary Ann's mother says.

"Mm."

The traffic isn't mean really, because how can traffic be mean, and it isn't old; anyhow no older than other traffic. Old is just a word Mary Ann's mother uses about things she doesn't like. And Mary Ann isn't hot. Only cozy, with the windy warm air blowing over her, and the engine music speeding and slowing and speeding up again, and ahead and behind and all round it other engines, a whole automobile band playing in different tunes. She can smell gasoline and motor oil and dust and her mother's toilet water, like fading flowers, and feel Theodore Ilgenfritz's furry face against hers. And even with her eyes shut she can imagine-see the fuzzy gray car roof over them with the round white light in the center, and above that the shiny black top of the car, and above that miles and miles of blue air with clouds piling and unpiling far far up away into space.

Against her other cheek she can feel the scratchy-soft back seat, and under it bouncy springs, and then car machinery shaking and drumming, and wheels going round around, and under the wheels the Saw Mill River Parkway curling and uncurling uphill and downhill like the roll of adding-machine tape in her father's office when she dropped it. And under the Parkway is dirt and rocks, deeper and deeper and thicker and thicker until finally you get to the other side of the earth where the Pacific Ocean is stuck on upside down by gravity, so that if she could open her eyes now and look straight through she would see sand and salty seawater and the white slippery bottoms of fishes and boats floating upside down. And the wet waves round them, and then miles of air and clouds and space going on forever and ever.

"What Ah'd like to know is, where did all these old cars come from?" Mary Ann's mother's voice says.

"It's Independence Day weekend, Honey."

Honey is Mary Ann's mother's name; not her polite name on letters, which is Honoria, but what everybody calls her that doesn't call her Mrs. Hubbard. Mary Ann's father is named William and called Bill. And ever since last fall, when she started Eastwind School, Mary Ann calls them Honey and Bill too. It felt funny at first, but now she is sort of used to it. At Eastwind all the kids call the teachers by their first names, and most of them call their parents by their first names. Honey explained to Mary Ann that the idea was for her to think of her parents as people not things. That for her to call Honey "Mummy" was like them calling her "Daughter" or "Child," as if they didn't know what her name was or that she was a separate person.

And it sort of worked out that way. Before she went to

Eastwind Mary Ann didn't notice much what her parents were like; they were Mummy and Daddy. Now she notices all the time. But maybe that would have happened anyhow just from getting older.

"Eight miles to Poughkeepsie. Ah thought we already passed Poughkeepsie," Honey says. "At this rate it'll be dark before we-all get to Anna's." Her voice goes up high and gets even more different from most people's.

"We're making pretty good time," Bill says.

Honey talks different from most people because she was born and raised in the South. The only other people in Larchmont who talk like her are cooks and maids and gardeners who mostly come from the South too, like their maid Precious Joy. They and their families had lived in hot climates for a long time and got sort of slowed down, the way most everybody gets slowed down in very hot weather, when it's hard to hurry or to speak fast and make all your words clear. Only they sort of got stuck that way. If your family lived in hot places for a really long long time, hundreds and hundreds of years, you also got darker and darker from the sun till you were shiny black all over like Precious Joy, all except the inside of your mouth and hands and the bottoms of your feet that the sun couldn't get to.

Honey isn't dark, but an ordinary light-pink color, and she can talk like other people in Larchmont if she wants to, because her family didn't live in hot places for all that long, but it tires her out. The more tired or cross she is the slower she moves and the more Southern she sounds. Mary Ann sometimes practices moving slow and talking Southern, but she doesn't do it anymore where Honey can see, because Honey gets mad. She thinks Mary Ann is making fun of her.

"We are still just about crawling," Honey says. "But what can you expect, with this damn old jalopy?"

"We're making pretty good time," Bill says again. He steps on the gas to prove this, so that the engine of The Franklin roars up loud; then he eases it back down, because driving too fast wastes gas and is against the law.

The Franklin is named after Benjamin Franklin who was a great Revolutionary patriot and inventor with his picture on the *Saturday Evening Post* every week, fat and gray with little square glasses. He was very good at saving money and discovered electricity with a kite and a key and wrote an almanac full of dull wise sayings.

Now he is their car and he doesn't mind that. He likes driving around the country and seeing what's become of it since he died and how much electricity there is everywhere. When you are lying down in his fat gray back-seat lap you can hear his engine saying the same dull things he said in history. —A pen-ny saved is a pen-ny earned, he says, over and over again.

The Franklin likes Bill, who understands him and takes good care of him. I understand this car, he says often; he has a collection of sayings too, though usually different ones. —Dirty hands make clean money, he says, and —The more you see of some people the better you like dogs.

The Franklin loves Honey because she is so pretty. When she gets dressed up to go for a Sunday drive in him she looks just like the smiling ladies who sit in new automobiles in ads. But Honey doesn't love The Franklin. She thinks he is ugly and ordinary looking, and also now she thinks he is too old, five years old, which is middle-aged for cars. Like cats. A year for a cat or a car is the same as seven for a person, and when they get to be more than ten (times seven is seventy) without dropping dead or having to be Put Away (like Tallulah when she wouldn't eat and kept spitting up on the rug) then everybody is surprised. It isn't fair because The Franklin is really only (seven times five is) thirty-five, five years younger than Honey. But she wants to get rid of him anyhow and says so even when he can hear it. "Ah would just adore to trade in this darn old jalopy for one of those beautiful new Buick roadsters," she says. So it is no wonder The Franklin gets discouraged sometimes and lets Honey down in emergencies.

Mary Ann doesn't exactly like The Franklin all that much; he is too square-shaped and black and his lap is too scratchy. But she feels sorry for him. She hopes he lives to be a hundred and stays just as strong and healthy as he is now, which can happen with cars if they are taken really good care of, though not with cats or people. (Minus thirty five is sixty-five; divided by seven is nine years and two left over.) Mary Ann will be nearly a grown-up lady when The Franklin is a hundred, and she will keep him in the garage mostly resting like Greatgrandma in the old ladies' home, but sometimes on nice days she will get all dressed up as pretty as Honey and take him out and drive around in him

"It's going on six already," her mother complains. "Ah don't understand why we couldn't have started sooner, and avoided some of this crowd. . . . If you would have quit work early for the holiday like most people, we'd be there by now. Ah really don't understand why you couldn't do that, considering you're the boss of that whole old office.'

"It's because I'm the boss that I can't leave early, Honey. I have to set an example."

"Ah don't see why. Mah father never fussed about examples down home. He took off whenever he felt like it to be with his family."

"Yeah, I bet he did."

"And you needn't throw aspersions on Daddy-Jack. He was one of the best . . ."

Mary Ann stops listening. She has heard this conversation before and probably she will hear it again. After a while, if it goes on long enough, Bill will say that Daddy-Jack (who died when Mary Ann was a baby, so she never really met him) was a hopeless alcoholic who couldn't even stay sober for his only daughter's wedding, and drank so much bourbon whiskey that morning he nearly fell down in the aisle of the First Presbyterian Church. And how Honey had to hold him up, looking cross and far away like a movie star the way she does in the silver-framed photograph on Mama-Lou's piano, in her white lacy wedding dress with her knees showing and a big bouquet of lilies of the valley.

Then Honey would laugh a special mean little laugh and start saying things about Grandpa and Grandma Hubbard up in Maine. She would say that Grandpa Hubbard knew how to pinch a nickel so hard it squealed and that Grandma Hubbard was so darn respectable she made Honey feel like the Original Scarlet Woman, whoever that was. Probably it had something to do with scarlet fever and was a fancy way of saying that Grandma Hubbard made her sick.

Honey talked much faster than Bill in these conversations and said worse things. In a way she was a lot madder than him; but in another way she was just kidding, and she always got over being mad much quicker. Pretty soon she would start to laugh at something she'd said and her laugh would get all bubbly, and she would lean up against Bill and say, "Aw, sweetie. Ah'm sorry. Ah don't know what got into me. Don't pull that long horse face. Ah'm sorry Ah lost mah temper and said all those awful things." "That's okay," Bill would say; but his face would look long and horsy for hours afterwards, sometimes for days.

Mary Ann must have slept some, because they are out in the country now. She can tell that even without sitting up. The road is bumpy, and there is no noise of other cars, and the wind goes past in a close steady rush, except when there are fence posts: then it comes in short breaths like somebody working hard. Besides, it's cooler, and she can smell cut grass.

"Something I'd like to make sure of right now, Honey," Bill is saying. "I don't want to have to play any of those games Anna always organizes at parties. She and her friends are supposed to be so smart, real intellectuals, but they're always hunting around trying to find where some damned ashtray is hidden, or making lists of ten animals that begin with the letter B."

Mary Ann knows that game already; it isn't ten with the same letter but one for each different letter in a word, and not just animals. Categories, it is called, and they played it when Anna came to their picnic only it rained. She hopes they will play it again, because she is very good at it.

"You said that already, darling," Honey tells him, which is true. "Ah told Anna you don't like playing those kind of games. Ah said they made you feel silly."

"Well, they do. Anyhow, I've got to work. I've brought all the figures for last month's report with me, and I'd like to get a draft written by Monday."

"Aw, Hubby," Honey says. "Ah want for us to have a good time this weekend. Can't you forget that old report?"

∘ ∘ ∘

Hubby is a special private name Honey calls Bill sometimes, that nobody else can use, because besides being short for Hubbard it means Husband. Bill's private names for Honey that she likes most are Kitten (because she is supposed to look like one) and Beautiful. Sometimes when dinner is late, which it usually is on Precious Joy's day off, he calls her Mother Hubbard. "Come on, Mother Hubbard," he says. "Time to go to the cupboard and get this poor dog a bone." So Honey goes to the cupboard and to the stove and to the refrigerator, but she doesn't like to. She doesn't like being called after Mother Hubbard, who is an old woman in a baby bonnet, even more than she doesn't like being called Honoria. "That name practically ruined mah entire childhood," she said once. "Ah wanted to make darn sure Ah gave mah little girl a name nobody in creation could make fun of."

But she hasn't. "Mary Ann, Mary Ann, washed her face in a frying pan," they sang at her on the playground at recess. Soon as she grows up she is going to change it to another one, sort of like it maybe, but nicer, more like books: Marian, or Marianne. Or maybe Miranda.

"I can't do that, Kitten. If you knew what the situation in the city was now, you wouldn't ask me to. There was a case I heard of just this afternoon, a family with five children. The father was hurt in a factory accident and he's been out of work two years, and the mother has TB, and they're living in—"

"Aw, Bill, darling. Ah want you to get your mind off all those miserable people, just for a couple of days—"

"I will, Kitten. Soon as I get my report done. I hope it won't take all weekend, but I'm going to need some time to myself at first, and a quiet place to work. I'd like you to explain that to Anna and everybody."

"How come you can't explain it yourself, darling?" Honey says in a sharp dragging voice like running your fingernails over cloth.

"It'll sound better coming from you."

"Ah don't think it matters who it comes from," Honey says. "Ah think it's going to sound pretty damn rude."

"Please," Bill says after a while.

"All right, sweetie. Ah'll tell everybody to leave you alone, and you can just sit upstairs in the bedroom all day. Only Ah don't know why the hell you insisted on coming along with us today if that's all you're planning to do."

"I wanted to get out of the office. Besides, I couldn't let you drive for three hours through this traffic."

"Sure you could. Anyhow, if we'd left earlier—"

"You mean you wish I had."

"No, sweetie. Honestly. Ah think it's real nice of you to drive us up, only . . ."

Mary Ann stops listening again. Whenever her mother says "honestly" it means she is lying. Like crossing your fingers behind your back, only fairer in a way because anybody could notice it once they caught on. "Ah've got some real tiresome news," Mary Ann heard her saying into the phone yesterday morning when she came in from playing hopscotch to get a glass of Ovaltine. "Mah hubby's decided he has to drive us up to Anna's place himself tomorrow, 'stead of taking the train Thursday, and he doesn't want to leave till about five, so Heaven knows when we'll get there. Honestly, Ah'm furious. . . . Ah suggested that, but he's so pigheaded." Honey gave a disgusted little laugh, as if Mary Ann's father's head had really turned into a big pinky-white bristly pig's head. "Ah guess he's worried that if he's not around the rest of us might not behave ourselves." Then Honey started giggling and whispering into the phone so that Mary Ann got tired of listening and went back outside.

Bill always wants everybody to behave themselves and act grown-up. Honey doesn't care about that so much; usually she is nicest when you don't, especially if you are really hurt or sick or scared. Then she puts her arms all round you and rocks you and smooths your hair and never says to stop crying now or don't be such a baby. But if Bill gets angry at somebody in the newspaper or the man at the garage or Honey or Mary Ann or Precious Joy or anybody, the worst thing he can think of to say is that they are babyish or childish or "immature," which means the same. He is always worried that Mary Ann might not act her age and that Honey might not behave in a serious grown-up Northern way, especially when he isn't around. Which is silly really, because when Bill isn't around Honey is much more grown-up and Northern, but of course if he isn't there he can't ever notice this.

Also Mary Ann's father doesn't want to get out of his office. He loves his old office, like Honey says, and is always staying late in it or going back to it when he doesn't have to on Saturdays. When Mary Ann visits him there he looks happier and more important than he does at home.

Bill's office is in a building near Times Square with sooty stone ladies standing each side of the doorway. You go up in an elevator like a big dirty gold birdcage and down a hall and through doors with the kind of bumpy glass in them you can't see through. Inside are a lot more halls and rooms but Bill's room is the biggest. It has two wide windows with glass fences at the bottom to stop drafts and keep things and people from falling out. From one window you can see parts of Broadway and the Thanksgiving Day parade, but from the other you can only see roofs and pipes and a brick wall that says in fat curly chocolate-milk letters

Fletcher's Castoria was a medicine sort of like castor oil, only it was supposed to taste nice, Bill explained, but she couldn't have any because she wasn't sick and because it wasn't good for her and because they didn't make it anymore.

The inside of Bill's office is all brown with a dark dust-colored carpet and walls and brown leather chairs and a shiny dark-brown desk as big as the dining-room table with a thick piece of greeny glass on top. On the glass are important papers you mustn't touch and a lot of interesting things made of dark-green leather. When she was very young Mary Ann used to think that this green leather and the red leather of her mother's pocketbook came from green and red cows. Mrs. Johansen, her father's secretary, always remembered this, and whenever Mary Ann came to the office she would ask if she had seen any green cows yet. Otherwise she is all right, a fattish lady with stiff waved gray hair who usually has a roll of Necco wafers in her top drawer.

In her mind Mary Ann has made a list of the green leather things on her father's desk. She likes organizing things into lists, and plans and schedules, and so does Bill, but Honey hates it. When Honey goes shopping she usually leaves her list home and buys something else. Then if Bill asks her where she has been and what she has done that day she usually can't remember, and sometimes she gets very very cross about it. "Ah honestly don't know what time it was when Ah got home," she says in a tight pulled-out-taffy voice. "Ah can't account for every single minute of mah day, Ah'm not a time clock."

The green leather things on Bill's desk are:

A cup for pencils, with different kinds of very very sharp pencils in it, including a special magic one that writes red on one end and blue on the other.

A blotter that goes back and forth like a rocking horse.

A sort of can for paper clips, with a magnet in the top that makes the paper clips jump up and try to get out.

A little flat round box full of aspirins.

A case for scissors, with a long pair of very heavy silver decorated scissors in it.

Another case with a heavy silver letter opener in it shaped like a fancy sword from the Metropolitan Museum.

A clock without any numbers, just twelve square shiny dots.

A calendar with a special page for each day.

A folding photograph frame with a picture on one side of Mary Ann last Christmas and a picture on the other side of Mary Ann's mother in a tight feathery hat a long time ago.

Anybody who saw this desk would know right away that Bill is an important person who every day has a whole page of different important things to do that give him headaches. Pencils and paper clips jump up to help him and blotters rock giddyap for him and when he opens letters or cuts things out he uses decorated weapons like the knights of old. Also he is so smart he can tell time without any numbers on the clock.

At home Bill is not so important. He uses ordinary pencils and scissors like anybody else and doesn't take up so much space. He mostly sits in his special chair with sides like a horse's blinkers and reads the newspaper or papers out of his briefcase and doesn't like to be disturbed. Or else he is in his shop out in the garage making things and fixing things that have got broken like Greataunt Honoria's candelabra or the toaster. Which is better because Mary Ann can watch and help and ask questions. Bill never says "How should Ah know?" or "Ah'm not an encyclopedia." He likes to explain what he is doing and always speaks slowly so you can understand what made the toaster quit working or why you should always sandpaper wood the way the tree grows.

Bill explains other things too, whatever you want to know, in a slow even voice the way Precious Joy irons sheets. Even scary confused things like volcanoes and ghosts get ironed out white and smooth while he talks, and either they aren't real or else they have rules that scientists have found out, and you can fold them up flat and put them away in your head. If he didn't know something he would look it up and tell you later.

Bill also explained his job, which is about taking care of poor people for the government. Lots of people in American are poor now because of the Depression. They lost their jobs and couldn't pay their rent and had to go live in shacks made out of rusty gasoline cans and old tin Lucky Strike signs on the wasteland by the railway tracks, and sell apples or matches or pencils. Like the awful man with the gray squashy cap and no legs who sits on a wooden tray with wheels outside the bank in New Rochelle sometimes. Mary Ann hates it when her mother gives him some of the money she has just got from the bank, and he flops his face to one side and smiles up at her with wet broken yellow teeth and says "Bless you, ma'am." "How's the little lady today?" he says sometimes but Mary Ann won't answer. Mary Ann's father doesn't like the squashy man either. He says he is a damned fraud who is probably quite well taken care of already by some relief organization, and if he isn't he could be, and that beggars like him siphoned away funds that ought to go to reputable institutions.

They had a siphon once in science class. You sucked on the rubber tube and it made a vacuum sort of like a vacuum cleaner and whooshed up water instead of dust. But it was a trick, it wasn't natural, because water doesn't run uphill and Nature abhors a vacuum whooshing dimes and quarters out of Honey's red pocketbook.

Bill's job has something to do with giving money away to poor people too, nice ones who really need it; but these poor people never come into Bill's office to get the money or even into his building. And he will never lose his job and have to sell pencils, even if the Depression gets much much worse. The more people that live in shacks and need the Government's money, the more important he will be. "It's an ill wind that blows nobody good," Grandma Hubbard said. Which means that whatever happens in the world usually turns out nice for somebody.

Once when Bill was repairing the playhouse roof Mary Ann asked him what would happen if the Depression got much much better or went away. Would they have to go live in a tin-can shack instead of their house in Larchmont? No, certainly not, Mary Ann's father said; but his office might get smaller. How could it get smaller? Mary Ann asked, imagining all the office rooms shrinking to the size of playhouse rooms, and Bill's big glass-topped desk and the green leather things on it shrinking, and even maybe Mrs. Johansen and the Necco wafers in her drawer, which of course couldn't really happen. What could really happen would be that fewer people would work for Mary Ann's father and his office would need fewer rooms. Especially if the Republicans won the next election. Republicans are on the side of Big Business, which is a lot of rich men in top hats who don't believe in helping poor people. They are mean and selfish and let farmers burn wheat and pour milk off trains into the mud to keep the price of bread and milk high when babies are hungry.

Mr. and Mrs. Parker down the street are Republicans, though they look just like ordinary people, with two little girls and a puppy named Brownie. They let Mary Ann use their sandbox any time she wants even if they aren't home, but last year when the election came they stuck Republican stickers on their Ford that are still there. Why are they Republicans? Well, probably, Mary Ann's father said, because Harold Parker is a romantic sap who doesn't know any better than to believe every word he reads in the *Herald Tribune*.

Anyhow even if he did lose his job because of Republicans, he could always get another one, Bill explained, because the poor are always with us. That didn't mean they were with Mary Ann and Bill in the garage, which would be awful; just that they are always hanging around somewhere nearby, like in front of the bank, or on the stone benches by the library, out of work and hungry and miserable, wanting Honey's and Mary Ann's new clothes and money and groceries and Hershey bars. But they can't follow her to Anna's farm. They might try, but their old beat-up car would run out of gas and break down.

So she shouldn't worry, Bill and The Franklin said Shouldn't worry, shouldn't hurry . . . Shouldn't scurry . . . blurry . . . furry . . . Mary Ann blinks her eyes hard She doesn't want to go to sleep now, she wants to see Anna's farm coming from away far off down the valley, the way Lolly Zimmern says you can. Mary Ann has heard all about the farm from Lolly, who is her new best friend at Eastwind School and will be there too this weekend with her mother and her father and her brother Lennie who is fourteen years old and a real meanie. The only good thing about him is that he isn't Lolly's real whole brother, only half. He has a different mother from Lolly and lives in New York City most of the time, thank goodness. Which makes Lolly sort of an only child too. Only children are supposed to be spoiled brats, which isn't fair at all, because if there is only one of you it is much harder to get away with anything.

When she was younger Mary Ann used to wish she wasn't an only child, so she would have somebody to play with besides Sliver their Welsh terrier. She wished it on stars and on birthday cakes and whenever she and somebody spoke at once and joined their little fingers and said "Needles, pins . . ." She wished that she would have one brother and one sister, and she would be older and tell them what to do. But then she thought, suppose they just messed up things and cried all the time like Erica Parker's baby sister, or suppose she had an awful brother like Lolly's. So she decided not to wish that anymore.

"Let me look at that map again, Kitten," Bill says, stopping the car. The sun is getting bigger and lower and when Mary Ann sits up she can't see anything out the window but the same old trees and hills, so she lies down again. "I wonder if we missed the turn?"

"Ah don't think so," Honey answers. "Anna said fifteen miles past Cowskill. It beats me why anybody would start a big farm way up here in the hills, where there's not a flat piece of land in sight."

Anna's house isn't a real farm now like when Anna was a little girl, with cows and horses and chickens, but there is still a barn full of hay and an old buggy and a tire swing and an orchard and a swimming hole and lots lots more. Lolly says it is the nicest place in the whole world. She also says it is enchanted and magic, but Mary Ann doesn't believe in magic, anyhow not that soppy kind.

Lolly believes there are fairies living in the woods behind her house in White Plains, tiny ones with silver and pink moth wings and sparkly wands. She is always drawing pictures of them and building little houses for them out of stones and leaves and flat pieces of bark everywhere—in the rock garden between clumps of sedum and round the perennial bed and between the roots of big trees. Lolly's fairies have names like Mossy and Daffodil, and they aren't good for anything like granting wishes or changing your enemies into stones. They mostly just fly around watching over plants and helping them to grow. Even if they were real they would be sort of dumb, but Mary Ann doesn't say that to Lolly anymore because she always starts looking as if she was going to cry.

If there is magic, then Anna is probably magic. Even Bill said something like that once. He said it took some kind of miracle to get a place like Eastwind going when most private schools in this country were failing like banks. Of course Eastwind is special. It was named that, Anna explained in a speech at assembly, because in America most of the time the wind blows from the West. Only once in a while it changes round and blows from the East, off the wild stormy Atlantic Ocean. She wanted everybody to know just from its name that Eastwind was different from other schools. It is Progressive, which means "going ahead." In the front hall there is a big picture of a ship sailing over a stormy sea, instead of George Washington and Abraham Lincoln like at public school. They had games in class to teach you things and you could move your desk around if you wanted, and there was a microscope and mice in her classroom, and they took you on trips to factories and museums to see how Oreo cookies and ball bearings and Egyptian pyramids were made

Anything Anna did was special and wherever she was at Eastwind was the funnest place to be, and the most crowded. Once she taught their class for a day and it was just like a party. Even stupid boring spelling that Mary Ann usually hates, because Anna told them about spelling bees. They aren't bees who can spell, which would be nicer in a way, but sort of contests they used to have in country schools, like the one Anna went to up in the Catskill Mountains long long ago. The whole town came to them and the noise and excitement sounded like a hive of bees buzzing, and the winner was as famous afterwards as a World Series star. Then Anna gave them that day's list of words to study, and then they had a spelling bee. Everybody stood up on their chairs and shouted out the letters, and when you missed you had to sit down, and Mary Ann came in second.

Anna is a big tall strong lady with bright wrinkly blue eyes and shiny thick hair the color of horse chestnuts wound round her head like a braided crown, or made into a twisty sugar-bun shape in back. Everybody likes her, even Mr. McCarty who said before their picnic that Honey had to sit by him and protect him because he was afraid of old-maid schoolteachers. But after he met Anna he changed his mind and kept sort of following her around. He latched onto her because she is such a good listener, Honey said afterwards. Which is true. When you talk to Anna she looks at you instead of at things behind you like most grown-ups, and she waits until you are all finished explaining things, for instance why you are under the table in the front hall of Eastwind instead of out at recess, without interrupting or saying what she thinks unless you ask her.

Anna is a good talker too. She can tell about when there were foxes in Central Park, and horses pulling delivery wagons and fancy carriages through the streets; and about how she went round the world twice. How she bought a little gray monkey named Sancho in Spain, but she had to give it away to a friend in Arizona because New York is too cold for monkeys; and how she rode on a camel in Arabia and a royal elephant in Ceylon. She said it was sort of like being in a ship on the ocean. When the elephant went fast a Canadian lady that was with her got seasick, but Anna didn't. Mary Ann wouldn't either, because she wasn't sick on the Hudson River ferry even when the waves went slosh over the deck and some ladies had to go lie down. The elephant would be big and square and gray like in the circus, with a fringed red-and-gold playhouse on top, and it would rock up and down like the ferryboat, and back and forth, swoosh splash. Swoosh. Splash.

Half an hour after sunset in the Catskill Mountains. A rose-gray light saturated the windless air, fading the already faded colors of the curtains and carpet in the west front bedroom at Anna's house. It dimmed even the bright Art Deco print dress of the young woman unpacking a suitcase into the tall wardrobe between the windows, and blurred her features nearly to anonymity.

Some people attract and focus attention; others, like Celia Zimmern, seem to repel or diffuse it. In a crowd they are invisible; even when they are seen alone the casual glance merely registers the presence of someone neither large nor small, neither fair nor dark, neither fashionable nor eccentric in costume, and passes on. Yet as Celia moved through the warm twilight, stooping and rising, reaching and lifting, her gestures were graceful, her face and figure lovely. Lovely, but in monochrome—the sepia photograph of a beautiful woman, all velvety beiges and browns.

As she turned from bed to wardrobe again with her arms full of clothes there were rapid resounding steps in the hall, and another sort of person entered the room: the sort whose voice carried in public places, whose features were distinct even in twilight. Dan Zimmern, Celia's husband, was a floridly handsome man in his late forties; tall, athletic, with ruddy tanned skin. He sported a luxuriant piratical mustache and thick dark curls to match, only partly subdued by an expensive hair tonic.

"All stowed away." Dan smiled, showing large strong white teeth. "God, am I tired!" He launched himself onto the four-poster bed with an energy that belied this exclamation, flinging himself back against the bolster; then bounced up again to pull off his perforated shoes.

"I hope Lolly's going to be all right up there," his wife murmured, turning from the open wardrobe with a limp filmy nightgown over her arm.

"Oh, sure. She'll be fine." Dan threw his jacket toward a chair and began to loosen a scarlet-striped tie. "Hey, did you pack my new shirt?"

"Yes, it's right here." Celia gestured. "You know Lolly's never slept up in the attic before," she persisted. "And it's so big and . . . dark. Especially at night."

"Don't worry, love." Dan yanked off his tie and opened his shirt collar. "Lolly will be okay. Anyhow, if she should wake up, her pal Mary Ann's right there in the next bed. Ahh." He lay back on the patchwork spread, quilted fifty years earlier by Anna's mother in the Wild-Goose pattern. He folded his arms behind his head and looked at Celia through the rose-madder dusk.

"How's your headache, Cilly?" he asked. "Any better?"

"A little." She smiled wanly.

"It'll go away fast, now we're not driving over those

bumpy roads," he predicted. Celia said nothing.

"We're going to have a great weekend. Not a chance of rain, the *Times* says. And it'll be fun for Lolly to have somebody to play with up here."

"Mm," Celia said. "I wish there were someone here for Lennie to play with," she added, feeling in the side pocket of the suitcase. "I wonder . . . if we asked Anna . . . if there might be any neighbors who would have—"

"No thanks," Dan interrupted. "Remember what happened on Cape Cod? I'm through trying to find friends for that picky kid."

"Those Stockwell boys weren't Lennie's type," Celia said, with the air of having said it before. "He's not awfully athletic, and he's never been to a private school . . . Maybe if—"

"Listen, darling: no kids are ever going to be Lennie's type. He thinks he's too smart for any fourteen-year-old that ever lived. Just let's leave it alone, all right?"

"Mm," Celia remarked; not obviously a negative response, but Dan treated it as one.

"I don't want you to speak to Anna. She's got enough on her mind. There's plenty for Lennie to do around here, if he had any initiative."

Celia, shutting a drawer, gave the faintest of sighs hardly more than a breath.

"Dan," she said presently in her soft, colorless voice

"What, love?"

"Did you . . . suggest to Anna that she might invite the Hubbards for this weekend?"

"Not me." He laughed and shook his head. "It was strictly her own idea. You know we voted to ask him to join the Eastwind School board. I guess she wants to get a closer look at him, in case he accepts. Or maybe try to scare him off if she doesn't like him."

"I don't know . . ." Celia's voice faded.

"What don't you know?"

"Well . . . They . . . don't seem really the sort for a weekend in a farmhouse with no indoor plumbing. Especially not Honey."

"Aw, they'll love it. Nobody minds roughing it for a few days. Makes them feel like pioneers, all healthy and patriotic." He began to hum: " 'My country, 'tis of thee—' "

"What I don't get," he added, breaking off, "is why Anna puts up with it herself. Staying alone up here the whole damn summer."

"Mm." His wife shook out a striped silk bathrobe. "Anna's always lived alone though, hasn't she?"

"Yeah. Most of the time."

"It's odd, you know." Celia lined up two rows of toilet articles on the oak washstand. "That she's never married, I mean. A woman like that, with so much . . . energy. And so many friends. And she seems so sure of herself. Though I suppose that might frighten men off . . . And she must have been quite attractive, when she was younger, I mean." Celia set two toothbrushes on end in a china mug.

"Yeah. She was."

"And she hasn't ever been engaged or . . . had a suitor, in all that time?"

"God, I don't know." Dan yawned. "She might have. I kind of lost touch with her after she left the city, up until we moved out to Westchester and Lolly started at Eastwind." He glanced out the window into the fading sky. "She was going with a man when I first knew her."

"Oh? You never mentioned that. What was he like?"

Dan hesitated, shifting his position on the bed. "Well, it's a long time ago now, must be, what? fifteen years. I didn't know him too well. He was kind of a bohemian; a Village radical." His tone was casual, scornful. "Didn't do much; called himself a writer." Like many persons who deal in words, Dan could control his voice far better than his face; it was not by accident that he had now turned the latter away. Had it been visible, a far less sensitive and concerned observer than Celia might have guessed that he was describing someone he did know too well. "It didn't last very long. Anna was offered a job out of town, and they broke up."

"That's sad." Celia drifted back toward the bed through the thickening dusk. "And since then she's been alone. All those years." She shook her head slowly.

"Don't waste your sympathy," Dan said, his voice louder. "Anna's not like you. With her the job always comes first. If she'd given a damn for that guy she would have stayed in New York." He laughed shortly and raised his knees between himself and Celia as a further barrier.

"Yes . . . I suppose she would. Of course she would, if she'd loved him. I wonder if it's some kind of psychological thing. Or maybe she just never met the right man." She smiled fondly at her husband's knees; then, approaching closer, at him.

Dan responded in kind, but only for a second; then, as if the gentle intensity of Celia's gaze made him uncomfortable, he shifted his smile toward the window. "Look at that sunset, Cilly," he said.

"Oh, yes. Lovely."

"We're going to have a great weekend," he said for the second time.

"Mm." She stooped to take an armful of carefully folded underwear from the suitcase.

"And the greatest thing about it is, I don't have to go near that goddamn lousy office for four days."

Celia, arranging the underwear in a drawer, turned. "Was it very bad today?"

The usual Osborne shot down Jeff's whole new soap campaign. Said he didn't feel it was happy enough. One of these days somebody's going to murder that phony bastard. And if I don't get out of there soon, it just might be me." He laughed harshly.

"You know, darling," Celia said, hesitant but earnest, gliding back across the room toward her husband, "what I said last week . . . I really meant it. If you . . . want to resign, I think you . . . should go ahead . . ." Her voice faltered, was extinguished.

"It ain't worth it, Cilly," Dan put on the accent of a stage yokel. "Every agency in New Yawk City is full of phony bastards; that's the type our business attracts, the same as some flowers attract bugs. We've got fewer of the nasty critters than a lot of outfits do."

"But you . . . You don't have to stay in that business," Celia said. "You used to be a reporter, and you did . . ." Her voice faded again. "Reviewing . . . for magazines . . ."

Dan gave a loud horselaugh. "You mean you'd like for us to sell the house in White Plains," he said. "And get rid of Corinne and the gardener, and take Lolly out of Eastwind School, and move into the kind of cheap Village apartment I had when I was married to Irma. And do your own laundry and live on corned-beef hash and canned beans, while I try to drum up some two-bit newspaper job. If I could even get one, the way things are now in New York."

"Yes . . . if you want it." Celia looked at him softly, steadily, over the raised lid of the large suitcase. Because of their relative positions, or perhaps because of his superior volume and definition, she seemed to be begging for some concession rather than offering one. "I could manage . . . Really."

"You don't know what you're talking about," Dan said

roughly. 'Even Irma couldn't take that life, and she was brought up to it. You wouldn't last a month.''

Celia moved her lips as if speaking, but no sound came from them.

"It's a waste of time to go on talking about it, love," he said with forced cheerfulness. "Anyhow, I'd be nuts to quit." His voice soured. "I'm too goddamn good at turning out the kind of shit they want. It's one of my few real talents." Dan was speaking to himself now, in the manner of a man beating himself with a stick he has used before and which has begun to soften with wear. "Great job for a socialist." This blow seemed to sting; his face in the dusk was contorted for a moment with pain and disgust.

"But . . ."

"Let's forget it, okay?" Dan glanced out the window again. The sunset had dimmed to a smoky lavender, against which trees stood out in inky silhouette. The bedroom was still filled with a gray haze of light that blurred shapes and washed out colors like the newspaper reproduction of a painting. Dan's white shirt and smile, his dark eyebrows and mustache, remained distinct; but Celia's subtler features were smudged, her expression impossible to discern.

"Come on over here, baby," he said in a caressing, mock-tough voice. He flashed a smile and held out his arms. Celia, shadowy, drifted toward him between the furniture.

"Come on. That's right." He seized one white wrist, pulling her down.

"Oh, Dan." Celia sank onto the bed and lay close beside him.

"Cilly, baby." Dan caressed her, disarranging the tight-waved feathery brown hair. "You're so lovely. So good to me." He rolled heavily toward her.

"Mm." Celia did not resist as she was pressed into the Wild-Goose quilt, now a faint pattern of grays; but neither did she respond in kind. Almost invisible in the dusk next to her husband, she grasped him in a close, feverish, but less than sensual embrace—sighing, stroking his cheek and shoulder, kissing his face all over with mothlike fluttering kisses as if she were some passionate ghost.

"Darling." Dan began to ease her clothes apart.

"Oh Dan . . . darling. I don't know if . . . enough time . . . Anna . . . back from their walk . . . not polite . . ." she whispered, but almost inaudibly. Dan, at any rate, did not appear to have heard her.

A cool, calm summer's night, broken by occasional distant pale flashes of lightning and the slow following sound of thunder. The mountains lay about in loose dark heaps, sparked here and there with clustering points of electric light, or (on the remoter slopes) by the softer glow of gas or kerosene. Anna's big brick farmhouse winked south over a broad upland valley. Its downstairs rooms shone yellow; the rest were dark, save for a single lamp in the arched window directly above the front door.

Most of the light came from the two windows on the right. Behind them was the long sitting room, scattered with faded chintz sofas and easy chairs like cows lying down, heaps of cushions, hooked rugs, tables piled with books and papers, hanging ferns and tall Chinese vases of day lilies or dried pampas grass—all warmly, obscurely lit by two oil lamps and a flickering, quickening blaze in the wide fireplace, round which Anna and three of her house guests were gathered. Over by the windows, Celia Zimmern and her stepson Lennie sat facing each other across a low table.

"Your move," Lennie said impatiently.

"What?" Celia turned. "Oh yes. I'm sorry." Chin propped on both hands, she studied the game, which was set out on an antique inlaid board with an elaborately carved but incomplete set of Indian ivory chessmen. Two of the pawns, borrowed years ago for some other game, had been replaced with aluminum salt-and-pepper shakers, and the white queen was an empty cut-glass scent bottle.

"Take your time." Lennie's voice was sharp with adolescent sarcasm.

Celia advanced a piece. Then she looked away from the board, her glance moving rapidly here and there, like one of the small, winged half-transparent night insects that flittered erratically about the sitting room; yet drawn always toward her husband, as if he were the lamp in which it would finally expire.

"Your move," Lennie repeated, following the direction of her gaze with jealous irritation.

"Sorry." She glanced down, then pushed her salt-shaker ahead one square, causing Lennie to give his characteristic short laugh—half child's crow of triumph, half sardonic adult chuckle.

"Oh, dear. That was a mistake, wasn't it?"

"It sure was." Lennie took the salt-shaker with a knight; then he shoved his horn-rimmed spectacles up what was already a prominent nose and peered suspiciously through them at Celia. Though he would never be as large as his father, Lennie had inherited his strong, handsome Jewish features; but the heavy eyebrows, the glowing dark-lashed eyes, the full curved nose and mouth were as yet too large for his thin face, and blurred by youth and acne; and Lennie's habitual expression was sour and critical rather than good-humored.

"What's the matter with you tonight?" he said, his voice

breaking from bass to alto. "Are you letting me win? I'm not interested in playing with you if you let me win."

"No, honestly," Celia said. "I just wasn't concentrating. Wait a sec." She studied the game again, while Lennie, scowling, studied her. "There." She moved another piece.

"That's better." Lennie sat back, looking at the chess board. "Yeah, but you loused it up already, you know. Look at where my rook is. You haven't got a hope in this game now."

"Really?" Celia smiled vaguely.

"Not a chance. Want to play again?"

Celia's glance flickered across the room once more, barely lighting on the elegant heavy curves of Dan's nose and cheek, the dandelion fluff of Honey Hubbard's bangs, Anna's large hands on the poker as she leant forward to turn a log. "All right," she said. "One more game."

MaryAnn half-wakes from a dream full of banging nd flashing into a confused darkness. She is in bed somewhere but it isn't her own room: it's some awful big black empty place. She wants Teddy but he isn't there anymore. There is a door far away partly open and a slice of light pointing across the floor to another bed with a humped-up scary dark shape in it. She wants to scream but she can't breathe enough to scream, it's all gasping choked inside.

But she can move and she squirms away from the snaky covers and jumps wide out of the bed which could have spookies under it that grab at your feet in the dark, that could have grabbed Teddy away. She runs across the bare cool wood floor, into a strange hallway place, beginning to

breathe, to make a noise—"Aow, aow! Mommy, Mommy!"
—and down twisted wooden stairs to another big dim place
with a little fire in a glass vase and a window seat and a
square gold-framed picture of square white cows—Anna's
house. She is at Anna's house, in the mountains; but still
crying, going on down down more wider stairs to the front
hall, and a door open into a room full of light and grown-
ups.

"Mommy!"

"Why, it's Mary Ann! What's the matter, ducky? Come
on over here . . . Did you have a bad dream?"

"I had a bad dream, Mommy." Mary Ann gives another
sob, louder than she has to because she is safe now, leaning
against her mother, and the strange grown-ups are only
Anna and Lolly's parents and Lolly's brother Lennie.

"It's all right, darling." Honey gathers Mary Ann into
her warm lap.

"And I couldn't find Teddy, and there's an Awful
Thing in my room."

"There, there. What kind of an awful thing?"

"Like a—like a sort of a black lump of blankets in a
bed." Mary Ann gives a last sob.

"That's just Lolly, darling. You were asleep when she
got here, just a little while ago, and her mommy took her
up and put her to bed in the attic with you." Honey laughs.

"I thought it was a spookie."

"Aw, ducky. There."

"There is no such thing as a spookie," Bill says, shaking
his head at them. He always gets cross whenever anybody
talks about spookies, or ghosts or bogeymen or anything
that probably doesn't exist. Because of this Mary Ann was
the first kid in kindergarten to find out that Santa Claus
was just your mommy and daddy, and so were the Easter

Bunny and the Tooth Fairy, even if you got in trouble with the teacher for saying so.

"Of course there isn't," Honey says. "Would you like a glass of milk and a cookie, chickie, and then Ah'll go back upstairs with you, and you can see it's only Lolly?"

Mary Ann nods.

"Is that all right, Anna? . . . Come on then, baby. We'll go look in the kitchen."

Anna lifts one of her old-fashioned lamps off a table and carries it into the big kitchen. Then there is milk in a tin mug speckled blue and white, creamier than the milk at home, and a flat square crumbly cookie that tastes of gingerbread.

"That's a good girl," Mary Ann's mother says. "Drink it up. . . . Now we'll go back to bed. Where's that flashlight you gave us, Anna? . . . Oh, thank you. Come on, baby, this way. . . . It's all right, everybody. She's half asleep already."

"I'll carry her for you," Lolly's father's voice says. "Then I can take a look at Lolly and see if she's all right. . . . Up you go."

They are climbing, the ceiling turning. It feels different from Bill, who always carries her stiff and careful like an important package. Lolly's father just sort of hugs Mary Ann to him warm and close, and doesn't notice when extra parts like elbows get bumped against a wall.

More steps. They are in the attic, high and shadowy, with a bright circle of flashlight sliding down the roof boards to land on Lolly, curled in a nest of sheets.

"You see, darling. It's only Lolly here, asleep in bed. And tomorrow morning she'll wake up and play with you. . . . What? . . . Oh, your Teddy. Here he is, hiding down under the covers. . . . Good-night now, chickie. Sweet dreams." Honey kisses her cheek. Mary Ann moves her mouth sleepily, kissing the air.

"Safe in the arms of Morpheus," Lolly's father's voice says. The yellow circle slides away across the ceiling.

Morpheus is in a book of myths Lolly has. He is the god of sleep, a tall invisible person with big soft wings like clouds, who comes at bedtime and takes you in his arms and holds you very gently and flies away with you into the Land of Nod. That doesn't exist really. But it might. Because maybe you just never . . . remembered it . . . afterwards.

In the attic of Anna's house a light flashed, darting from one gable-end to the other. It vanished and appeared again, a little lower down, in a round window cut like a pie into panes of old bubbled glass. Here it illuminated a narrow spiral of steps, and two sets of shoes descending them: one pair of high-heeled peach silk sandals, women's size 5; one pair of brown-and-white perforated brogans, men's size 10 1/2.

"Hey, baby," Dan Zimmern whispered in the same caressing, mock-tough manner he had used earlier in another part of the house, stopping Honey with one heavy warm hand on her neck. "When am I going to see you?"

"Why, just anytime. Ah'm going to be here this whole weekend." Honey looked up at him out of wide gray eyes shaded in green and lined in sooty black.

"That's not what I mean, and you know it." He twisted her fingers loosely in her fluffy curls. Honey giggled and tossed her head, tightening his grip.

"Just watching you across that room is driving me wild," Dan said. He descended another step and moved in on Honey, crowding her into the angle of the stairway. "You're so goddamned pretty."

"You're not so bad yourself," Honey said in a lazy, purring voice. For a long moment she seemed to lose herself; then she turned her mouth aside, smudging lipstick onto his cheek.

"No, Dan!" she whispered, pushing at his arm so that the circle of flashlight rocked up the wall. "Not here—For heaven's sake—Not now."

"All right, damn it." Dan moved back. "When?"

"Honestly, Ah don't see how we can manage it," she whispered, breathing a little hard. "Not with this house full of people, and mah hubby watching me the whole time like a blasted chicken hawk."

"Come on," Dan said, in a different, cooler voice. "You promised me that this weekend we were going to get together."

"Ah said maybe this weekend." Honey brushed softly against Dan, turning up her face. He stared at her for a second or two, then kissed her hard but briefly and drew back.

"You can get away for an hour if you want," he whispered persuasively. "Just say you're going for a walk tomorrow sometime. Say after lunch, soon as you can get away. We can meet down the road. There's an old hay barn the other side of Anna's orchard, nobody ever goes there." He leant over Honey and finished the kiss slowly, with her cooperation.

"Just up from the road, the other side of the orchard," he said presently. "You can't miss it. I'll be waiting for you there. Okay, baby?"

"Ah'll try."

"You do that."

Honey giggled. "Here, let me wipe your face." She

pulled a filmy handkerchief from her dress and wadded it into a ball. "You're all over lipstick."

"Well, was everything all right?" Bill asked as his wife and Dan came into the sitting room.

"Just fine." Dan grinned. "Now where the hell is my drink? Ah, there you are." He lowered himself onto a sofa and raised his glass.

Bill looked from Dan to Honey, already curled up again on the hearthrug like a little plump blonde cat. "Honey, you know I don't think it's a good idea to indulge Mary Ann the way you just did," he said. "We don't want her to learn that she can get up at night and come downstairs to interrupt adults and demand something to eat whenever she wants to."

"She didn't demand anything, darling. We offered it to her." Honey looked up at Anna for confirmation.

"That's exactly what I mean. It wouldn't occur to Mary Ann to want food in the middle of the night, if you didn't suggest it."

"She was scared and in a strange place." Honey's purr had changed to a mew. "Besides, she'd lost her Teddy."

"I realize this might be an exception," Bill conceded "But I mean, as a general rule. If she tries the same thing again while we're here, for instance. We mustn't encourage her acting childish."

Honey turned round toward Bill, arched her back, and spat. "Why in tarnation shouldn't Mary Ann act childish? She's a child, isn't she?"

"I just meant—" Bill's manner became both stiffer and more apologetic. "Coming downstairs in the middle of the night crying for a teddy bear. She's not a baby anymore after all; she's almost nine. And I think usually she's pretty mature for her age. That's all I meant."

Honey smiled, stretched, and gave a little feline yawn. "You're always fussing about Mary Ann being too old for a Teddy." She turned to the rest of the company. "Why, Ah kept mah Teddy till Ah was years and years past her age. Ah took him with me to boarding school, and to college, and Ah probably would have him to this day, except that he was spitefully kidnapped from me in mah first year, by Landon Clay, one of mah crazy beaus."

"Kidnapped?" Dan asked, laughing.

"Uh-huh." For the first time since they had re-entered the room, Honey gave Dan a quick sideways glance. "Landon said he was crazy jealous of Teddy, sleeping up so close to me in mah bed every night. So he plotted and schemed with a mercenary stonehearted nigro maid that we had in our sorority. Ah believe he gave her as much as five dollars, and she kidnapped mah Teddy while Ah was out and slipped him to Landon. Then he sent me a ransom note, swearing Ah would never see mah sweet Teddy again unless Ah complied with his ransom demands." Honey allowed a dramatic pause.

"What was the ransom?" Anna asked.

"The ransom was, Ah had to promise to spend an hour with him in his old jalopy at midnight down by a lake near the University named Loon Lake on the map, only everybody called it Spoon Lake. Landon swore on his honor as a Southern gentleman he wouldn't make the tiniest attempt on mah virtue. Ah positively refused. Ah told him Ah wasn't worried about mah virtue, Ah could take care of that; Ah was worried about mah reputation." Honey giggled. "Ah said he knew perfectly well mah reputation wouldn't be worth a hope in Hades after every brother in his fraternity heard Ah'd been with him at Spoon Lake after midnight. Well of course Landon said he wouldn't tell a single living soul, on his honor as a Southern gentleman and a descendant of General Clay. He said he knew Ah was mad at him, but he hadn't been able to make a date with me for five weeks, and he loved me so much he was just plain desperate. Well, Ah said, if he really loved me that much he would give mah Teddy back to me right then. But he downright refused.

"Well, then Ah lost mah temper, which was a real bad mistake, and Ah told Landon that he was no gentleman, but just a common thief and sneak. And Ah said that if his great-uncle that he was always taking the name of in vain knew what he'd been up to he would positively rotate in his grave. Ah told him Ah would definitely never go out with him again, and Ah said that if he didn't bring mah Teddy back directly Ah would never speak to him again either, and Ah would tell every girl in Rose Manor the whole story and they would all despise him like Ah did. That was real dumb, because Landon Clay said he didn't care what the other girls thought, the only one he loved was me, and if Ah wouldn't speak to him, at least he'd always have Teddy to remember me by. . . . Ah could use another little drink," Honey added, holding out her glass as the laughter subsided. "Ooh, thanks."

"So did you ever get your teddy bear back again?" Dan asked, replacing the bottles of gin and ginger ale on a side table.

"Uh-uh. But Ah did hear, a long time later, that when Landon Clay joined the Army and went overseas he took mah Teddy with him, only he left him in France somewhere. . . . Ah have to cry even now, when Ah think of it, mah poor sweet Teddy abandoned in a foreign country. Ah just hope the Huns didn't get him, like they did silly old Landon."

July 4

"Lolly?. . ."

Blobby sun patterns sliding on the cool kitchen table. Yellow round spots. Pointed shadow spots the shape of? Of hands, Lolly thinks—greeny half-transparent leaf hands pressing against the kitchen window. Hands round all the windows. Anna's whole house covered in vines, woven over, knitted and? Crocheted.

—Virginia Creeper, Anna told her once. —My great-grandmother planted it, over a hundred years ago.

Years, a hundred years; Lolly says the words inside her head. Creeping Virginia patting the walls with her green hands as she climbs up and round and all over Anna's house, stretching out long pale butterfly antennae, digging her nails into the sandy folds between the bricks. Wrapping and winding her arms and stems up the chimneys and drainpipes, pulling at the windowsills and gutters with her greeny fingers until they sag.

—She stuck two slips of vine into the ground; if you look, you can still see them, one each side of the front door.

Virginia and Virginia. Old old lady trees now, leaning against the front of the house, with twisted gray rope legs. Reaching their twisted rope arms along the sides, clasping hands in back. Years of twigs and branches cut back in a thick bristly green square around each window, except

"Lolly . . . not eating . . . your nice scrambled .
except one window was missed this year; a curtain of green
hands hangs over it, moving in the breeze, stroking the
screen. Love. Because everything growing here loves
Anna. Grass comes crowding up to her walls, big puffy
rosebushes spill Ivory Soapflakes petals round her. Forget-
me-nots jump out of the flower bed and run across the
terrace between the stones toward the house, to be remembered by Anna. Moss makes her wide marble doorstep
velvet at the edges and climbs toward the fan-shaped window over the door, up the cheese-white stone.

". . . no more appetite than a bird . . ."

Virginia loving Anna's house, surrounding it holding it
hugging it safe forever. Green-veined soft hands, hundreds
of them. Virginia and Virginia, grandmothers, greatgrand-
mothers, digging their long root toes gently into the earth
under the rosebushes. Wrapping their arms round. Love.

"Lolly! . . . Lolly, dear, you're not listening," her mother
says. "Look at me, dear. I said, if you're finished with your
breakfast, wouldn't you like to take Mary Ann down to the
pasture and pick some black raspberries? You know where
they grow. . . . If you find enough, Anna can make raspberry tarts for supper."

A bird's voice. A pigeon voice, cooing and clucking, or
a hen, ruffling its feathers, shut in the kitchen.

"It's getting real warm out already, girls, so you'd better
be off right away. Ah think maybe Mary Ann ought to have
a hat if you've got an old one round somewhere, Anna, she
burns so easy, just like her poor daddy."

Mary Ann's mother's voice is another bird, a soft high
feathery trilling one. Bunches of sound, stop, another
bunch of sound—sweet and sticky like her name.

"I don't want a hat," Mary Ann says. Quack quack.

"I know just the thing," Anna says. "You can have my

Greatuncle Charlie's Chinese coolie hat, Mary Ann. The great big straw one that's hanging on the wall in my bedroom. He bought it from a Chinese boatman with a pigtail who ferried him across the Yellow River."

Anna's voice isn't a bird, it's—

"Don't let her wear that, Anna. Ah'm sure it's much too valuable."

"Hats are made to be worn."

—It's a wise-woman's voice, a fairy-godmother voice, deep, a little cracked, a queen's.

"She'll be careful of it. Won't you, Mary Ann?"

"Of course I'll be careful. How could I not be careful?"

"I want a special hat too," Lolly says.

"All right, chickie. Mmm . . . I know; you can wear my mother's pink sunbonnet, that she sewed herself. Wait, I'll get them."

She swishes out, the room is emptier, the way all rooms are without Anna, though bird voices go on chirping and quacking, and then she is back.

"Here you are, Lolly. Hold up your chin now, so I can tie the strings. That's right."

Everything shuts in around her face, like looking through a pink tunnel. Or the drainpipes stacked along the road before the WPA men came to dig it up. Only Lolly can move this tunnel around with her head: up to a round section of ceiling—white with flakes of another white. Or down to her hands holding a white enamel pan with a blue rim, the faded brick floor, half a brown braided rug. Or move it sideways, so you put the rug into

"C'mon, Lolly."

the center of the tunnel picture. Or the pan and hands. Or Mary Ann, but she keeps moving, spoiling it. It is nicest straight down with mostly flat braided stripes and the pinky-red floor and a bit of round white pan and

"Lolly! Come on!"

The tunnel follows Mary Ann's back out the kitchen door sucking in bright leafy trees and bushes and red brown barn, across a grassy space with yellow dandelions to the road. Dust rises into the picture from Mary Ann's sandals and sagging white socks.

"Okay, here's the stone wall like Anna said." Mary Ann turns in a whirl of dust, her face freckled with points of light by the Chinese straw hat. "How do we get over into the field?"

"There's a special secret way. Round here."

Lolly leads Mary Ann behind thick bushes, higher than they were before. There is the ghost of a wagon-track, sunk in long grass, curving up to the gate. Gray split splintery rails. She climbs through them, ducking the pink tunnel between the bars. But Anna's Chinese hat is too big. Mary Ann has to climb the gate, wobble on the top rail, jump down into the tall rough grass.

"Come on," she calls.

Grass that will be hay, thick now with flowers. White thin daisies with yellow cornmeal centers. Chickory like scraps of blue tissue paper stuck untidy on greeny-brown stems. Tall Queen Anne's lace umbrellas in thick creamy snowflake designs with a speck of dark-purple or dark-brown or navy-blue velvet at the center of each one. Queen Anne, Queen Anne, she washed her lace, and hung it out to dry . . . Queen Anna's lace. Anna in a lace queen's dress, powdery white, walking through the field surrounded by flitting lace fairies.

"Come on, stupid. Show me where," Mary Ann says.

"Right here, stupid." The black raspberry bushes are all round them, pouring over the stone wall, everywhere, thick with fruit. In bunches like half-spread hands, ladies' hands with painted nails, strawberry-red shading to ripe shiny black.

Eating and picking. Picking and eating. Lolly puts a ripe berry on each finger of her left hand, and eats them off. Little beehive hats, hot and sweet in the sun.

The white enamel bowl fills slowly. Ahead, Mary Ann moves down the field, wading through high hay grass in the greatuncle's hay-colored hat. It has a point on top, curving down and out to a wide brim, with Mary Ann's skinny white neck and two wispy orange Chinese pigtails beneath.

"You look like a Chinese house," Lolly says. "A Chinese pagoda house, like on the Asia map at school."

Mary Ann turns, her small smiling Chinese mouth jam-magenta. "Well, you look kind of funny too. You look—uh —like those sunbonnet twins on the scouring-powder box. You know. The Dutch Cleanser Twins."

Dutch Twins. Lolly's hands stop picking, her mouth stops eating. She doesn't want to remember; she remembers. Under the kitchen sink, an orange-and-gray box. In a cupboard not to open or go into the kitchen when it is open because the Dutch Twins are there and other awful dirty things.

"I don't want to." Lolly shakes her head hard. She puts down the pan of berries, she tries to drag the tunnel sunbonnet off, but it won't come! won't!

"What's the matter with the Dutch Twins?"
because it's tied onto her. Tied in a bow. She pulls one end, the other. The bow loosens, explodes; the tunnel slides apart, opens up into a wide calm picture of fields and hills and sky.

"What's the matter with the Dutch Twins, anyhow?"

"They haven't got any faces." Lolly drops the collapsed sunbonnet into a pool of grass, where it floats, harmless and empty.

"Of course they've got faces, silly." Mary Ann stops picking. "You just can't see them in the picture. They couldn't clean things if they didn't have faces; they couldn't see to clean anything." She giggles. "I bet whoever drew them on the box just can't make faces very well. Like when you can't draw hands for paper dolls so you make them going behind their back."

"I can too draw hands," Lolly says.

"Or maybe they don't draw them because the Dutch Twins have stupid goopy faces. Like this." Mary Ann crosses her eyes and sticks out her tongue.

Lolly stares, trembly; then the bubble of fear rises in her, breaks, and she is giggling too.

"No, like this," she says. She rolls her eyes and tries to make a fish mouth. "Silly faces."

"Oogy googy!" Mary Ann, giggling louder, squints and puffs her face up with air.

"Oogy googy," Lolly says too, safe now, safe always from the Dutch Twins. "You look funny Chinese. Chinese twins!" She bulges out her own cheeks, trying to stop laughing, to go on laughing; she pulls up the corners of her eyes.

"And you look—ker-azy."

"Kerazy twins!"

Giggling, helpless, they fall in the long grass.

As morning advanced, the sun swung west over the Catskills, slanting into the front bedrooms of Anna's house and across the Victorian pedestal table that Bill Hubbard was trying to use as a desk. Twice he moved this heavy table and a matching chair away into the shade; the sun pursued, opening its blinding yellow fan sideways, steadily crowding Bill into the corner. Finally he blinked, sighed—defeated. He stubbed out his cigarette laid down his red, blue, and black pencils, sorted his sun-stained papers, and stood up: a tall, somewhat overweight man in his early forties, with long pale features and thinning reddish hair, dressed in his usual white shirt, narrow dark tie, and trousers held up by brown striped suspenders. He descended the wide creaky stairs and walked back through empty sun-checked rooms to the kitchen, which also seemed empty until Anna, in a long apron, backed out of a cupboard carrying a stack of baking pans.

"Oh, excuse me."

"Hello. Come in." Anna dealt out pie and muffin tins on the kitchen table. "How's your report going?"

"Okay, thanks. Thought I'd take a break. Where is, uh, everyone?"

"Let's see." She dipped her hand into a bin and dusted the other end of the table with flour. "Celia's reading *The Waves* out on the terrace, Lennie's gone for a walk, and Dan and Honey and the girls have driven into the village to get groceries and buy more fireworks for tonight."

"Oh. Well, I don't want to bother you." Bill began to drift away toward the hall.

"You're not bothering me. You can help me, if you want to." She laughed, seeing his face. "I don't mean with the baking. But I'd like to get some more wood cut up, so we can have another fire tonight if we need it."

"Sure. Glad to help."

"Let's do it now, then, before it gets hot." Anna took off her apron, uncovering shapeless jeans and a faded man's workshirt.

"There's some big logs already sawed," she explained, as Bill followed her out the kitchen door into the sun. "If you could drag one of them over here by the shed— Watch it, they're pretty heavy . . . **Thanks**. Now I think the best method is to stand the log up on one end— Yes, like that, and then we can start it with the hatchet."

"I know. I used to split firewood up in Maine when I was a boy."

"Then we can hammer in one of these wedges here, and — **Sorry**." Anna stopped and looked at Bill. "I didn't mean to lecture you. I get in the habit of it, talking to children so much."

"That's okay. You sound like a real expert," Bill said, smiling for the first time that day, though stiffly. "Who cut up all that wood we burnt last night?"

"I did." She met his skeptical look; then took a step back, raised the ax, and made a neat deep gash in the end of the log.

"Not bad."

"Thanks. I enjoy it." Anna fitted a metal wedge into the split. "Where's that sledgehammer? Ah." She struck lightly to release the ax; then harder, driving the wedge down into the big log. "It's best when you're angry with someone or something. When I get really riled up, I like to come here and take it out on my woodpile. I name the logs after my enemies."

"Enemies?" Bill began to drag another log over. "Do you have enemies?"

"Lots of enemies." Anna punctuated her words with blows. "Well, some. Enough." The log fell apart. "Now, this one—" She stood a fat, knobby log on end. "This is Mrs. Norman Wright. You know **Midge Wright**?"

"Never met her."

"You're lucky." Anna grasped the ax again. "I hope you'll never have to." She started to raise the ax, then lowered it. "No, I take that back. If you come onto the

Eastwind board you'll have to meet her sometime."

"Come onto your board?"

Anna nodded.

"I haven't been invited to be on any board." Bill's face, expressionless at the best of times, was blank, resistant.

"Oh, hell. Well, never mind." Anna grinned. "Larry Arnold was supposed to ask you this week."

"Oh, yeah? Honey said he called, but I've been so darn busy— I thought he just wanted to fix up a golf game."

Anna squinted against the sun, regarding Bill with her sea-blue eyes. "You were proposed at the last meeting," she said without animation. "Almost everybody wanted you."

"Oh, really?" Bill smiled briefly.

"We've got to find someone who knows something about planning a budget and running an organization but is still a liberal. There's so many parents like Midge Wright, who say they're all for progressive education; but when it comes down to it they object to every new idea because it might cost too much, or it hasn't been tested yet somewhere else."

"Yeah," Bill said noncommittally.

"We have a lot like that. Midge is just the noisiest. And then there's all the ones who want to turn Eastwind into Rye Country Day, only with lower tuition." Anna smiled. "They keep trying to persuade me to have dancing classes, and build a tennis court, and arrange for riding lessons over at that stable in Mamaroneck. All at an extra charge, of course, for children whose parents can afford it. The ones who can't can watch the others riding and dancing and playing tennis," she added with some indignation.

"I see what you mean," Bill said. "But I'm so loaded with work right now; I really don't think—"

"If you won't come on the board, they'll probably ask Ben Trager instead."

"Trager? Yeah, I heard him talking at your last parents' meeting," Bill said with ill-concealed contempt. "I forget about what."

"He's interested in reviewing our financial situation."

"Aw, come on. He can just about count to twenty if he takes his shoes off. You can't put that booby on the East-wind board."

"We don't want to." Anna smiled, shrugged. "But he's been awfully persistent; always offering to help, and he's given us all that expensive athletic equipment that we didn't need."

"I'm very busy now," Bill said again. "I'll have to think about it."

"Yes, do." She gave him the look of a woman used to, indeed hardened against, refusals, and stooped to retrieve the ax.

"Here, let me have that." Disregarding Anna's protests, Bill seized the handle from her. "Stand back," he ordered. He rolled up the sleeves of his shirt, spat on his large pale freckled hands, and split Mrs. Norman Wright clean down the middle, exposing the raw corrugated yellow wood.

"Nice work," Anna said, giving him, for the first time, a glance of unqualified approval.

"Enemies," Bill repeated to himself, then laughed loudly and suddenly. "Yeah. I get the point. Let's have another."

Anna upended a smaller log. He took a step back and looked at it. "Yeah . . ." He murmured a name. "Guy in the commissioner's office," he explained. "Mean little reactionary bastard, belongs to the American Legion. Okay."

Bill struck this time with an excessive violence that not only split the wood but buried the blade of the ax in trodden earth. "Take it easy," he told himself. "Hm. That fat receptionist in Ed's office— No, hell, she's probably just got sluggish bowels. Benito Mussolini . . ."

"Father Coughlin . . ."

"Martin Dies . . ."

"That's grand," Anna said, stacking the last of the split logs. "Thank you." She looked at Bill, who was breathing a little hard. "Well, you probably want to get back to your report now. But maybe sometime later you could help me saw up the rest of that dead apple tree."

"Let's do it now, if you've got time. It's good exercise."

"Fine. Wait, I want to move this thing into the shade. It's getting hot." Anna dragged the old sawhorse across the grass. "Now, if we could hoist up one end of that big branch there."

"Sure." Bill, breathing more easily now, helped her raise the branch and wedge it between the arms of the sawhorse. "No. Hold on! This way more."

Anna shifted the branch as instructed, but with the delayed response and slightly sour smile of someone neither accustomed to nor fond of taking orders.

"Okay. Give me the saw now."

Again Anna hesitated; she frowned and seemed about to speak sharply, but merely said "It's faster with two people," and passed him the other end of her antique wood saw, which was about a yard long and shaped like a barred gate. "All right," she added, taking up position.

Instantly there was a struggle as to who should set the rhythm; both Anna and Bill pulled back on the saw; then both pushed, causing its steel teeth to rasp on the rough bark.

"Goddamn it," he said under his breath.

"Let's start again." Anna laughed briefly. "No, wait a moment . . Oh, hell. The trouble with us is we're both used to being in charge. We'd better try counting."

"Okay. One, two. Right?"

Anna laughed, then nodded.

"One, two," she repeated. A thin spray of sawdust fell from the log.

"That's it." Bill grinned. "One, two."

"Now that I know we can work together, I really hope you'll decide to come on the board," Anna said presently, deadpan.

Bill gave her a look, then laughed. "Thanks.... Whoops. One, two. I'd like to help Eastwind out, if I had the time. It's a fine school, from what I hear."

"Thank you." Anna smiled unguardedly. "Of course, there's lots of problems still. And we're so small."

"That's no disadvantage. Hell, I wish I was in charge of some reasonable-sized organization that was on its way up, instead of spending my whole damned life looking after one sick elephant or another, fighting the city bureaucrats and the state regulations and the inspectors from Washington. And half my own staff."

"Yes; but if you're helping people who really need—"

"A few, maybe. For every case we help there's a dozen we can't do anything for, and maybe another dozen we never even hear of."

"Still. It's serious work. Even when Eastwind's doing well I feel ashamed of myself sometimes. I think, what right have I got to stay in Westchester County running a school for privileged middle-class children, taking them on trips to see dinosaurs and cookie factories, when there's children in this country who can't read and don't even have enough to eat."

"Yeah, well—" Bill paused awkwardly, searching for something consoling to say. "You got to do what you can," he mumbled.

"Of course that's only sometimes," Anna said. "Other times I look out of my window at recess and tell myself that some day, maybe after I'm dead, one of the kids I see playing out there is going to change the world, because of what they learnt at Eastwind." She laughed and began to saw again.

"Sure. Why not? One, two." He pulled the saw back. "It's a good school. Done a lot for Mary Ann."

"That's nice to hear."

"She's been much happier this year." Bill spoke in rhythm as he sawed, each stroke and phrase of equal length. "Last year when she was in public school, she came home almost every day, complaining about something, throwing temper tantrums, upsetting Honey and our maid."

"That's hard."

"Yeah; it was kind of tough, living with two nervous females." Bill gave a sideways wrench to the saw, then corrected it.

"I wouldn't call Mary Ann nervous," Anna protested. "Sensitive, maybe. Imaginative."

"I didn't mean her. Mary Ann isn't nervous." Bill pulled the saw through the last splinters of bark and set it down. "She's going to grow up to be a good strong woman, like my mother.

"She's a real pioneer type, my mother," he added, with a sigh that seemed to belong to this statement rather than to the effort he and Anna were making to drag the branch along the sawhorse. "She'd just love this place of yours. There." He stood back; Anna passed him the other end of the saw.

"One, two."

For several minutes they worked in companionable silence, cutting through the dry, dense white apple wood.

"The thing about Honey . . ." Bill said. "She's not nervous, exactly. She hasn't got a complex or anything like that. But she's a Southern girl; and you know Southerners are brought up different from us, at least the women. It's a kind of foreign culture, really."

"You may be right."

"Southern girls, well, you have to admit they're way out ahead of most other women in America for charm, and looks, and pretty ways—" Bill glanced at Anna, who was sawing steadily with an expression which, while attentive and sympathetic, did not quite admit this. "In general, I mean. On the average. But they're sheltered from the world all their lives, and waited on. They aren't educated to stand any kind of trouble or frustration. When they see something pretty they want it the way a child would, and they genuinely don't understand why they can't have what they want. And when things go wrong they just—" Bill broke off, drawing the saw back, so that its shrill rasp seemed to complete the sentence.

"Mm-hum." Another log fell to the grass; Anna pushed it aside with her shoe.

"That's one reason I'm glad Mary Ann's at Eastwind; it relieves a big potential source of trouble.... And another thing, I think it's been good for Honey to meet some intelligent women, educated women, like, well like you and Celia Zimmern. Most of her friends are pretty empty-headed."

"Oh?"

"You remember that Bitsy McCarty who came to our picnic last month?"

"The one who ate the ant and couldn't get over it?"

"Yeah. You saw the way she carried on about that. And then when it began to rain a little, she wouldn't even get out of the car."

"I missed that." Anna laughed.

"Now, Honey wouldn't have acted that way. She's got better manners, for one thing. Sorry. One, two . . . And she's a lot smarter than Bitsy. But she's always having her over to our house, and her stuffed-shirt husband. Even though she knows they drive me round the bend, and she doesn't like Ken any better than I do. Or so she says. Only he's always there, for some reason, drinking my gin and boasting about the latest dumb expensive thing they've bought that we can't afford, and telling me that Roosevelt is really a Jew. Well, you were at the picnic, you heard him."

"Yes; I can see how having Mr. McCarty over too often might drive anyone round the bend."

"That's what I mean. But Honey keeps on inviting them. She likes Bitsy because they were at school together, and they have these schoolgirl jokes. She's like a little girl in some ways, younger than Mary Ann, even though she's forty. I mean thirty-seven." Bill stopped sawing and gave an awkward half-laugh. "Forget I said that, will you? You know how women are. They all like to fib a little bit about their ages."

Anna said nothing.

"Come on. I bet you do it too." He looked at her weather-roughened skin and wide thin mouth, free of any trace of lipstick. "Well, maybe you don't anymore."

"I haven't yet." Anna pulled the saw back. "And I'm fifty-two next month. Why should that be a secret? At any given time somebody in this world's got to be fifty-two. And everybody's got to be fifty-two sometime; if they live that long."

"Yeah," Bill said.

"It's not a social disease."

He guffawed. "Honey would say that's just what it is." He gave a final pull on the saw, blinked, and set it down. "There. That should do it. The rest's just kindling."

"Good." Anna glanced at Bill. His pale, partly bald head was damp and mottled red with heat; his white shirt stuck to his body in sweaty patches. "Thanks very much," she said. "Are you feeling all right?"

"Sure. Little dizzy."

"Let's go in. I'll get Dan and Lennie to stack the rest of these logs and fill the woodbox."

"I can do that." Bill lifted a stick, set it down. "Uh—what I said just now. I don't want you to think I'm complaining about my wife."

"No, of course not." She smiled warmly but a little ambiguously.

"I love Honey. Matter of fact, I'm crazy about her."

"I noticed that."

"Funny way of putting it," he added, setting his load down against the wall of the shed with a sigh.

"What?" Anna turned, her arms full of twigs.

" 'Crazy about her.' Everybody says that; it's in all the popular songs. 'I'm just crazy over you,' or 'mad about you,' or whatever. Nobody thinks what it really means, which is that some woman is literally driving you out of your mind." He shook his heat-blotched face from side to side as if in demonstration.

"No." Anna looked full at him.

"Just poetic license, I guess." Bill laughed. "Okay; where do you want me to take that firewood?"

"**Come on,** girls, let's go!" Lolly's father calls, whurring the engine of his shiny red De Soto so it sounds as if it wants to go too and is panting like a horse to gallop away down the road. Mary Ann and Lolly run across the grass and scramble on the running board and into the back seat, and Honey gets into the front one, all out of breath and holding her hat on with one hand. The doors slam. Lolly's father whurrs the motor again for real, and they bounce out of the yard and swing round and off along the road with dust puffing up behind them just like in the advertisements for shiny new cars on the walls of Lolly's father's office in New York City.

"Hey, we made it!" he shouts, and he and Honey laugh.

"Why are we in such a big hurry?" Mary Ann asks, sliding forward on the red-leather seat. "What's going to happen?"

"We're not in a hurry," Lolly's father says, slowing down for the curve at the bottom of the hill and even more as the road straightens out again and Anna's house vanishes in dust and trees. He begins to sing, marking time by stamping on the gas pedal:

> *Ta-ra-ra Boom-de-ay,*
> *Ta-ra-ra Boom-de-ay.*

The De Soto jumps ahead in a funny way when he sings "Boom." Mary Ann once asked Bill if he could make The Franklin do that, but he said "Certainly not; it ruins the engine." Well maybe Mr. Zimmern might not care about his engine, Bill said when she asked why he did it all the time then; because he got a new automobile cheap every year from the company he wrote advertisements for, and some poor sap had to drive his used one. But it is fun anyhow.

> *Ta-ra-ra BOOM-de-ay.*

The De Soto is bouncing along the dirt road, and Lolly and Mary Ann are bouncing with it up and down on the wide back seat, singing and giggling, and in front Honey is giggling too, sort of as if they were all kids playing hooky running away from the grown-ups.

It is like this a lot of the time around Lolly's father. He is quite old really, older than Bill even, with deep creases by his eyes and under his big cowboy mustache, but he seems much younger. He tells silly jokes like Knock-knock who's there, and stories which weren't always funny, but you had to laugh anyhow because of the faces he made and because everyone else was laughing. If he feels like it he can turn somersaults and walk on his hands, and he can airplane swing you round and round by one hand and foot with the grass and flowers and Lolly's big house swirling past. Sometimes he plays funny tricks, like dressing up as a Wild West outlaw for Lolly's ninth birthday party with a red bandanna over his face and an old toy gun of Lennie's and a pillowcase sack over his shoulder rushing in at the end of the party shouting "This is a stickup!" and then he opened the pillowcase and gave everybody gum and candy.

He took Lolly and Mary Ann to the circus in Madison Square Garden, which wasn't square or a garden, and bought them Mickey Mouse balloons with balloon ears, and pink spun cotton candy that everybody else said was bad for your tummy but he ate some of it himself. Afterwards they all went to his office, which was very very different from Bill's office. It was on the other side of New York City in a tall new building with four elevators like shiny silver closets, and they went up so fast her ears hurt. The front room of Mr. Zimmern's office was more like a hotel lobby with rugs and sofas and rubbery-looking plants and great big colored advertisement pictures on all the walls. Behind it were a lot of hallways with telephones ringing and doors opening and people running in and out, and the secretaries looked like movie stars, only they had different voices from movie stars. There were free samples of things Lolly's father's office advertised, not cars of course but smaller things like soap and gum and talcum powder and yummy toy packages of cereal.

Bill said once that writing advertisements was no job for a self-respecting grown man. Self-respect meant treating yourself like you would treat important people you didn't know very well, for instance mayors and kings and presidents. Respectfully. It wasn't all that much fun, but it made you feel important.

They have turned onto a real road now, with a white line painted down its middle. Lolly's father steps on the gas, and pretty soon the De Soto is going faster and faster: forty miles an hour; forty-five miles an hour.

"Here come the Burma-Shave signs!" Lolly calls, and Mary Ann sees them too, white on red growing out of the hay one behind the other. As the car swooshes past, Lolly and her father begin to chant, and she joins in:

NO LADY LIKES
TO DANCE AND DINE
INVITED BY
A PORCUPINE
BURMA-SHAVE!

"That's the way," Mr. Zimmern says, laughing. "Great advertising idea, those signs, hm?"

"Bill says," (Honey is giggling) "Bill says they just make people mad, 'cause they spoil the scenery."

"Aw, what does he know about it?" Lolly's father laughs again. "He couldn't sell ice water in hell."

Mary Ann imagines Bill trying to sell ice water in hell (which doesn't exist), with a big tin bucket and a dipper and a lot of little red devils with tails running around not paying any attention to him. But he wouldn't do that anyhow, he would just give it away.

The pointer on the speedometer moves up: fifty miles an hour, fifty-five—

"Dan, slow down!" Honey shouts. "For goodness' sakes!" But he doesn't slow down and you can tell from the way she is laughing and gasping that she doesn't really want him to.

"Just opening her out a little," he shouts. "Just want to see what she can do."

Honey laughs even more. She likes going fast. And so does the De Soto; she doesn't cough at all, even when it's uphill. Probably she has extra horsepowers in her engine, the kind Bill said were completely unnecessary. It was ridiculous the way automobiles were being designed now, he said. An automobile should be a reliable machine, cheap and easy to repair and able to get you where you want to go, and that's enough. Everything else like the De Soto's bouncy red-leather lap and chrome trimming is just showing off. What is the point of manufacturing an engine that can exceed the speed limit?

But you can tell that Lolly's father loves exceeding the speed limit, and so does the De Soto. Probably she knows she won't belong to him for very long, and wants to have a good time before the poor sap gets her.

> *Oh my darling,*
> *Oh my darling,*
> *Oh my darling Clementine,*

Lolly's father has started singing again, one of his favorites, and Honey joins in:

> She is lost and gone forever,
> Dreadful sorry, Clementine.

It is a funny kind of song: the words are sad but the tune is happy and sort of who cares; maybe the way it would be after the De Soto was lost and gone forever. Maybe her name is Clementine, and that's why Lolly's father always sings it.

> How I missed her, how I missed her,
> How I missed my Clementine,

He bounces the gas pedal again, making the car sing too, and then everybody, they can't help it, Honey, and Lolly, and Mary Ann:

> Till I kissed her little sister,
> And forgot my Clementine.

It would be fun if it was like this always, she thinks. Roaring along the road singing and laughing and who cares and the sun and wind blowing through the car like a warm hurricane.

Lolly's father slows down as they come into the village. He pulls up by the porch of the store and gets out and runs around to open the other door for Honey.

"Here you are, ma'am," he says, bowing. "Welcome to Saks Fifth Avenue." Mary Ann giggles, because the store is only a sort of white wooden shed with two red Esso gas pumps in front of it and tin ads for chicken feed and Drink Coca-Cola nailed to the wall.

It is dark inside and smells of spices, and pickles from a big wet barrel by the door. When her eyes start to work right again she can see around her every kind of store in the world, all jumbled up together. On the floor is a row of burlap bags full of oats and rice and dried beans, and sacks of flour stacked up, and a wire stand of newspapers and another of the *Saturday Evening Post.* Higher up are shelves of canned peaches and chicken-noodle soup and floor wax and milk of magnesia and ink and soapflakes. On the other side are bins of nails and screws, and hammers and saws, and balls of brown and white and green string, and rolls of screening and linoleum and brown paper and . . .

"Let's see that list," Lolly's father says, and he and Honey start walking toward the back of the store where a stringy old man in overalls and a cap is sitting. "Howdy, pardner," he says in his Western voice. "We've come to clean out your store."

"Okay by me," the old man says in an ordinary voice not smiling or even hardly moving his face at all, just making a little slit in it for the words to come out.

"Ready?"

The old man gets up slowly out of his rocking chair.

"Okay. Here we go. Two pounds of brown sugar. . . . One dozen oranges . . ." Mr. Zimmern goes on reading the list while the man takes things off shelves and out of bins. "And have you got any fireworks? We want to really set this town on fire tonight," he says, and he and Honey laugh some more.

The old man doesn't laugh or even smile, just points to a big cardboard carton on the floor. It is full of strings of little red firecrackers like birthday candles, and bigger red-and-white striped ones, and fizzy snakes and bundles of thin black sparklers and big fat red rockets and Roman candles with pictures of explosions on them.

"Staying up to the Judge's place with Miss Anna, eh?" he says while they are all deciding about the fireworks. Mr. Zimmern looks up and says "Yes." And Honey giggles and says "How ever did you know?"

The old man goes behind the counter to get some paper bags and then he says "I just figured it."

This counter, which is in the darkest part of the mixed-up store, is low and wide and made of old smooth wood and on it are big round glass jars of candy. Looped-up licorice like black spaghetti, and red spice drops, and sticky yellow sourballs, and pale pink and cream and white heart-shaped mints with mottoes printed on them, and a rack of all different kinds of candy bars including Mary Ann's very favorite kind, only she's already spent all this week's allowance.

"Can I have a nickel for a Forever Yours?" she asks Honey, not that there is much chance of it. Most of the time it was no use asking for anything in stores. Honey would just say No, or not even answer, like now. And it was worse than no use asking again, or looking sad, or saying how awfully hungry you were, because that always got her very mad.

Honey hates sniffling and what she calls a Long Face "Now don't you pull a Long Face," she says to Mary Ann sometimes. "Don't you put on that Pore Little Old Orphan Annie act for me," she says, for instance last month when Mary Ann didn't feel like giving any of her toys or books away to the White Elephant Sale for Eastwind School. "You've got more old books in here than you know what to do with." She did too know what to do with them, Mary Ann said. Anyhow White Elephants were supposed to be ugly things that people didn't want anymore and all her toys and books were perfectly good Gray Elephants and if they were old it wasn't their fault.

Behind the counter and the stringy man there are shelves with rolls of cloth and piles of folded shirts and underwear and overalls and men's hats. Nothing interesting, except for a big rubber ball hanging up, colored red and blue in sections like an orange.

"Hey, Lolly, come over here," Mary Ann calls.

Lolly can usually get anything she wants in a store just by asking for it, except candy and stuff; but mostly it doesn't come into her mind to ask for anything. Her mother won't buy her candy because she is afraid of cavities; she knows that if you tell Lolly she has to go to the dentist she will hide in her closet and cry, even though he is a nice man who keeps goldfish in his office.

"Look at that blow-up ball," Mary Ann says. "Don't you just wish we had that? . . . If your father bought that ball for you we could play catch."

But Lolly doesn't answer. She never wants to play catch much anyhow. She has lots more toys than Mary Ann has, but she practically never uses them except for her paints and crayons and the big dollhouse. Probably her mother could go into her room and take most of her toys away and she wouldn't even notice.

A lot of the time when she is home Lolly doesn't do much of anything. She lives in a big house with trees all around it way out in the country where there are no sidewalks to roller skate on or play hopscotch and no neighbors next door or across the street and no other kids. When her father isn't there, which is mostly, it is very very too quiet really. There are a lot of big rooms full of silence and furniture, and the Zimmerns' maid Corinne doesn't sing or shout "Praise Jesus!" or have friends visiting in the kitchen like Precious Joy. Lolly's mother doesn't ask ladies to tea, or talk and laugh on the telephone every day like Honey. She and Lolly and Corinne just sort of drifted through the house as if they were walking in their sleep, and it was never any special time of day, and sometimes they drifted outside into the big garden.

Lolly's mother's name is Celia, but Lolly's father calls her Silly. She isn't silly exactly, but she isn't like a real grown-up either. She is scared of things most grown-ups aren't, like spiders and the dark; and when she plays easy games like Lotto and Snakes-and-Ladders with Lolly and Mary Ann she doesn't get tired of them. And she doesn't always notice when they do things they aren't supposed to —for instance climbing out the bathroom window onto the roof of the garage, or eating fruit from the silver bowl in the middle of the long dark shiny dining-room table—even when she is looking straight at them.

Mostly she sits in the corner of the big white squashy sofa in the sitting room looking out into the woods at nothing; or else reading grown-up books from the library, or sometimes children's ones from when she was a little girl, the kind that are full of long words and keep telling you how to be good. Other times she lies down in her bedroom with the door shut trying to sleep because she couldn't the night before, and they have to be specially quiet.

Mary Ann follows Lolly along the counter. At the end behind a rack of seed-packets there is a kind of humming noise that turns out to be a freezer with yummy colored pictures of ice cream pasted on the side. Well, it's worth trying.

"Hey, they've got ice cream! Can I have a Dixie Cup?"

"No," Honey says without even turning round, and she goes on laughing at something Lolly's father is saying.

"Aw come on. Can't I just have a popsicle then? I'm hungry."

"Stop nagging at me," Honey says. "Ah don't want you to ruin your lunch." But she says it in a sort of lost silly way.

"Please, Mommy. Please!"

"What's the trouble?" Lolly's father says.

"We want some ice cream."

"Sure, why not? What kind? . . . Two Dixie Cups for the ladies, please."

"Oh Dan, before lunch, you shouldn't." Honey giggles and pulls his arm, but he goes on holding out the dime, and the skinny man takes it and opens the freezer. White cold steam comes out and two Dixie Cups covered with snow, and the man puts them on the counter along with the flat little wooden spoons in their envelopes of waxed paper. "Well, take them outside then," Honey says.

It is so bright and sudden on the porch that Mary Ann and Lolly have to squinch up their eyes, and when they try to sit on the steps the hot gray paint burns the underneaths of their legs.

"Come on," Mary Ann says and they move around to the side part of the porch where it is shady and sit on the edge under the railing, swinging their legs. Mary Ann pulls off the top of her Dixie Cup by the cardboard tab, and licks the circle of paper on the other side. Then she peels it away to see what movie actor's face will be underneath, printed blurry blue and surrounded by blue stars.

"Who'd you get?" she asks Lolly.

"Tom Mix."

"I'll trade you for Myrna Loy."

Lolly shakes her head. "I don't like Myrna Loy," she says. "She has a sly smile." She finishes licking Tom Mix clean and puts him away in the pocket of her dress.

Mary Ann looks at Myrna Loy. What Lolly said is true, but she might as well keep her anyhow to trade at school. She pushes the wooden spoon out of its paper and begins on the vanilla half of her dixie cup so as to save the chocolate. It is cold and sweet and creamy with ice crystals frozen into it, and sugar to make cavities, but Lolly's father wouldn't think of something like that.

One reason Lolly can always get things in stores is that her father earns more money than Bill does, even though he isn't the boss of his own office and doesn't do anything but make up advertisements. Mary Ann asked Bill about this once and he explained that it was because America was organized wrong. It was organized in the Capitalist System, which meant that the people who ran the country wanted to sell things much more than they wanted to help the poor.

Years ago some very rich people grabbed everything in America, and now they own most of the land and all the factories and other people have to work for them while they sit around and collect all the extra money. Really there ought not to be any extra money; things in stores shouldn't sell for more than it costs to make them, but they do, because of another part of the Capitalist System called Supply and Demand. The way this works is, the fewer things there are to go around the more people want them and the more expensive they are. That's why mean farmers burn wheat and pour milk away, so what is left will cost more.

The rich grabby people fixed the Supply that way, and then they tried to fix the Demand too, by getting everyone to want things more, especially things they didn't need in the first place like chewing gum and De Sotos. So they got Lolly's father to write advertisements and convince people to want a De Soto, and if he was good at it the grabby people who make De Sotos would pay him lots of money.

It wasn't that way everywhere in the world, Bill said. For instance in Russia everything belonged to the government and was shared out fairly, and they wouldn't ever have a Depression. Well, Mary Ann asked, why didn't we go and live in Russia then? Because we weren't Russians, Bill said. Our job was to stay here and work to make our own country better, and when she grew up Mary Ann could help. Anyhow, he said, they weren't doing so badly. Right now they were richer than most people in America, and Mary Ann had as much of everything as was good for her. Which must mean that Lolly has more than is good for her.

Not that she ever gets much fun out of it, Mary Ann thinks, looking at Lolly who is stirring her ice cream slow and dreamy into a whirlpool shape with the vanilla and chocolate all smudged together so you can't really taste either of them.

The screen door twangs open and then bangs back. "Where am Ah?" Honey cries. "Ah can't see a thing." She is blinking and giggling and sort of leaning on Lolly's father, who is carrying a big paper bag of groceries and laughing too.

"Neither can I," he says. "Whoops!" He bumps them into a post sort of accidentally on purpose. "Sorry."

"Where's the girls? . . . Oh, there you are. Come and get into the car, ducky, we're going."

"Steps here. Careful!" Mr. Zimmern says, and he and Honey go down the only three steps as if they were much more, blinking and holding onto each other and laughing as if they were drunk, but of course they couldn't be.

Mary Ann and Lolly follow them. Out in the sun it is so hot now her sandals stick to the tar, all soft dull black rubber except where a bubble has popped and the tar shows its sticky licorice insides.

"Nice day," Lolly's father says as Clementine turns off the highway onto the dirt road. "Nice day for a little roll in the woods, I mean stroll in the woods."

"Dan, for heaven's sake!" Honey squeaks.

"Aw, they aren't paying any attention. Lolly never listens to anything."

"Well, Mary Ann surely does," Honey says.

"So what'd I say?" Lolly's father asks in a surprised voice. Honey only giggles. Slowing Clementine, he looks back over the seat "What'd I say, Mary Ann?"

"You said it was a nice day for a walk in the woods," Mary Ann tells him, thinking how dumb grown-ups are.

"Right you are, sweetie. And it's just about time for one now." He stops Clementine by the side of the dirt road "You see that path, kiddies? It goes across the field there, and through those trees, and straight up to Anna's house. Comes out just across from her barn. You can't miss it."

"So you can get out here," Honey says, smiling, "and walk back."

"No thanks," Mary Ann says.

"Aw, go on. It'll be fun." Lolly's father reaches over the seat and opens the back door.

"It will not be fun. It's too hot, and it's too far."

"It's not that far, for heaven's sake," says Honey, who has stopped smiling.

"It is too."

"Anyhow, you need some exercise, both of you," Mr. Zimmern says. "You've been lazing around the place ever since we got here."

"We have not," Mary Ann says. "You've been lazing around much more than us."

"Mary Ann." Honey's voice gets real slow and loud. "Ah want both you girls to get out of this car, right this minute."

"Why do we have to? It's not fair. We never said we wanted to take a walk. Mr. Zimmern said that. We don't have to go on a long stupid hot walk just because Mr. Zimmern feels like it!" she shrieks in the special high voice that always makes her mother put her hands over her ears.

"You're a very selfish, aggravating little girl!" Honey shouts with her hands over her ears.

"And you're a very selfish aggravating old mother!" Mary Ann shouts back.

"Don't you get smart with me," Honey says, and she rises up out of the seat and leans over as if she was going to slap Mary Ann, but then she stops maybe because other people are watching and she knows perfectly well she isn't being fair. Probably she couldn't have reached Mary Ann to slap her anyhow, the back seat is so wide.

"Ah guess we'd better forget it, Dan," she says, in her lazy company voice again, all soft and drawly, and she sits back down.

"Not on your life," Lolly's father says, smiling at her and then turning the same smile toward Mary Ann. "Why are you making so much fuss? It's a great day for a walk. Lolly wants to go for a walk, don't you, Princess?"

Lolly, who has already got out of the De Soto, because she practically always does whatever she is told, doesn't look up at her father. But she shakes her head so hard her dark curls flap.

"No? Why not?"

"The woods," she says in a voice you can hardly hear.

"Woods? What about the woods?"

"Scary," Lolly whispers.

"There's nothing scary about these woods, Princess," her father says, smiling under his cowboy mustache. "They're beautiful and shady and cool." Lolly just stands in the grass and stares at him. Her mouth is open and her eyes look wet and empty.

"Don't make her go, Dan," Honey says. 'She's really frightened."

"All right, Princess," Lolly's father says, laughing in an impatient but cheerful way. "You don't have to if you don't want to. Climb back in."

People have the wrong families, Mary Ann thinks, as Clementine purrs on up the dirt road. If she lived with Lolly's family they would never yell at her like Honey, or tell her to stop bothering them. Lolly's father would laugh all the time and tell jokes and everything would be lots more fun, and she could eat ice cream and candy before lunch, and have Lolly's Southern Colonial dollhouse to play with and Lolly's De Luxe Junior Microscope that she never used anyway except when Mary Ann came over.

And mean old Honey could be Lolly's mother. She wouldn't ever yell at her or slap her, because Lolly never did anything wrong or asked for anything or contradicted grown-ups or got her nice clothes dirty or was rude to company, mostly because she never said anything to company anyhow. And Bill would never get angry at her the way he was at Mary Ann after breakfast because she was making so damn much noise he couldn't do the important work he had brought in his briefcase. Lolly wouldn't make any damn noise, she would just creep around like a mouse they way she did at home. And Bill wouldn't have to be bothered explaining anything to her, because she never wanted to know anything. So there.

•   •   •

"Here we are," Lolly's father says, turning into Anna's yard beside the lilac bushes. "All right, girls, out you go." He opens Clementine's back door. "What are you doing this afternoon, baby?" he says to Honey.

"Ah don't know really," Honey says, sort of giggling. She never gets mad when people call her a baby the way Mary Ann or most anybody else would. "What are you doing?"

"Well, I thought I just might go for a walk," Lolly's father says. "Go on, kids. Run and tell Anna we've brought the groceries."

"**A**nna, I want to ask you something," Celia said as she stood by the kitchen stove, ladling hot water into a battered tin pitcher. "About Lennie . . ." Her voice faded.

"Yes."

"I'm afraid he's not having a very good time here . . . He didn't want to come, you know, but it was Dan's turn to have him, and . . . I thought, once he sees how nice it is . . ." As always when she was nervous, Celia began each sentence with a rush, then trailed off into inaudibility, like a shy child making a dash into a room and then retreating. "I just don't know what . . ."

Anna, used to this style of discourse, said nothing, but continued soaping the thick white ironstone plates one after the other and standing them in the dishrack.

"I do worry about him lately; we used to get on so well, but now . . . He's still friendly when we're alone, but other times he's so sulky, and hard to please, and mean, even . Dan says it's because he's spoiled . . . He says Lennie thinks the world ought to revolve around him, the way it does at home . . . In New York, I mean, with his mother."

"Is that so?" Anna said dryly. "The pot and the kettle."

"What?" Anna did not repeat her comment. "But I really wanted to ask you . . . Do you think it could be a psychological problem?" Celia carried the steaming pitcher to the sink. "I mean, do you think he's . . . disturbed? You must have known lots of boys his age, and I haven't ever really . . ."

"I don't think Lennie's any more disturbed than most fourteen-year-olds," Anna said, pouring a rush of rinse water over the soapy plates. "And you can see he's got a good mind. I'm sure he'll make something interesting of himself. He's not going to have an easy life, though."

"I suppose not." Celia sighed. "Dan expects so much of him, he's . . . unfair sometimes, and he doesn't realize how harsh he sounds when he's disappointed . . . Like just now at lunch. When Lennie said he'd left that delivery job because they didn't pay him what they'd promised . . . And of course I can't say anything."

"Why can't you say anything?"

"Well. Because it's none of my business. Lennie isn't my son." Celia began to refill the pitcher. "And then, well, you know, Lennie's not very fair to Dan either. Dan does so much for him—trips, and clothes, and expensive presents. And Lennie hardly says thank you, even though I do keep reminding him—"

"You keep reminding him?" Anna interrupted.

"Yes, I try . . . What do you mean?"

"You can talk to Lennie about Dan, but you can't talk to Dan about Lennie."

"Oh no, I wouldn't dare, I—" Celia stopped ladling out water. She stared into the simmering kettle, then blinked and refocused.

"I don't know," she said. "Perhaps you're right." She finished filling the pitcher and brought it to the sink again. "Tell me where there's a clean dish towel, Anna, and I'll start on those plates."

"Certainly not." Anna smiled. "It's a waste of time, drying dishes. If you rinse them with hot enough water, they dry themselves. I worked it out once, how much time you could save that way; it came to something like ten days a year. Now if you multiply that by the number of women in America, you'd get—God knows what." She laughed.

"I rather like drying dishes," Celia said. "It's kind of, you know, soothing."

Anna turned to look at her friend. A morning in the country had not warmed Celia's voice or her complexion, and faint lavender bruises of insomnia showed beneath her eyes. "Second drawer down on the right," she said, lowering another stack of plates into the dishpan.

"I'm always a little uneasy when Lennie's around," Celia admitted, unfolding a striped dish towel. "I keep worrying that something's going to go wrong; that there's going to be some awful scene . . . Because quite often there is." She gave a faint false laugh. "And essentially it's my fault."

"Really? How could it be your fault?" Anna asked, almost impatiently.

"Well." Celia dried a plate with a repetitive circular motion. "Because if it weren't for me, Lennie and Dan might still be living together, and then they might get on better "

"Or they might not," Anna said.

"Yes— Do you mean, might not get on better, or might not be living together?" Celia took another plate.

"Both."

"Yes, I suppose . . . I don't know. If I could have had more children, it might have been . . . Of course I know Dan's first wife is an impossible woman, that's one reason I feel so sorry for Lennie. But still, I can't help thinking . . . Suppose she loved him too? I mean, even impossible women can love someone."

"Oh, yes," Anna admitted.

"I'm sure she must have, because who could be married to Dan and not love him?" Celia smiled slightly, fondly. "And then, when she found out that he didn't love her . . . It's awful to imagine that." She shook her head. "If I knew Dan didn't love me, I'd—I'd go out like a candle." She smiled again, more wanly. "Or suppose she wasn't an impossible woman to start with, because if she had been, Dan wouldn't have married her, would he?"

Anna did not offer an opinion.

"He says she changed," Celia went on, continuing to dry the same plate monotonously. "And what I keep thinking is, suppose that was what changed her, finding out he didn't love her . . . You know he never did love Irma really," she added. "He only married her on a sort of impulse after he'd broken up with some other girl he cared more about."

"Really," Anna remarked in an oddly neutral voice, pausing with her strong browned arms up to the elbow in soapsuds. "He said that?"

"Yes. It's awful what people do sometimes, isn't it? The mistakes they make . . ." She sighed. "Did you know Irma back then?"

"What? Oh yes, a little," Anna answered almost distractedly.

"What was she really like?"

"Irma?" Anna stared out at the long red barn and the darkening fields behind it, as if looking back over fifteen years. "She wasn't such a bad sort. A little noisy and emotional. And jealous, of course—very jealous. But you know how people exaggerate each other's faults after they've split up. I expect Irma's not such a bad sort even now."

"I'm jealous," Celia said, as if to herself. "I love Dan so much, I can't bear it when he pays attention to other women. There was a girl who used to work at the agency —She's left now, thank goodness. She was always calling him up at the strangest times, to ask about some layout or something, and Dan would laugh and kid with her . . . I couldn't bear to hear it; I had to go and shut myself in another part of the house, though of course I knew it was harmless."

"Mm." Anna's murmur was not quite an assent.

"Or the way he put his arm round Honey today at lunch. I realize he was just being friendly; it didn't mean any more than if he'd been sitting next to you and put his arm round you. But she played up to him so, as if there were some private joke between them . . . I felt all trembly and frightened, Anna; I could hardly eat . . . Of course I know that's weak of me." She gave a little laugh. "Honey's so lightheaded, I'm sure she jokes and flirts that way with everyone; and besides she and Dan hardly know each other. But I love Dan so much, I couldn't bear it if they really had some secret, even a silly one." Celia noticed that she was drying a dry plate and added it to the pile on the counter. "I don't ever want to have any secrets from Dan, or for him to have any from me." She turned away to set the stack of plates on their shelf in the cupboard and shut the door on them, thus missing the involuntary tensing of Anna's features, as of a child suddenly accused of cheating. "That's what marriage means, I think."

"Maybe that's why I never got married," Anna said, after a marked pause. "Could you bring over some more hot water, please?"

"Oh, of course." Celia returned to the stove and took up the dipper. "Sorry."

"There was a man I knew once who used to talk that way to me," Anna said presently, in a tone eased by the change of subject and also by the removal of Celia's immediate presence. "He was always quoting poetry, or what sounded like poetry, to me when I was in college. 'Marriage is the complete merging of two souls,' he used to tell me. 'I want to know everything about you: all your thoughts, all your dreams, all your secrets. I want you to give yourself to me completely.' "

"Oh, Anna." Celia gazed across the room at her friend, her face softening. "But you didn't ever marry him."

"Certainly not." Anna laid a heavy iron skillet on the drainboard and began scouring it with steel wool. "I can't imagine anything more terrible than being completely owned by some other person. Or owning them. That's what the Civil War was all about." She laughed.

"Oh, Anna," Celia said with another intonation—motherly, impatient. "That's just because you weren't in love. It's so different when you're in love."

"Maybe so," Anna said in the unmistakable manner of one who rejects a statement but wishes to be polite.

"If you'd ever really known . . . If you'd only met a man like . . . the right man . . ." Celia's voice trailed off again.

Scruff, scruff went the steel wool on the iron bottom of the pan, but Anna said nothing. She finished scouring the skillet and set it in the dishrack, then glanced toward Celia. "If there's still some hot water left—" she said.

"Yes, lots. Sorry." Celia finished filling the pitcher and brought it across the room. As she set it down beside Anna on the sink, their glances met through the steam, and both smiled, full of generous and affectionate pity for the other.

body else in the orchard now; and anyhow, so what if they did?

"This is a ship," Mary Ann calls down. "It's a big old sailing ship, and I'm up in the crow's-nest, looking out over the sea-green sea for other ships." She braces one foot against the trunk, which is smooth up here like a mast, shades her eyes, and leans away from the ship, feeling it bend and rock as the waves dash against it. "Come on!" She puts her foot up on another branch to make room for Lolly in the crow's nest, but it isn't strong enough and cracks with a noise like a BB gun. "Whoops! Don't come up any farther, Lolly, the rigging isn't strong enough." She looks down at Lolly's face, white among the apple leaves. "Why don't you climb that other tree, over there, and it can be another ship."

"I don't want to play just ships," Lolly says. 'I want it to be a castle."

"Okay. Yours can be a castle, on the seashore, and I'll be a ship sailing over the ocean to visit you."

"Okay." Lolly begins to climb down again. Through the green sails, Mary Ann watches her curly dark hair and yellow dress cross the grass.

"This is Princess Elinore's castle," Lolly calls out, putting her hand on the trunk of the other tree. "It's one of her extra vacation castles. Not the main one, because that's on a mountain in the middle of a forest surrounded by a howling desert." She pulls herself up into the tree. "This is a tall green castle on a rocky piece of beach that sticks out into the ocean. It's made of green marble studded with emeralds and it has a high wall and pointy towers. At night the moon shines on the castle over the dark dark green sea, and mermaids swim up to sit on the rocks and comb their green hair, and little merbabies play in the foamy waves."

"Okay." Lolly might get lost sometimes, but when she

came back she could make up things better than anyone outside of books.

"Now I'm in my highest tower. I'm looking out over the ocean to see if a ship is coming from Princess Miranda's country. . . . I don't see it yet. I see lots of little fishing boats full of green and silver fish, and way out on the horizon there's a big gray whale, look, over there." The whale is the gray slate roof of Anna's house, spouting smoke-water from one chimney.

"Thar she blows!" Mary Ann cries, like Grandpa Hubbard on the beach in Maine.

"And I see white swooping beaky gulls, and now—"

"Shut up, it's my turn. I'm Princess Miranda up in the highest crow's-nest of my ship, looking out for land."

"That's not right," Lolly calls. "Princesses don't climb their ships themselves."

"They do so. Princess Miranda's sailors always ask her, I mean me, to go up to the highest crow's-nest and help the lookout sailor because I can see farther than any of them. I can see the whale, and the fishing boats, and now I see a big fish swimming along, I think it's a shark."

"Where?"

"Right down there, coming along fast by my ship. It's your father."

Lolly's father must have heard them, because he stops walking and looks around the orchard in every direction but up.

"Lolly? Is that you?" Princess Elinore and Princess Miranda giggle. "Oh, there you are! Hello, Princess." Lolly's father doesn't know about the game, of course, only sometimes he calls her that. If he does it while they are being Princess Elinore and Princess Miranda it counts as sort of magic. "Hello there, Mary Ann. Having a good time?" He always says this, or else sometimes he says, "Have a good time."

"Uh-huh."

"That's right." The shark swims off through the orchard, without telling them to please come right down or be careful not to fall or for heaven's sake don't get your clothes dirty again, the way Lolly's mother or Bill or Honey would have.

"My royal father the king goeth a-hunting," Princess Elinore says. "He hunteth the deer in the greenwood."

"I don't want him to hunt deer." Mary Ann hates anything being killed, even mice in mice traps, but especially deers, like Bambi's mother and the poor dead stags tied onto the fenders of automobiles in Maine at Thanksgiving time.

"All right. He's going hunting, but not to shoot anything really. He's just going to ride around in the greenwood and blow his horn, for fun. . . . Do you see any land yet?"

"I'm looking for it. No. Yes. Land Ahoy! Can you see my ship?"

"I can see a ship, but it's just a black speck on the far horizon. I have to get my silver telescope carved with dolphins." Lolly screws up her fists and looks through them. "Ship Ahoy! Lo, I can see it now. By my troth, it is the ship of my dearest friend, Princess Miranda, the—What's the name of your ship?"

"The, uh, Flying Horse."

"It's the Flying Horse! Lo, I can see its green silken sails and its golden ropes, and its decks full of sailors and ladies-in-waiting and people. It's coming nearer and nearer. I must fain descend into my royal kitchen and bid my royal cook prepare the feast. Did you save anything from lunch?"

'I've got an orange," Mary Ann says. "And some potato chips."

"I saved two Oreo cookies. I'm going down from my tower to meet your ship now, okay?"

"Okay." Princess Miranda, from the crow's-nest, directs her captain and sailors to bring the Flying Horse into harbor by a secret channel known only to her.

"Greetings and welcome, O Princess Miranda of the Larch Mountains!" Lolly calls from under her tree.

"Greetings and thank you, O Princess Elinore of the White Meadows," Mary Ann replies, jumping down and stepping stately onto the dock. "Let's make some gold and silver crowns for the feast. There's lots of gold and silver growing over in that field where we were this morning."

"There's some much nearer here, right along the road. Follow me to my royal treasury, dear Princess Miranda."

"Okay."

They climb the stone wall at the edge of the orchard, and there is a high sunny bank deep in long grass and so many daisies you can pick practically all you need for a crown just sitting in one place. Below the bank is the narrow dusty road that runs past Anna's house, with nothing to see on it except Mary Ann's father and mother going for a walk. As they get nearer you can see that they both have mean closed-up faces on, and Honey keeps looking over the wall into the orchard as if she were looking for Mary Ann, though Mary Ann hasn't done anything wrong lately that she can think of. But you never can tell. She stands up in the tall grass so her mother can see her, to get whatever it is over with. "Hi," she says.

"Oh, hello, chickie." Honey looks at Mary Ann in an ordinary uninterested way and keeps on going.

"Hello, girls," Bill says, and goes on after Honey.

"They're mad about something," Mary Ann tells Lolly,

but of course Lolly doesn't say anything. She is never interested in what people do or why they act funny, especially not grown-ups. And probably Honey and Bill are just mad at one of the dumb things grown-ups care about like money or what happens in newspapers and at school is called Current Events.

At the far end of Anna's orchard a long narrow hayfield thickly embroidered with field flowers rose toward the horizon. A cart-track led from the road up one side of the field to an old barn, gray and sagging, open to the warm summer wind.

The field and the barn were empty. Then Dan Zimmern pushed his way through the screen of branches at the edge of the orchard. Smiling slightly to himself, he halted to look at his watch, which showed five minutes past three. Then he climbed the overgrown stone wall with some grace and dexterity, beat his way through burdock and milkweed to the cart-track, and sauntered up to the barn.

"Hello?" He glanced into the shadowy, light-split interior, and finding himself alone, looked round, smiling again as he noted that the uphill and more sheltered end was heaped almost to the rafters with sweet-smelling new hay, and that a long wooden ladder rested conveniently against this hay.

Dan brushed the seeds and twigs from his sharply pressed tan trousers and bright red polo shirt. He checked his watch again: nine minutes past. Then he strolled outside, leant against the sunny side of the barn, and gazed downhill toward the road. He folded his arms across his chest and began to whistle idly:

The air was thick with the sounds and odors of summer. The gentlest of breezes ruffled the standing hay; midges and flies buzzed nearby, and a bird somewhere in the orchard squeaked rhythmically. Dan felt his hair; then he took out a pocket comb and ran it through the dark thick curls, subduing them to the currently fashionable formal wave. He checked the shape of his luxuriant mustache, stroking it with a slow, idle fondness, as if it were some expensive but familiar pet. Then he looked at his watch again, still smiling. Twelve minutes past.

A small cloud the shape of a one-legged chicken slid over the sun, dragging a chicken-shaped patch of shadow behind it. Dan watched this chicken cross the hayfield and vanish into the orchard, darkening the trees. He began to whistle again, more deliberately:

Hinky-dinky, parlez-vous.

Sixteen minutes past. The side of the barn, full in the afternoon sun, was too hot to lean against with comfort. Insects had begun to circle Dan, attracted by the dampness collecting on his forehead and neck and in his armpits, in spite of a recent application of antiperspirant cream. He retreated into the shade of the barn and stood just inside the entrance, folding his arms in such a position that he could both smoke and continually see the face of his wristwatch.

Twenty-two minutes past. Dan shifted his position, alternately stepping out into the sun where he could observe the whole length of the cart-track as it descended to the road, and retreating into the barn. "Making me wait, huh, baby?" he said aloud. He had ceased to whistle, and the expression on his face was no longer a smile.

Twenty-eight minutes past three. Inside the barn, Dan began to pace back and forth, stirring the chaff on the uneven floor. He slapped at a horsefly that had followed him there, and missed. He paced again and stopped, listening, scowling. Then, treading lightly, he approached the empty downhill end of the barn and peered through a gap left by a fallen plank.

Below the field, half-hidden by flowering brush, two figures were coming along the road: a man and a woman, talking and laughing. Though their faces could not be seen, Honey's characteristic high giggle sounded out through the summer air as clearly as a bird's call.

Dan watched Mr. and Mrs. Hubbard until they had passed by and continued out of sight down the dirt road. Then, swearing, he left the barn, descended the cart-track, and crashed his way back through the weeds and briars. He climbed the orchard wall with considerably less elegance than before, and disappeared between the apple trees.

MaryAnn sits beside Lolly in the grass and goes on with her braid of daisies. It is just like braiding hair once you get started, and she can do that since she was seven and a half without even looking. All you have to do that's different is put in another daisy every inch or so and keep going. She will be finished long before Lolly, who doesn't have any braids to practice on, and keeps stopping to pick other flowers for jewels in her crown: bachelor's button sapphires and Indian paintbrush rubies that aren't ruby-colored really, too orangey; or she stops to watch a line of red ants climbing a stem, or to pull the petals off one of her daisies for magic:

"One he loves me, two he loves me not, three he loves a little, four he loves a lot, five not at all. Six he comes, seven he tarries—" She stops because the daisy is finished.

"Who tarries?" Mary Ann asks.

"Nobody—anybody—I don't know." Lolly starts on another daisy. "One he loves . . . Six he comes, seven he tarries, eight he courts, and nine he marries." She smiles and rubs the egg-yellow velvet center of the daisy against her mouth.

"If it's nobody, why say it? Anyhow, it doesn't count if you do it twice," Mary Ann says. "Like wishing on stars. You can't say 'Star light, star bright, second star I see tonight.'"

"It's not nobody." Lolly begins braiding again.

"Who is it, then?"

"It's my prince. Princess Elinore's prince." Lolly looks down the road to where it sinks between two hills. "I'll tell you about him," she says, pushing the green stems of rubies and sapphires into her braid.

"Okay."

"He's going to come riding on a black horse to my castle from the far blue end of the world, and I'll know he is the only true one because nothing can stop him. He'll cross over the hot burning desert where everybody else who tried to get to the castle without being invited lies dead, all turned into sandy skeletons with their clothes blowing around in the burning wind. And he'll ride through the spooky dark forest and the ghost wolves and bears won't be able to hurt him, and he'll ride straight up the rocky icy mountain. And I'll see him coming and order the drawbridge to be let down over the bottomless chasm for him, and tell my royal trumpeters to blow their horns. And he'll ride in through the gate and get off his horse. And he'll put his arms around me and say, 'Lo, I have come at last, my only beloved Princess Elinore.' And we'll be married with a great feasting and party and live happily ever after."

"Mm." Lolly has told this story before, and it is always sort of the same, and sort of dull too because nothing much ever happens, except sometimes the prince has to fight the ghost wolves and bears but of course he always wins.

"Now I'll tell how it will be for Princess Miranda," she says. "I'll be all grown-up and very beautiful with long long dark red hair like Anna's. I'll live in my castle and hundreds of princes and kings and poor farmers' sons and rich businessmen and doctors and dentists and soldiers and sailors and baseball players will ride there from all over the world and sail in ships and fly in planes. When they come I'll make them do a lot of hard jobs for me and ask them riddles, and we'll have races and contests and make magic. And they'll help me go and fight armies and kill horrible giants and build towns in one day."

"And then you'll find out which one is the very bravest and handsomest and wisest and strongest and marry him," Lolly finishes.

"Maybe," Mary Ann says. "Maybe I won't marry any of them."

"Why not?" Lolly stops braiding.

"Maybe I just won't feel like it," Mary Ann says in a kind of mean don't-care voice. She gets tired of how Lolly is always going on in that dumb way about princes and beloveds.

"Everybody gets married," Lolly says. "If you want children, you have to."

"I know that, stupid." Princess Miranda is going to have four children, two of each kind. Their names will be

Theodora, Anna, Arthur, and Edward. Arthur and Anna are twins.

Mary Ann knows all about sex and babies; Honey told her. A man and a lady get married, and then they decide they want to have a baby. So the man takes his wee-wee thing and puts it inside a special hole in the lady's bottom and squirts a baby-seed up into her stomach, and it meets another baby-seed and they go pop together like popcorn and start to grow into a baby. She wouldn't like that, it would be dumb and sort of ucky. She's glad she doesn't have a silly little wee-wee thing stuck on her stomach, like a fat pink worm. Or like part of your private insides hanging out, the way poor Woozle's did after the truck hit him on Weaver Street.

Every time you wanted a baby you would have to do that dumb ucky thing. Suppose she was married to Theodore Ilgenfritz; the real one, not her bear, of course. Well, probably they would just do it, like going to the dentist. It didn't hurt, Honey said, except sometimes the first time, and then not very much or for very long. So they would only have to do it three times, and Edward and the twins would be easier.

Having babies used to hurt a lot in olden times, but it doesn't anymore because they give you gas. Honey didn't like it though because it made her all fat and swelled up for months and she couldn't wear her pretty dresses or go out dancing and no man looked at her twice. "Ah'm not going through all that again, thanks very much," she said once to Mrs. McCarty, which is why Mary Ann is an only child. But Mary Ann won't care beans about dresses or dancing or being looked at.

Lolly said Lennie told her that people did sex all the time because it was fun, even if they didn't want babies or weren't even married, but that probably wasn't true. Lennie was always teasing Lolly and picking on her and trying to fool her with lies that only a dope would believe anyhow.

Lolly has finished her crown now finally, and it is getting too hot by the road, so they climb back over the wall to have their feast in the shade of Princess Elinore's castle. They have roast chicken arranged out of sections of orange on a big dock leaf, and potato-chip french fries, and a four-layer devil's food cake for dessert.

"There comes your father again," Mary Ann says as Lolly is cutting the cake with a golden twig knife.

"Hi, kids," Lolly's father says, smiling down at them.

"Hail, O noble father," Lolly says.

"We're playing princesses," Mary Ann explains, so that Mr. Zimmern won't think they are crazy.

"And you're my father the king, and you've just returned from the royal hunt."

"Oh, yeah? That's nice," her father says.

"Only you didn't catch anything," Mary Ann tells him.

"Oh, yeah?" Mr. Zimmern asks again in a different way, and for some reason he gives her a funny look. "Well, have a good time," he says.

Evening. The sun had set, and the still air was heavy with a lustrous summer twilight which veiled outlines but intensified colors; the grass outside the kitchen windows and the dandelions that spangled it glowed like neon. The same thick light soaked through the screens of the open windows over Anna, Honey, and Celia, as they cleared up after supper. The women were alone in the house; everyone else had gone down across the road into the south field where Dan and Bill were setting up the fireworks.

"—So she said to me, 'Why should Ah divorce him?' " Honey continued the story she was telling. " 'Ah've got him just where Ah want him.' Those dry? Ah'll take them." She stood on tiptoe and put a stack of plates away in the cupboard—with some difficulty, since she was a good six inches shorter than Anna and about forty pounds lighter. "And the very next day she went into Bonwit Teller and charged herself a Persian lamb coat exactly like the one he sent that girl. Well, that was kind of a mistake, Ah think; it wasn't her style, made her look sort of chubby. If it'd been me, Ah would have got one of those pretty new silver foxes. Or maybe—What was that?" Honey turned toward a noise in the front hall already noted by Anna and Celia; the screen door opening and slamming, loud overlapping voices.

"This way," Dan cried, dragging his son with him into the kitchen. "Over here!"

Lennie, his face sour with fright and pain, allowed himself to be pulled toward the kitchen table by one arm. He held the other out stiffly before him, with the blackened remains of a plaid shirt-sleeve dangling from it.

"Oh, Dan!" Celia wailed, clutching a dish towel to her chest. "What is it?"

"Burnt himself with a firecracker. All right, pal, this way! Get out of the light, damn it, Celia, so we can see," he added, his voice still loud and shaky; then, a little more steadily, "Okay; hold still. Hey, it doesn't look too bad. What do you think?"

Anna bent over the table, where a tall kerosene lamp had begun to color the twilight. "No; it's not serious. He'll have a blister. But it must have burnt his shirt mostly."

"Thank God," Dan exhaled. "You're going to be okay,

kid." He grinned and squeezed his son's narrow shoulders. "But you sure gave us a hell of a scare."

"It was his fault." Lennie, who had not previously spoken, opened his mouth to announce this to Celia, then instantly shut it, choking a sob.

"Aw, come on. You know that's not true," Dan said easily. "I told you five times at least to leave our stuff alone, but you—"

"I didn't touch your darn stuff!" Lennie shouted, his voice breaking from alto to baritone. "I was testing one of my own crackers. Nothing would have happened if you hadn't tried to grab it away from me."

"I said not to light any fireworks, Lennie."

"I didn't light any of your stupid damn fireworks!" Lennie was half sobbing. "I was testing one of my own, that I bought with my own money."

"Don't swear at me, okay?" his father said, his tone cooling rapidly.

"Aw, go to hell," Lennie gulped.

Dan raised his arm, then let it fall, unwilling to strike an injured and smaller person. "Dan, really, Lennie's hurt—" Celia cried simultaneously.

"Goddamn it, I know that!"

His wife shrank. She looked up, not quite meeting his eyes, then lowered her glance to the table again. There was an uneasy, electrical pause.

"We'd better wash off that arm and put on a bandage, ' Anna said. "Celia, I think the first-aid box is in the dining-room cupboard, on the top shelf. And you'll need some water." She took a pan from a shelf and looked round. "Dan? Could you hold this for me?"

"Sure thing."

Anna turned to the sink and began to work the cast-iron handle of the pump. It creaked, coughed, gargled, and at last spat out a jet of cold water.

"Fireworks sure are the dickens," Honey said in a forced conversational tone. "Ah remember one Independence Day celebration down home they blew up a henhouse and five chickens."

"Is that so?" Dan, registering Honey's presence for the first time, gave her a quick grateful, slightly conspiratorial smile. "Okay, here you are, kid," he said to Lennie. "Just put your arm—"

"I can do it myself," Lennie said sourly. He jerked the pan nearer along the table, splashing water. "Just leave me alone, okay?"

"All right." Dan spoke casually; his face, however, was that of someone who has just been slapped. "But I don't want you near those fireworks again tonight. Do you hear me?"

"You said I could let off one of the Roman candles."

"Well, I've changed my mind. For God's sake; you could have killed yourself, you know that?"

"You said—Ow! That hurt," Lennie exclaimed, as Celia, dipping a wad of cotton in the water, began to wipe the soot from his arm.

"I'm sorry," she said.

"I'm going to light my own crackers anyway, that I bought myself, and you can't stop me," Lennie said, gulping.

"You are not." Dan had lost his temper again. "You're not old enough to be trusted with fireworks. You can sit up on the hill and watch, and that's all."

"I won't sit up on the hill with the stupid little girls. I don't want to see your dumb fireworks anyhow." Lennie and his father, so similar in feature, looked at each other with almost identical expressions of rage and hurt; then Dan smoothed his out.

"That's okay by me," he said.

"And you'd better not light any of my crackers," Lennie wrenched his arm away from Celia, making the hand into a fist. "You just better not."

Dan began to reply, then stopped. He stood back. "Well, girls," he said, forcing a smile. "It looks about dark enough out." His glance moved toward the window, where the sky had now faded into a smoky lavender, then back toward the three women, lingering last on Honey. "If Bill's ready we can start the show as soon as you-all get yourselves out there." He mimicked her accent.

"Why don't you go ahead?" Celia said. "We won't be long."

The screen door squeaked, then slammed. Celia pulled Lennie's arm gently back toward her and continued to wash it, soothing him meanwhile with a soft monotonous clucking. "Here now. Hold still, dear. That's right. Just a second more . . ." Slowly his public scowl relaxed, easing into a private smile.

"There." She pushed the basin away and began to pat Lennie's arm dry with quick fluttering touches.

"Ow," Lennie said without emphasis.

"I'm sorry." Celia flinched as if she felt the pain herself. "Burns do sting so."

"It was all his fault," Lennie repeated, jerking his head toward the hall.

"Oh, no. You mustn't say that. Dan was trying to keep you from hurting yourself."

"I wouldn't have hurt myself!" Lennie cleared his throat and lowered his voice to its future pitch. "I know how to light fireworks, for God's sake. I've done it about a hundred times."

"Mm." Celia twisted open a tube of Unguentine and

began to spread his arm with thick, strong-smelling yellow ointment.

"He doesn't think I know how to do anything. He thinks I'm a baby, a jerk."

"Dan loves you very much." Celia said this as if it were part of a prayer in which she still devoutly believed, but which had become dulled by repetition.

"Ow." Lennie made no other response.

"Sorry." She squeezed out more ointment, leaning close over the kitchen table in the glow of the oil lamp. Anyone seeing her look of apprehension, Lennie's of faint but evident satisfaction, would have assumed she was the patient, he the doctor.

"Listen, when are we getting out of this dump?" he asked presently.

"We're leaving Sunday afternoon. Don't you like it here, Lennie? I think it's really lovely."

"Oh, sure," he said with heavy sarcasm. "This is a wonderful house. There aren't any electric lights or any hot water or phone or anything. They haven't even got a real bathroom, just a smelly old wooden shed outdoors like greenhorns. Why don't they do something about this dumb old house? What's the matter with Miss King, is she very poor or something?"

"I think she likes it this way," Celia said, centering a gauze pad on his thin arm. "There. Hold that, dear."

"She must be some kind of nut."

Celia opened the roll of adhesive tape and pulled out a length.

"I never wanted to come here in the first place," Lennie went on. "Dad said it would be so great out in the country, ha ha. What's so great about the country? It's just a lot of old dirt and grass. He never told me Miss King wouldn't even have a radio, for Pete's sake. How am I supposed to hear the Yankee game tomorrow? You know I have to hear that game."

"Maybe there's a radio down in the village . . . The general store, you know, where we got gas yesterday, they might . . . They might have one you could listen to."

"Yeah. Maybe," Lennie said in the tone of one unwilling to abandon a grievance.

"Mr. Hubbard . . . He might like to go down there and hear the game himself. He was talking about baseball before supper." Celia stuck a final piece of tape on Lennie's arm. "There you are . . . I'll ask him, if you like."

"Okay." Lennie's mouth remained open, forming the shape of the word "Thanks," but no sound emerged. "Mr. Hubbard's a Giant fan," he said instead. "All those guys that work for the city are Giant fans."

"Oh, really." Celia began repacking the first-aid box.

"It's not as bad as being a Dodger fan. Only a moron like Dad, that didn't know anything about baseball, could be a Dodger fan." Celia made no comment. "You could come too if you want. Uh, I mean if Mr. Hubbard feels like driving down to the village, you could go with us, and then you could hear the game. It's a double-header, and Red Ruffing and Lefty Gomez are pitching."

"Thank you," Celia said, rising. "I don't know if I can, Lennie. I'll have to see what Dan's planning to do tomorrow. He was talking about taking the car over to Cowskill to have its engine looked at, and if he wants me . . . We might go to some antique stores." She smiled anxiously. "I'm sure you could come along, and maybe—"

"I don't want to go anywhere with him," Lennie said, also standing. "And I don't hafta, either. I don't hafta go anywhere he says or come to White Plains ever again if I don't feel like it. My mother said so."

"Oh, Lennie. Don't talk that way."

Lennie turned his head aside, staring toward a cupboard. "What do you care?" he muttered in the sore, resentful voice of a young and unfavored lover. "It doesn't make any difference to you."

"That's not so." Celia looked nervously at him through the blurry dusk. "I'd miss you very much if you never came to visit us. I'd wonder what was happening to you and . . . how your life was going."

Lennie's acned complexion reddened. "Oh, yeah," he said, his voice breaking.

"Really, I would. We all would."

Lennie said nothing. Crickets could be heard outside, and another less familiar sound: light, crackling, explosive.

"Listen; I think they're starting," Celia said. "You'd better go up and put on another shirt. And throw that one away—no, wait, Lennie. Let's see." She took the scorched, hanging sleeve in her hand. "Leave this in our room, and I can cut it down into a short-sleeved shirt. And then you can come out and watch the show with us."

"I already said I don't want to. Are you deaf or something? Anyhow, that isn't a real fireworks show, it's just a baby fake one." He slouched toward the hall. "I was at a real fireworks show last year at Coney Island."

Celia stood for a moment in the kitchen hearing his footsteps go down the hall and up the stairs.

"Lennie?" she called.

No reply. She sighed and followed him.

"Lennie?"

Blam! A nearer explosion; the slam of a bedroom door. Celia paused on the landing and looked down the shadowy tunnel of the back hall. "Lennie?" she repeated, hardly audibly.

There was no answer. She stood there for another moment in the flickering light, a flickering expression on her face, then retreated.

Outside, the night was navy blue behind the elms. As Celia crossed the grassy yard toward the road, two fireflies approached her between the dark tree trunks: Lolly and Mary Ann, each holding a sparkler, a tiny fizzing firework on a wire stem.

"Mummy, Mummy, you've got to hurry!" Lolly cried, pulling at her arm.

"They've started," Mary Ann said. "You missed a real good one already."

"All right, dear, I'm coming." As Celia crossed the road with the children and descended the field, there was another burst of fire, visible as a chain of rising green sparks against the night. She turned to look back at the house; but Lennie, crouched on the window seat in one of the front bedrooms, staring out through the leaves, was only an indistinct blur.

July 5

Early morning. Sunlight like pale oil poured into Anna's big farm kitchen, coloring the white plaster walls, the long scrubbed pine table, and the bare faintly tanned arms of Celia Zimmern, who stood at the table breaking eggs into a yellow bowl. Over her cotton dress she was wearing one of Anna's mother's aprons, a voluminous ankle-length pinafore with a high bib and straps crossed in back.

Across the room, Honey Hubbard leant over the big black stove watching a rack of brown bread turn to toast under the broiler. Honey had rejected another similar apron, declaring that it was about the most hideous old thing she'd ever seen in her life and must have been designed by missionaries trying to lower the birthrate. She wore only a pink-and-white ruffled sundress, too flimsy for serious cooking, but most becoming. A red-checked dish towel was tied round her waist, more as a decoration than for protection.

"Ah don't see how Anna stands it," she said. "Making all her toast this way." She turned three slices of bread over with a fork and some difficulty, dropped a fourth through the rack, and reached into the oven for it. "Ow!" She stood up, sucking one of her pink manicured fingers. "It's just plain ridiculous. Not to mention having to heat up every single blessed drop of hot water she ever needs on this dumb old stove."

"I think she likes it that way," Celia said for the second time that weekend. She poured a little milk into the bowl and began to beat up the eggs.

"Well, maybe. Ah suppose it's kind of fun for a while, camping out like this. If you go in for that sort of thing. But it would drive me out of mah mind." Honey stooped to check the toast again. "Ah don't even want to mention the sanitary arrangements. But imagine having to wash yourself standing up, out of a pitcher and basin, the whole time, just a lick and a promise before the water gets too cold, like the poor white trash down home. Ah couldn't ever get used to that. Ah just don't feel right if Ah don't get mah hot bath with lilac salts every night. Ah like to lie in the tub a real long time and feel all my sins and errors float away. Ah guess Ah should have been born a Baptist."

"Ss." Celia made an indistinct noise; hardly a reply, certainly not a laugh. Or perhaps she had not spoken at all, and the sound was only the scrape of her wire whisk against the sides of the bowl.

"Anyhow, Ah certainly couldn't put up with these kind of primitive conditions for a whole darn summer," Honey continued, spearing the finished pieces of toast with her fork and lifting them onto a plate. "For instance those old-fashioned oil lamps. They're kind of cute, and Ah admit they're most as flattering as candlelight. But they smoke up the place so, and you can't really see anything by them. And even if they gave enough light, do you realize there's not one mirror in this entire house where you can see to comb your hair or put your face on straight?"

"Mm," Celia said. She gave a brief, almost involuntary glance at Honey's snub profile; there was, in fact, a tide-mark of unblended pinky-white powder along the line of the small jaw. "I usually bow to necessity and leave off most of my makeup when I'm here," she suggested.

"Ah couldn't do that." Honey began to butter the hot toast generously. "Ah'd feel positively naked." She giggled. "Even in Anna's own room," she went on. "All she's got is that big antique mirror that's turned all blue and moldy, makes you look like a ghost with the mange. Of course Ah guess Anna's past caring about that sort of thing. And you know she's really magnificent looking in her own way."

"Oh, yes."

"When she lets all that chestnut hair down and ties it back in a scarf, and with those gold hoop earrings, and that long striped skirt she got in India, that she had on last night, she's like some old-fashioned gypsy queen. If Ah just threw mah clothes on that way Ah'd look like something out of a rummage sale." Honey smoothed the fabric of her dress across one of her small high breasts.

"Another thing," she went on, buttering more toast. "If Ah had a big country place like this, Ah'd make sure Ah had some help running it before Ah asked a lot of company up. Even if it was just getting some local farm girl to come in for a few hours a day to do the heavy work. Ah guess maybe she can't afford it, though."

"I don't think it's that," Celia said. "I think Anna just prefers to do things for herself." She lifted a heavy iron skillet down from its hook and set it on the stove.

"People sure are different." Honey put the toast on the table. "Mah idea of heaven is never to have to make another bed or sweep another floor." She giggled.

"Mm." Celia smiled faintly, politely. "I understand how Anna feels," she added. "I don't like having servants around myself . . . I feel sometimes that my house doesn't really belong to me, it belongs to Corinne, because she takes care of everything and knows where everything is. And my garden doesn't belong to me either, it belongs to the gardener." She paused, tilting the pan to melt a lump of butter in it, but Honey remained uncharacteristically silent. "I didn't grow up with servants, you know. Perhaps that's why I can't get used to them."

"Ah thought you were a banker's daughter and lived in a mansion," Honey said.

"I was . . . But my father died when I was just a little girl, and after that we were quite poor. I hardly remember the big house at all."

"You went to college." Honey had two voices: one light, childish, and drawling; the other plainer and less inflected. It was this latter voice, seldom heard by anyone except Mary Ann and Precious Joy, their cook, that she used now.

"My uncle paid for it," Celia explained. "I was twenty years old and I still wasn't married, so he sent me away to the university. He wanted to make sure he wouldn't have to support me the rest of his life." She poured the beaten eggs into the hot skillet.

"Ah see." Honey looked at Celia, and then past her out the window and across the hills. "Ah could have gone to a real college like you," she said. "Ah was smart enough: Ah got A's in school whenever Ah tried, only mostly Ah didn't bother. It took too darned much time off your social life, and of course the boys didn't like it. But Ah thought about it. Ah even decided at one point that Ah was going to go to college, to the University in Chapel Hill, Ah mean, not Rose Manor, which was nothing but a fancy rinky-dink finishing school. Ah wanted to be a chemist, it was mah favorite subject, can you believe it! Like cooking, only more exciting. Go on, laugh at me." Honey had slipped back into her usual frivolous manner.

"I wasn't laughing," Celia said, stirring the eggs in the pan.

"Well, mah Daddy surely did. He said to me, 'Honey

darling, who ever heard of a lady chemist? You can't tell me you really want to spend your life in some dirty old laboratory,' he said, 'getting smelly chemicals all over those pretty little hands.' Ah got real irritated at him. Ah screamed and Ah threw the crystal flower vase right across the sitting room, the one that Mama-Lou inherited from mah Greataunt Honoria that Ah was named after. There was glass and pink chrysanthemums everywhere, but Daddy-Jack didn't even get angry. He just laughed and said it looked to him like Ah was going through some kind of female trouble, and my mother should take me to the doctor for a checkup. And Mama-Lou told him not to worry, Honeybunch was just hyper-dramatizing herself because she'd had a spat with her current beau. Well, Ah admit Bobby Jackson and Ah weren't speaking that week, but that wasn't all of it by a long shot." Honey sighed, then giggled. "Probably Ah would have simply despised college anyhow. You have to grind at your books so hard, isn't that the truth?" She began to set places at one end of the kitchen table.

"It depends," Celia said. "It was the happiest time of my life, in a way. I love reading books."

"Yeah; you used to be the librarian at Eastwind, Anna told me."

"Well." Celia turned the flame off. "Only for a few months."

"You couldn't stand it, huh? Ah can understand that. Ah can't think of anything more awful and boring than being shut up in a stuffy old library with nobody to talk to all day."

"I enjoyed it," Celia said. "And there were plenty of people to talk to; too many for me sometimes. But Dan didn't like my working, so . . ."

"You mean you quit just for that?" Honey said, surprised into her other voice again.

"Well, you see, I had to stay after school for meetings with the teachers, and so I couldn't always come home with Lolly. And then they wanted me there in the evenings too sometimes, and of course he said no to that."

Honey paused, a bunch of spoons in her hand, and stared at Celia's averted profile. "How often did they want you to go back in the evening?" she asked.

"Oh, I don't know. Once or twice a month, at least."

"For the love of Pete," Honey remarked, almost to herself. She began to lay out the spoons.

"You don't know Dan very well," Celia said, smiling as if she took pleasure in this. "You have to understand what it means to him . . . Coming from his background. His mother worked all her life, and it wore her out. And his sister too. And his first wife, of course. He's not against women working, if they have to. But he says that one of the greatest luxuries a man can buy in America, if he's successful, is a wife who doesn't belong to anyone else, or have to take orders from anyone else, even for a few hours a week. Someone who can give all her time and all her care to him. I know that sounds old-fashioned." Celia smiled again.

"It sounds like my Greatuncle Harper, if you want to know," Honey said.

"Oh?" Celia remarked politely.

"Greatuncle Harper, he was a real old Southern Gentleman. Owned a lot of country." Honey began laying down the knives. "Had four children by my Greataunt Honoria that left us the flower vase Ah broke that Ah was telling about, and never did a day's work in her whole life. And three more by a big fat nigra laundress that lived on their place, only nobody was supposed to notice them. Course, that was down in Alabama, before Emancipation. Greatuncle Harper used to say, "The only proper places for a Southern lady to be seen are church and her husband's drawing room."

The screen door banged and shut; Mary Ann and Lolly came into the kitchen.

"We're hungry!"

"All right, chickies. You can sit right down. Breakfast's almost ready."

Lolly gives the packed ground beneath the hammock a push with one bare foot, and falls back onto the rough stretched gray canvas next to Teddy and Mary Ann. The leaves, foaming, rise and fall above her, rise and fall. Green lace waves, and the clouds rocking sideways past in bigger white waves, rise and fall.

"What'll we do this afternoon?" Mary Ann says. A bird peeps somewhere, sleepy. Bob-white. Far down the road there is the hum of a car going away taking Danny and Lennie and Mary Ann's daddy away to the village. Rise. Fall.

Bob-white. Another bird, nearer, behind the barn. They are calling for an old man who once lived up in these hills, Anna said. A hermit; yes, a sort of magician. He wouldn't have much to do with people, but he used to feed all the birds. Striped sunflower seeds and crumbly white suet, and fat worms he dug for them, and shiny buzzing bugs he caught in a special bug trap. Every kind of ordinary bird came to his cabin in the hills, and rare unusual kinds too: wild geese and hummingbirds and herons. They still fly all over the Catskill Mountains looking for him, calling his name. Bob

White. —Do they ever find him? —Yes, sometimes, Anna says.

Rise. Fall. The sky is a sea, and Lolly floating flying over it. Up is down and down is up, like when Danny swings her, airplane swing. He holds her by one wing and tailfin and it is wonderful scary exciting, the grass dipping and circling, a green blur. And round and round faster till she isn't a plane or Lolly anymore, she is nobody nowhere nothing, a speck of air whirling, a wind crying Ooooh round Danny who is the center of everywhere, with trees and sky and house and road just shapes pouring round him. Swinging out wide and then at last in toward him, gathered in, hugged warm and close to the center of everything, crying Ohh.

But then, too soon, he puts her down, almost drops her to the grass, dizzy and breathing loud, a crashed plane. He laughs and goes away. Even sometimes still holding her he suddenly isn't there anymore—only someone else looking like her father pretending to hold her but not caring, laughing with other people, gone away. Or suddenly he says something awful. —Lolly wants to go for a walk, he shouts at her, a walk into the woods, where the trees are dark, tangled and unfriendly, hiding danger, not like Anna's tame lacy trees.

—Don't ever go into the woods alone, Lolly, Princess, darling, he says other times. —Don't go too far down the road, stay close to us, baby, hold tight to Danny's hand, don't get lost. Especially downtown or in tall heavy New York City, don't don't. And if you should get lost from us don't don't talk to anybody except a lady or a policeman.

He doesn't say why, but Lolly knows why. It's because of gangsters, and robbers and burglars and kidnappers, the ones in the *Journal-American* that comes to their house on Sundays for Corinne, wrapped up in bright-colored

"Prince Valiant" and "Abie 'n' Slats" comics, but inside them are murders and attacks and the blurry gray pictures of gangsters and kidnappers that the policemen have caught and are taking away to jail or to death in Electric Chairs, with their heads bent down or covered with hats to hide their awful-to-see faces. Or no faces at all because they are FACELESS CRIMINALS with nothing under their hats but a horrible smooth gray space with a big black question mark in the middle of it.

But there are other ones that the policemen haven't caught. In the downstairs hall at Eastwind there is a red-and-black poster about them, WARNING in big sharp red letters DON'T get into an automobile with anybody you don't know, that might be planning to kidnap you and trade you for a ransom of a million dollar bills in bundles.

When Lolly said kidnappers Mary Ann said —Oh pooh. She said her father and mother told her not to worry about it, because they weren't rich enough for any kidnapper in his right mind to bother with. So Mary Ann doesn't worry. She is steady, safe, solid next to Lolly and Teddy in the hammock. As solid as Anna; always there when she is there and always the same, like a strong friendly kitchen chair. Mary Ann doesn't think and Lolly doesn't ever say to her what she knows, that some kidnappers and gangsters are in their wrong minds. At Thanksgiving dinner Aunt Rose was talking about the man who stole away the Lindbergh baby and murdered it and hid it in the greasy gray newspaper bushes. —You'd have to be crazy to do a thing like that, she said. —Out of your mind.

—Please don't frighten the child, Rose, Mummy-Celia said, her own voice frightened, watery, so Lolly knew it was true.

Or even if the kidnapper was in his right mind, he

might not know that Danny didn't have a million dollars, and after he found out he would be so angry he would kill her anyway.

Mummy-Celia isn't like Danny, or like Mary Ann either. She never goes away is never really there. She is unsafe, watery, pouring. Like bath water, soapy warm rocking you but giving way. You can sink into her, melt, dissolve, drown. She is melting drowning. When you go into her room sometimes she is half-sitting half-lying on the chaise longue and her face is all wet melting but she isn't crying. —I'm not crying, she says.

Mummy-Celia knows but doesn't talk about the gangsters and kidnappers, and the horrible crazy men who are everywhere looking for little girls, especially on trains and in railroad stations, that Auntie Helen told her about last summer when Lolly stayed overnight in Philadelphia and Danny and Mummy-Celia went to New York to see a play and the next day she took the train all by herself to Pennsylvania Station.

Before Uncle drove them to the train, Auntie Helen took Lolly upstairs into her tall bedroom with the slippery floor and the long windows wrapped in net curtains. She shut the door and made Lolly sit on her needlepoint stool with the four dog feet and asked her if she knew that she musn't ever talk to strangers.

—Because it isn't only people who want you to get into their cars that you have to watch out for, Lolly dear. There are other bad men looking for little girls traveling alone. You can't tell who they are on sight; sometimes they seem nice and friendly just like somebody's father or grandfather or uncle, and those are the most dangerous of all. Because little girls trust them, and take candy from them, which you must promise me you will never do,

Lolly darling, because you can't be sure what might be in it. What might be in it? Lolly was afraid to ask; the answer would be:—Poison.

So the safest best thing was for her not to speak to anyone on the train, and if any man or big boy tried to speak to her she mustn't answer him, and if he kept on she should tell some nice lady that was sitting nearby; and if he tried to bother her or touch any part of her body she should stand up and scream as loud as she could.

Auntie Helen didn't say how the bad men would bother Lolly. It is too awful to think about, she won't think about it. Only that day from the time Uncle drove them to the railroad station in Philadelphia until she saw Mummy-Celia standing in the station in New York she was thinking about it and watching watching every man that got on the train or was already in it, looking at them with fast sly little looks so they wouldn't notice her. Young men and old ones and fat ones and thin ones and smiling ones in new clothes and shabby sad-looking ones. Any of them maybe all of them wanted to grab Lolly and hurt her, and they all had a horrible huge hard red thing in their trousers that they wanted to take out and shove into her panties but nobody is supposed to talk about that. Lolly knows because of the drawing on the wall low down by the newsstand in the White Plains railroad station, the dirty dark tunnel part under the tracks. It is done in sticky red crayon, a drawing of something like a hard fat gun and two bags of ammunition. —Oh, nothing, it's just a design, Mummy-Celia said. But later, when Mummy-Celia was buying something in the drugstore in Grand Central, Lennie told her what it really was.

Nobody ever washed the awful drawing off the wall and it was always there afterwards whenever they took the train into New York City and again on the way home.

Lolly tried not to look at it. She turned her head sideways and held on to Mummy-Celia's hand or dress, but it was there. I'm here, it said. I'm coming to get you and hurt you, poking into you like the dentist, only worse. Like a Buck Rogers Space Disintegrator Gun, like a giant red firecracker I'm going to shove myself into your panties and explode and you will be blown up inside and disintegrated and bleed and scream. She won't think about it anymore, she won't won't. She hates railroad stations. And trains, all dirty and noisy. She doesn't want to go on a train alone ever again, she won't, nobody can make her. If they try to make her she will just scream and scream.

"What'll we do this afternoon?" Mary Ann says again.

There are no trains here, not for miles and miles. Only the trees and the sky, rocking. Birds squeaking softly. Mary Ann and Teddy. The castle in the orchard, and the fairies in the hayfield looking after the hay and flowers. Danny and Mummy-Celia. Anna. Anna's farm

"Let's dress up and play something," says Mary Ann. "We can use the stuff from that big trunk of old clothes you said Anna has in her attic."

"All right," Lolly says, swaying.

"Let's give a play."

"All right," Lolly says. "A fairy tale."

"What one?"

" 'Sleeping Beauty.' "

A cloud slides by like a big sheep with ears, feeding sideways on the elm waves, leaves.

"We did that last time, at your house," Mary Ann says.

Long fat ears, too long for a sheep, maybe it's a horse. A white fluffy curly horse, a magic one. Falada. " 'The Goose Girl,' then," Lolly says.

"Okay. Who do you want to be?" Falada slides up the

sky, his fur turning into feathers. "I tell you what," Mary Ann says. "You can be the princess, if you let me be everybody else. The queen mother and the wicked serving-maid and the prince and Hans and everybody."

"All right," Lolly says.

Alas, Falada, hanging there. Melting into white feathers and shreds.

"What about the horses?" she asks.

"We can make them," Mary Ann says. "Just their heads on sticks, you know, like hobbyhorses. Out of cardboard. Then we can put Falada's head up over the castle gate. We'll have to make a gate too, out of chairs or something." Mary Ann sits up all at once; a tilt and sag in the hammock. She puts her feet down and stops its slow small rocking. "Okay, come on. Let's get started."

In the vegetable garden, beneath a shimmer of sun and heat, two contrasting female figures squatted, picking green peas. One looked like some eccentric migrant worker—tall, long-limbed, wrinkled and browned by the sun, with a faded pinafore apron for a dress and a red gypsy scarf knotted round her head. The other, a pink-and-white blonde, wore dancing pumps, a low-cut pink-and-white sundress, and a wide pagoda-shaped straw hat, as if she were a chorus girl in some mock-Chinese musical comedy.

"Just like men, huh, to make themselves scarce when there's any real work to do," Honey complained, rising on her high heels with a tiny groan and stooping again a little further along the row.

"It does seem to happen that way," Anna admitted. "I

think it might be a good idea to make the lot of them clean up after supper tonight."

"Ah'm with you a hundred percent." Honey giggled and stopped picking, not for the first time, to scoop the bright green peas from an especially succulent-looking pod into her vermilion mouth.

"Actually, Ah'm real delighted Bill's gone somewhere for the afternoon," she said a few moments later, halting to retie her hat-strings in a perky bow. "Ah think the way he's been hiding out this weekend is perfectly rude and disgusting. Ah really ought to apologize to you."

"There's nothing to apologize for." Anna smiled at Honey through the chicken wire and curling vines. "I don't think either of the men, or Lennie, has washed a single dish since they got here."

"Don't be polite. It's not just the work Ah mean. Ah told Bill yesterday, either he should stay upstairs till he finishes that darn old report, or else he should just forget about it and enjoy himself with the rest of us. But he won't do either one." Honey tossed a handful of peapods into the bowl beside her.

"Look at the way he behaved last night after the fireworks," she went on. "Bringing his stupid papers into the sitting room, even though we all told him we didn't mind if he took both lamps upstairs so's he could see to work. But oh no he wouldn't do that. Wouldn't fish or cut bait, like mah Daddy used to say. He had to sit downstairs the whole evening; not being sociable, just fussing with his silly old report so's the rest of us couldn't talk naturally for fear of bothering him, and making us feel like criminals if we laughed out loud. Did you ever hear of a man like that?"

"I've heard of them, yes," Anna said. "And some women too."

"Yeh." Honey giggled. "Ah've met a couple of those.

Only most times 'stead of working they pass themselves off as invalids; at least down home they do. A friend of mine had an aunt like that. She was kind of good-looking, but she had a weak spine and a nervous constitution and a crush on the Congregational minister, so she never got married to anybody. They had this sofa in the parlor window with ferns around it, and Belinda's aunt used to lie there most all day knitting for the church missions or reading books of poetry, and giving a suffering lovesick sigh now and then, 'Oouh,' like so, and making everybody that came to call uncomfortable. Thought she was Elizabeth Barrett Browning, Ah guess."

Anna laughed and moved her basket along the row. "There are children who act like that too, you know," she said presently. "It's not really their fault, though. I see them at Eastwind sometimes, hanging round the edges of games at recess, too awkward and shy to join in, but not wanting to go off and play by themselves. The other children usually pick on them because they get in the way."

Honey, raising her head, looked hard at Anna for a moment. "Well, it's not shyness with Bill," she said. "It's more like he's forgotten how to play. He's always thinking about his darn job." She pulled a handful of pods and leaves off the vine resentfully.

"His job?"

"Aw, you know. Brooding about the Depression, and the bad condition this country is in, and the awful relief cases he keeps hearing about. He gets real desperate and low-spirited sometimes, much worse than he is now."

"I can understand that," Anna said.

"Well, sure. Everybody feels that way once in a while. After Ah read that book you lent me about the poor white families in Mississippi, with those terrible sad photos, Ah wanted to cry for a week, and Ah rushed out and sent that farm workers' school fifty dollars Ah should have paid Gristede's." Honey laughed. "But with Bill it's like he can't ever relax and enjoy himself anymore. Ah tell him, one man can't mend the whole world."

"Or one woman," Anna said.

"Lord, no." Honey giggled. "And besides, Ah don't see what good it does poor people for everybody else to go round with long faces the whole time." She lengthened and froze her own short heart-shaped face, then let it melt back into a smile as she caught sight of Mary Ann and Lolly approaching across the garden, both dressed in clothes from Anna's attic.

"Hello, kiddies," she called. "Time for your play?"

"It's not ready yet." Mary Ann held up a red flannel petticoat to hop over the rows of dark-green spinach and pale ferny carrots. "We can't find the workbox, to fix Lolly's skirt."

"I remember that dress." Anna sat back on her heels to gaze at Lolly. A pretty child, with Celia's fine features heightened by Dan's brilliant coloring and curly dark hair; in the old-fashioned white summer frock trimmed with fine tucking and rows of lace she looked like a late-Victorian valentine.

"Yes," Anna went on. "I wore that to Chautauqua when I was about your age. There was an Indian snake charmer there who played on a wooden flute; and a tremendous purple thunderstorm over the lake—" She interrupted herself. "You want the workbox? Isn't it in the dining-room cupboard?" Mary Ann shook her head. "Ask Celia then. I think she borrowed it."

"We can't," Lolly said.

"She's still having a nap," Mary Ann explained. "She said she didn't sleep very well last night so please not to wake her up until just before the play starts."

"Well, you might wait—" Anna began.

"That's okay," Honey interrupted, looking at her watch. "You can use my sewing kit, Mary Ann; it's in the side pocket of the big red suitcase, in our bedroom."

"Okay." Mary Ann and Lolly turned and began to hop back across the rows of vegetables.

"Ah wish you could have met Bill a few years ago," Honey said when the girls were out of earshot. "He used to be a real good-looking man, Anna, till he started losing his hair. He's only forty-two now, but you'd never know it. He doesn't take hardly any exercise anymore, so naturally he's putting on weight, getting kind of soft— Ah think that's a real pity. Ah think a man ought to keep himself in condition, the way Dan Zimmern does."

"Mm." Through the pea-vines, Anna gave Honey a sharp glance.

"And it's not just his looks." Honey sighed, and her small plump hands with nails like bits of sharp red shell moved even more slowly. "He's started thinking and acting old. Sometimes he reminds me so much of his father I could scream."

"His father?"

"Yeh. He's this hidebound old Puritan up in Maine, doesn't approve of anything anybody does that's fun. Bill wasn't like that before. Ah don't mean to say he was ever exactly the life of the party, but he used to be such good company, and a lovely dancer."

"Really."

"You should have seen him do the Bunny Hug." Honey smiled. "But it's like pulling teeth to get him to dance nowadays, even just to fox-trot. When we're at a party he mostly just hangs around watching me like a, like an old policeman or something. The way he did last night." She giggled. "And he's always interrogating me, and suspecting me, Ah honestly can't understand why."

"Honestly?" Anna moved a green curtain of vines aside to look at her.

"Well." An ambiguous expression crossed Honey's face under the freckled shadows of the Chinese pagoda hat. "You know how it is. A girl has to have a little fun sometimes. This is the twentieth century, after all." She giggled. "Ah admit Ah was flirting a little bit with Dan last night. But now really, Ah ask you, what harm was Ah doing?"

"Well, if you really ask me."

"Sure."

"You were causing Bill considerable misery, for one thing."

"Ah was just teasing him a little. Anyhow, he deserved it."

"And you were upsetting Celia."

"Aw, come on. She'd already gone to bed; she went right after the fireworks almost. If she was really jealous or bothered, she would have stayed up, now wouldn't she?"

"Not necessarily."

" 'Course she would." Honey sat back on the straw between the rows of peas. "Ah feel kind of sorry for Celia," she said. "She was telling me this morning how Dan made her quit working at Eastwind, just 'cause she wouldn't be home to wait on him a couple of evenings a month, is that right?"

"That's right," Anna said with feeling.

"Holy gee. Men are such babies, aren't they? Ah wouldn't have stood for that for one minute." Honey broke off another peapod and ripped it open with her vermilion nails. "You know what gets me is, Celia's graduated from college and reads all those heavy books, but that poor little old gal doesn't know the first thing about how to manage a man. Or her own self, for that matter." She shook her head and the pagoda hat. "Those clothes, just for instance. They don't do a damned thing for her. You know that awful lace dress, the one she always wears to parties?"

"Yes," Anna said. "I don't care for it either."

"It probably cost a lot, but it's just plain murder with her olive complexion, that pinky beige. Now it'd be okay on me— Ah did have a dress that color once, just after the war. It was double chiffon with satin piping and a handkerchief hem. Ah looked real cute in it, if Ah do say so mahself." Honey sighed and picked another handful of peas. "Ah'd like to tell Celia she ought to retire that old dress of hers, but Ah don't know if she'd take it right."

"No," Anna agreed.

"Maybe if you—"

"No," Anna said again, more firmly. "She told me once that dress makes her feel like a proper lady, old enough to be married to Dan."

"It sure does." Honey sighed. "It's a real shame, 'cause with her looks and his money she could be positively ravishing. Ah'd just love to take her through Lord and Taylor's with a hundred dollars to spend on clothes."

"Yes." Anna smiled. "I think we've got enough peas for supper now," she added, standing up.

"Good. Ah'm really steaming." Honey rose too, holding her half-filled bowl of green pods against the ruffled top of her dress.

"If you really want to know, Ah think Bill kind of gets a charge out of my carrying on," she said, looking out across the valley. "As long as it doesn't go too far. In mah experience, most men don't really like a good woman. What they like is a naughty little girl." She giggled and glanced at Anna. "Ah bet if Ah got all serious and reformed, Bill would divorce me."

"You know him better than I do," Anna admitted after

a moment's pause, lifting the loop of wire that held the garden gate shut.

"Anyhow, what if Ah did annoy him a little?" Honey asked crossly. "It's no more than he deserves, for spying on me all the time the way he does." Anna laughed, as if in spite of herself. "It's the truth. He wants to know everything Ah do, and everything Ah think.

"Ah really can't stand it sometimes," she added, closing the gate and following Anna across the sunlit grass. "Ah know he loves me, but Ah get to feeling like he wants to eat me up alive. Ah know that sounds kind of nutty." She giggled a little nervously.

"No, it doesn't," Anna said. "I've known people who made me feel like that." She held open the screen door.

"You have, huh?"

"Yes, I—" Anna fell silent.

"Well, then." Honey set her bowl of peas on the kitchen table. "That's why Ah have to kind of play around, you know what Ah mean," she said. "Nothing serious. Ah'm not planning to ruin mah reputation or end up in the divorce court. But it seems like sometimes if Ah don't have some private life of mah own that Bill doesn't know about, even if it's only going to Macy's and buying a hat without telling him, or kissing some fellow in the pantry at a party, well Ah feel Ah'm going to be swallowed up whole and just plain vanish."

Four kitchen chairs were ranged in a row on Anna's lawn beneath the golden-green shade of the elms. In them, facing the front door, sat Anna, Celia, Honey, and Theodore Ilgenfritz, Mary Ann's teddy bear. A white bedspread with yellow chenille dots hung on a clothesline between two ancient rosebushes. It swayed in a soft breeze, revealing and then concealing the bottom half of the front door and most of the wide moss-greened marble doorstep.

The bedspread bulged as some bulky object was moved into place behind it, then gaped at one side. Mary Ann's face, oddly marked in brown, appeared next to the right-hand bush. "'The Play of the Goose Girl,'" she announced. "Scene One."

The curtain settled, then was drawn back by seen hands, revealing three dining-room chairs placed together and draped with blankets and pillows to form a sort of chaise longue, on which Mary Ann reclined. She wore the long red flannel petticoat, Dan's maroon paisley bathrobe, and a large gaudily crayoned paper crown. Brown lines were drawn with eyebrow pencil between her pale eyebrows and on each side of her mouth to represent age.

"I am very sick," Mary Ann announced. "My head hurts and my stomach hurts and my heart hurts." She placed her hand on each afflicted part as she spoke. "I think I am dying. But before I die, I must speak to my daughter, the Princess. Princess, come here, so I can tell you something."

She beckoned with a queenly gesture, and Lolly came out from behind the curtain, wearing Anna's white dress and another, more modest (but more elegantly made and colored) paper crown.

"I'm probably going to die now," Mary Ann went on. "And I want you to be happy ever after. So I've fixed it up for you to marry a very nice handsome brave prince who lives in the kingdom next door, all right?"

"Yes, dear mother," whispered Lolly, who appeared to suffer from stage fright.

"I'm going to give you my magic horse, Falada, so you can

ride to the prince's kingdom and marry him; and my silver cup to drink out of. And you can take my serving-maid along to serve you and keep you company on the trip."

"Yes, dear mother."

"And I'm going to give you my silver— No, I said that already. I'm going to give you a piece of my hair." Mary Ann sat up, reached under the sofa pillows, and took out the kitchen shears; then she pulled one of her orange pigtails forward and cut off nearly two inches from the end below the rubber band.

"No, don't!" Honey, in the audience, gave a little shriek.

"Here you are," Mary Ann went on, ignoring the interruption. "This piece of my hair is a magic charm. As long as you've got it, nothing bad can happen to you. So don't be dumb and lose it, all right?"

"Yes, dear mother."

"You can go now." Mary Ann sank back on the sofa pillows. "Wait. Kiss me good-bye." Lolly bent forward. "Okay. Have a nice trip."

Mary Ann sighed in a theatrical manner and closed her eyes. Lolly, with some difficulty, drew the curtain shut along its sagging rope. The audience applauded. Honey looked at her watch.

There was a lengthy pause. Again the bedspread quivered with the shifting of objects. Mary Ann could be heard telling Lolly, in a loud whisper, to leave the chair there so the screen door would stay open. Anna and Celia commented on the unusual heat of the afternoon, and on its humidity. Honey looked again at her watch. Finally Mary Ann put her head round the edge of the curtain to declare: "Scene Two."

For a moment or two the stage was empty. Then Lolly and Mary Ann galloped out of the front hall on homemade hobbyhorses. Mary Ann had wiped most of the brown lines off her face and was wrapped in one of Anna's mother's aprons, pinned and tucked up so that it would not drag on the ground.

"Lo, we have been traveling many a weary mile," said Lolly, speaking with a bit more confidence, though not much more volume. "I am thirsty, and I would fain drink from yonder spring." She pointed behind the lefthand rose-bush. "Take my silver cup, and get me some water."

"I don't feel like it," Mary Ann said, pushing away Lolly's hand and the toothbrush mug it held out. "Get your own water."

Lolly dismounted, knelt down at the edge of the door-step, and pantomimed drinking from the mug. Then she mounted her hobbyhorse again and both she and Mary Ann rode off through the open door into the front hall, turned round in the kitchen, and galloped back out onto the stage.

"Lo, we have been traveling many a weary mile. I am very thirsty, and I fain would drink from yonder spring. Please fetch me some water."

"Oh, stop bothering me," Mary Ann said.

Again Lolly mimed dipping and drinking water, and then she cried, almost out loud, "Oh, I have lost my silver cup!" Mary Ann made no comment. They rode off into the house, and returned.

"Lo, we have been traveling . . ." Lolly repeated her speech.

"How am I supposed to get water without a cup, stupid?" Mary Ann said. "You'll just have to drink from your hands."

Lolly dismounted, bent low over the doorstep, and cried out, "Oh, I have lost the piece of my mother's magic hair, I mean the magic piece of my mother's hair. Oh, woe is me! What shall I do?"

"Nyah, nyah," Mary Ann said. "I'm going to fix you

now. I'm tired of being your maid. I want to be the princess myself. You have to give me your princess clothes now, and put on my ugly old maid clothes. And you have to ride my ugly old horse, and I'll ride Falada. And when we get to the kingdom next door, you have to tell everybody that I'm the princess and you're just my maid, so I can marry the prince instead of you. And if you don't do everything I say, I'll kill you, so there." Mary Ann struggled with the pocket of the apron and produced a table knife, which she brandished. "Okay?"

"Okay," Lolly said in a feeble whisper.

The girls now began to change their costumes on stage, Mary Ann acting out impatience, grabbing and pushing and crying "Hurry up, stupid!"; Lolly—either for dramatic reasons or out of natural shyness—remaining submissive. When the transformation was complete, Lolly got astride the serving-maid's horse, which had a plain brown cardboard head; Mary Ann mounted Falada, whose cardboard had been covered with white paper and sported a curly white-paper mane. They rode off into the front hall.

Nothing happened for a few moments. Honey looked at her watch again. Then Mary Ann reappeared. "You can clap now, if you want," she said. The audience obeyed. Honey leaned over and moved Theodore's plush arms in the gesture of applause. Then she stood up.

"Well, that was real lovely, Mary Ann," she said. "Thank you."

"You're welcome. Hey, where are you going? It's not over yet; there's lots more scenes. We haven't even got to the other castle. Sit down."

Honey, looking less than pleased, sat down. "Ah hope those scenes are short," she said. "Ah'm just about perishing with the heat."

Mary Ann pulled the bedspread shut and went back

into the house, while Anna and Celia began a conversation about theatricals of their own childhoods. Anna described a circus that she and her younger brother (killed nearly twenty years ago in France) had held in the barnyard, of which the feature attraction was an occasionally performing duck named Bluebell. Honey did not join in. She fidgeted, looked at her watch, patted her powdered face with an embroidered handkerchief, and sighed audibly. Then she excused herself and went off in the direction of the outdoor privy.

Above the bedspread, the top of a stepladder appeared, followed by the top of Mary Ann and the cardboard head of Falada, which she endeavored unsuccessfully to fix to the ladder with a piece of string; then both disappeared. A pause. Celia related to Anna the story of her own appearance in a Philadelphia Sunday-School pageant in 1909 as an angel with German measles.

"Hey." Honey came round the corner of the house, clutching her red pocketbook with one hand and holding the other to her abdomen. "Ah've got to drive into town and get me something," she whispered to Anna and Celia. "Ah've had a little surprise visit from my grandmother."

"Oh, that's too bad— Wait—I think I might have some Modess," Celia said, rising. "I'll look in my suitcase."

"Don't you bother. Ah might as well go now and buy me a whole darn box." She raised her voice, "Mary Ann!" There was no reply. "Listen, tell the girls Ah'm sorry to miss the end of their play, and Ah'll be back real soon."

"Ten more minutes," Dan said, glancing at his watch. He and Bill Hubbard were standing in the hot shade of the porch outside the general store, drinking beer and waiting for the baseball game to commence on the radio. From within, where Lennie and other boys and men were sitting or lounging, came a static-roughened voice recommending a different but similar brand of beer. "Crazy kid," Dan added, grinning and shaking his head. "Most boys his age would jump at the chance to drive a car, am I right?"

"A lot of them would," Bill agreed.

"Okay. Suppose he didn't feel like it. He doesn't have to act as if I was Mussolini or something." Dan gave a short, quite convincing, careless laugh. In spite of the increasing heat, he looked handsomer than ever. Sun-flushed, evenly tanned, lounging against the railing with a country landscape behind him, he might have been posing for a beer ad, or perhaps one promoting the sale of his crisp white shorts and open-necked yellow polo shirt. "Maybe I was a little rough on him last night. I figured okay, I'll make it up to him today. Show him a good time. Hell, after all, I only see him five days a month." He shook his head. "But Lennie's a weird kid. You try to be nice to him, you don't get anywhere, you know what I mean?"

"I thought he— Well—" Bill fell silent and drained the beer from a bottle which, like his heat-mottled face and neck, was dewed with sweat.

"What?"

"Well, it seemed to me maybe he was a little scared to drive your car."

"Yeah." Dan frowned. "He's got no nerve; that's what it is. Hell, I was sitting right next to him; I could have grabbed the wheel if I had to. I wouldn't have let him smash up my baby." He blew a kiss across the road to where the De Soto glowed red in the speckled shadow of a tree. "You know, I don't like the way she sounded today," he added. "Kind of a clunk in the engine."

"I didn't hear anything."

"I think maybe I'll run her over to that garage in Cow-skill now, see what they can find."

"You'll miss the game."

"Ah, the guy there probably has a radio. Anyhow, hell, it shouldn't take long. I just want him to give her the once-over. I'll be back in a couple of innings." Dan looked at his watch again, then toward the store, where an advertising jingle was being broadcast. "Like another beer?"

"Sure. Thanks."

Left alone, Bill mopped his face and the bald top of his head with an already damp handkerchief. His dress, unlike Dan's, was unsuited to the rural scene and almost equally so to the weather. Heat and exertion had creased his seer-sucker suit and white shirt, and the tie hung from his loosened collar like a brown-striped rayon rag.

"Here you are," Dan said, returning with two opened bottles. "Chicken-livered," he added, gesturing toward the store and continuing the last topic but one.

"I wouldn't say that." Bill shook his head. "I thought Lennie was pretty brave last night when his shirt caught fire. Put it out himself and didn't even cry."

"Yeah, he's okay in emergencies." Dan smiled, but only briefly. "He used to be such a great little kid, ready for anything. Now—" He looked at his beer with an expression that would have ruined any advertisement. "Well, what the hell can you expect of the kid, growing up in a house full of neurotic women, spoilt rotten."

"Lennie lives with a lot of women, huh?"

"Three of them. His mother, his aunt, and the old grandmother, who came over from Latvia in eighteen ninety-six, if you can believe it, and still can't speak English worth a damn. They're all of them yentas—complainers and nags. Always worrying and fussing over the kid. Ooh

Lennie darling, better you should take your rubbers, I felt a drop of rain. And his mother is the worst of the lot. I should have been warned. I should have known what I was in for as soon as I saw the grandmother, because a Jewish girl always turns into her mother in a few years. But Irma was such a good looker, I couldn't believe it would happen to her."

"You never do know what a woman is really like," Bill pronounced. "Not when you just meet her socially."

"That's the truth." Dan laughed again. "The more proper and polite a dame acts in public, the crazier she usually is when you get to know her."

"It's the way they're raised."

"Yeah, maybe."

"See, the women we know, they most of them grew up before the Eighteenth Amendment. They're usually pretty irrational, like children really, because that's how they were brought up to be. When they got the vote, and short skirts, and all that, it was too late for them. They might try to be like men, but they don't know what it means even."

"You've got a point." Dan looked away again, recalling the person who must have inspired these generalizations. Though a habitual womanizer, he had until now confined his attentions to women who had no husbands, or none personally known to him.

"Or when you do meet a woman who can think and act like a man, she's probably somebody like Anna who was raised to have a career, and never had time for anything else."

"I don't know about that. If you ask me, Anna's got more sex appeal than most married women her age. And probably more experience."

"Aw, come on." Bill lifted his bottle of beer.

"I'm not kidding. Still, there aren't too many like her."

Dan left the railing and began to pace the length of the porch as he spoke, away from and then back toward Bill, as if he saw him alternately as a future cuckold and as a congenial fellow sufferer from female perversity. "When you come to think of it, I've known damn few women who had any sense. I don't know why in hell we run after them and make so much trouble for ourselves."

"Because that's what we were raised to do," Bill explained, warming as usual to this activity. "Also, it's the result of natural selection. For thousands of years men who didn't chase after women had fewer descendants, or none. So eventually those genes died out."

"Yeah, I get it," Dan said, pacing. "You mean if you love your wife, but you can't resist a beautiful babe, it's just heredity."

"Heredity isn't everything," Bill said, giving Dan's back a look of sour suspicion. "Anyhow," he added, "my personal opinion is, it's going to be a lot different in the future. For Mary Ann, say, and Lolly, their generation."

"I'm not so sure." Dan tossed his beer bottle in one hand. "I worry about Lolly; she's so dreamy, just like her mother. When I think of the girls I grew up with in Brooklyn—tough little brats who knew their way around the streets from about age five, I wonder— Hell, not that I'd want her to be like them."

"I know what you mean."

"You can't win." Dan laughed, and leaned on the rail again, easier with this new subject. "If you have the money, you want to protect your kids, give them a beautiful safe place to grow up in, am I right?"

"You're right," Bill said, wiping his mouth.

"Okay. So I leave New York and move out to the country, find the best school in Westchester— So what's the result? The result is, I've got a little girl who thinks America is a beautiful safe country and everybody in it is a nice guy. What the hell is going to happen to her when she gets out into the real world?"

"Maybe the world will be different by then."

"After the revolution, huh?" Dan laughed. "I'm not so sure. Anyhow, until the revolution comes we've got to look out for our kids, right?"

"Yeah. Well, I don't worry about Mary Ann, not too much," Bill said. "She's a smart little girl, knows how to take care of herself better than Honey does already, in some ways."

"Hm," Dan said, frowning in the direction of Anna's house like a lawyer who refrains from questioning a statement about which he has contradictory but illegal evidence.

"I figure she'll do okay," Bill went on. "I'd like for her to have a career, if she wants one. But I wouldn't want her to take it so hard she'd miss her chance at a normal life, you know, the way Anna has."

"Hm," Dan repeated mechanically, not listening; it had just occurred to him that if he and Honey were to be found out, Bill would regard him as the responsible party.

"She looks a lot like you, Mary Ann does," he added, turning to regard Bill's thin orange hair and long pale freckled face.

"Yeah; I know." Bill sighed. "Oh well; maybe the men of the future will be different too. They won't care whether a girl is pretty and soft and cuddly."

"I wouldn't bet on it." Dan laughed.

Again, Bill sighed. "I always thought, if Honey had a girl baby, it'd take after her," he said. "Seems like a waste of genes otherwise." He shook his head. "I guess we none of us get the kids we wanted."

"You can say that again." Dan drained his beer and

glanced into the store. Lennie and the others were now regrouped around the radio, which had exchanged its tone of commercial eagerness for one of genuine enthusiasm. "Let's go in, okay? Sounds like the game's starting."

"Okay." Bill paused behind Dan, holding the sagging screen door open. "Aren't you going to take your car over to Cowskill?"

"Yeah, maybe, in a little while," Dan grinned uneasily. "She can wait."

A dusty, sun-blanched, weed-bordered country road; rippling hayfields rising to a wood on one side; on the other broken stone walls and neglected pastureland falling away toward the valley. In a shimmer of heat a solitary car, a Franklin, appeared round the bend, traveling faster than it had been built to travel on such a rough road; it coughed and wavered from side to side, striking against the verge and raising a cloud of dust. It slowed down unevenly, stopped, went into reverse, chugged ahead again, and finally tilted to a stop beside the road, its right side buried in weeds, not far from where, earlier in the day, Mary Ann Hubbard had called its present driver an aggravating old mother.

Now, inside the car, Honey rose in her seat and leant out, smiling enticingly at herself in the concave rear-view mirror known to Mary Ann as Little Land because it reflected everything in miniature. She fluffed up her blonde bangs, moistened and pouted her neon-pink lips, and sat back, clicking her nails idly on the steering wheel; then she turned one wrist to read her watch, which showed ten past three. She yawned a little catlike yawn, and waited.

Gradually, the temperature inside the parked car increased. Honey fanned herself with her red leather handbag; then she opened the car door and moved it back and forth like a larger fan. Finally she turned, hopped down into the dirt road, and slammed the door behind her.

Still carrying her handbag, she started along the road toward the shade of some scrub maples; but before she could reach them one of her high-heeled sandals caught in a rut; she tripped and fell forward with a loud mew.

"Aw, ow!"

No one replied. Honey got to her feet, hobbled back to the Franklin, and sat down on the running board to inspect the damage.

"Oh hell."

There were ladders in both her silk stockings; her lower legs and one arm were smeared with dust. There was dust all over her pink-and-white dress, and a raw, scraped patch on her knee was beginning to ooze blood. She stood up painfully and bent to look into Little Land, which showed a diminished road, fields, woods, and sky, haloing a cross, dirt-smudged painted face, which in the bright flat light was that of a rather middle-aged kitten.

"God damn damn it."

Honey sat down again on the hot corrugated-rubber running board of the car and tried without success to dust off her legs on the underside of her skirt. Then she stood up again, looked both ways along the empty road, and reached up under her dress to unhook her stockings from her garter belt. Still scanning the road, she rolled one stocking down to the ankle, then the other, grimacing as she eased it over her damaged knee. She unfastened the ankle-strap of her sandal, peeled away the stocking, and put the sandal on again. Then she began the same process with the other foot.

When she had finished removing her stockings, she wadded them up and threw them through the car window onto the floor of the back seat. She looked along the road, and then at her watch, which now showed fifteen minutes past.

"Wouldn't you just know," she said aloud. Then she opened the rear door, crawled partway into the hot car, retrieved one stocking, and backed out again. Stooping toward the projecting rear-view mirror, she spat on the wadded silk and began to scrub at her face, smearing the dust to grime stained with pink powder and patches of bare, flawed skin, a result faithfully recorded in miniature in Little Land.

"Aw, shit."

Honey stamped her sandal, looked along the road again, opened the front door of the Franklin, and got in, squealing with distaste and discomfort at the contact of the fusty gray upholstery against her bare legs. She started the engine and drove along the road to where it widened, turned the car round, and drove away in the direction in which she had first come, watching the scene behind her dwindle to a point in the rear-view mirror and vanish.

The sun soaked unevenly down through the elms into Anna's front yard. Celia, sitting in a splotch of hot light, shielded the sides of her face with both hands like someone trying to gaze out over a long bright distance. But her head in its tight-waved cap of brown hair was lowered so that all she could have seen was the trodden grass directly in front of her and a crack in the doorstep where a company of red ants was excavating. The candlewick bedspread was still drawn shut, though above it Falada's cardboard head had now been positioned atop the stepladder—supported by four volumes of the works of George Eliot from the glass-fronted bookcase in the sitting room. There was no sign of Mary Ann or Lolly.

"Celia?" Anna glanced with concern at her friend, who was now bent almost double as if with cramp.

There was an inarticulate noise, a sort of half sob.

"Celia, are you all right?"

"Yes . . . It's just . . ." She shook her head, then raised it to stare at Anna. "I know what's happening now, that's all. And you do too, don't you? You know where Honey's gone."

"I expect she's down at the store."

"She's going to meet Dan," Celia said in a pinched whisper.

"Well, of course she'll meet him, if she goes to the village," said Anna, a little impatiently.

"No, no, no." Celia clutched both sides of her kitchen chair. "They're meeting somewhere else, I know they are . . . I could tell at lunch, the way . . . The way they were looking at each other."

'Celia, you've got to be sensible about this." Anna's voice was soothing but firm. "Dan is at Meggs's store listening to the baseball game with Bill and Lennie and Mr. Meggs."

"Then why did she rush off that way, for nothing? I know there's something going on between them, Anna. I can sense it. Because I love him." She began to weep, then controlled herself. "I'm being punished, that's what it is," she said in a low, strained voice. "I'm being punished by God for having taken him away from Irma and Lennie."

"Celia," Anna exclaimed. "You can't really believe that. Not in nineteen thirty-five."

Celia gave an unconvincing laugh. "Of course I don't believe it, I suppose," she said. "I'm an enlightened agnostic." She stared at the ants and the grass. "I was looking forward to this weekend so much," she said. "I thought, it will be all right at Anna's, it'll be safe . . . Dan and I will be together all the time, and nobody can call from the office, because there isn't any phone . . ." She began to sob again. "I can't take it anymore, Anna!" she said in a painful whispered shriek. "I'm falling apart."

"Oh, Celia." Anna put her arm round her friend's shoulders. "I really don't think they're meeting now. And even if they were, I'm sure there's nothing serious between them. It's just a flirtation."

"Nothing serious! How kkn— aaoo—" Celia's voice began to come apart into bunches of vowels and consonants. "Everything hee— everything he ddd—" She choked and lost hold of language completely, clutching her elbows with her hands and doubling up again. "Oh, Anna," she wailed aloud from this stooped position. "I love him so much it's killing me, Anna."

"Scene Three," Mary Ann announced, putting her head round the curtain and observing the alternative scene in front of her.

Celia swallowed and sat up, wiping her eyes. "Sorry." She gave Anna a strained smile, then turned to the stage.

There was a pause after the curtain had been pulled back. "Come *on*," Mary Ann's voice whispered from behind it. Another pause; then Lolly appeared from the house, still wearing Anna's mother's apron, and now carrying one of Anna's father's canes, with a pink hair-ribbon tied round it.

"Oh, woe is me," she said in a rapid monotone. "I'm in the prince's country. But everything has gone wrong. My maid made me change clothes with her. And now everybody thinks she's me. And she's going to marry the prince. Oh, woe . . ." Her voice faded away.

Anna glanced sideways at Celia, who was sitting rigid in her kitchen chair, holding onto the wooden seat with both hands as if it were about to take off.

"Falada," Mary Ann prompted in a loud whisper from behind the bedspread.

"And she told the prince that my dear Falada was a bad wicked horse," Lolly went on. "And she got them to cut his head off and put it up over the castle gate, here." She pointed. "Oh, woe is me . . ." Another fadeout.

"Goose girl," Mary Ann hissed.

"And now I have to be a goose girl, and go out in the meadows and watch the silly white gooses all day." Lolly turned away from the audience and approached the step-ladder, looking up at the horse's head with its white fringed paper mane.

> *Alas, Falada, hanging there,*

she recited, raising her goose girl's crook.

Mary Ann, from behind the curtain, replied for Falada in an assumed deep voice.

> *Alas, Princess, how ill ye fare!*
> *If this your mother knew,*
> *Her heart would break in two.*

There was a sobbing, choking sound from the audience. Lolly stopped in the act of passing under the castle gate. She stared at her mother, who was still holding onto the seat of her chair, and also rocking back and forth on it, her eyes sticky with tears.

"I can't— I'm sorry—' Celia wailed. She let go of the

chair, stood up, and wavered off, half-running across the lawn and round the side of the house.

Anna looked after her, and then back at the stage, where Mary Ann was now also visible, peering round the bedspread. "I guess I'd better run and see what's the matter with Lolly's mother," she said, rising. "Why don't you go into the kitchen now, girls, and have some lemonade? It's in a glass pitcher in the icebox. And I'll be back to see the rest of your play as soon as I can." She strode across the grass after Celia.

For a few moments the front yard was empty and silent. Then the Hubbard's Franklin could be heard struggling up the steep hill beyond the orchard. It came into view and turned off the road rather too fast, so that it overshot the driveway and buried its hood in a tall stand of lilacs.

Honey, swearing, put the car into reverse and backed away from the broken bushes. She turned off the engine, got out, and limped round the lilacs onto the front lawn. No one was there; only the wide marble doorstep with the bedspread pulled aside to reveal a ladder crowned with a cardboard horse's head, and four kitchen chairs arranged in a row on the sun-spattered grass. In the furthest of them Theodore Ilgenfritz, with a bright-eyed pleasant expression and furry extended paws, sat watching the stage.

"**Pussy** wants a corner!" Lolly calls in the middle of the front lawn, and Mary Ann and everybody else rushes to change, stumbling and bumping into each other because it's getting dark. Mary Ann changes trees with Honey, who is gasping and giggling, and Lolly's father changes with Bill, and Anna changes with Lolly's mother.

Lennie doesn't change with anybody, which is against the rules. He didn't want to play in the first place, and he said "So who cares" when they told him he wouldn't get any lemon coconut cake, which would have been swell because there would be more for the rest of them and who wants him to play anyhow. But then Celia asked him "Please, just this once," and he said Okay. And practically the first thing he did was to knock Lolly over when he was changing bases with her, sort of on purpose.

"Pussy wants a corner!" Lolly calls, and Mary Ann starts to change with Lolly's mother but she runs in the other direction and Mary Ann has to change with Bill instead and it's too far and Lolly tags her before she gets there, and now she is It.

It is hard being It when it's so dark you can't see where anybody is or who is creeping out away from their bases crying Nyah nyah to tease you. Everybody is shouting and calling things at you and when you run after them as hard as you can they pretend they are already safe when they aren't really. Mary Ann has to call for them to change four times and is feeling sort of like crying before she finally tags Anna and gets her tree.

Grown-ups are really unfair, she thinks, leaning on the rippled rough trunk of the tree and trying to catch her breath. When you get invited to a party they always make you get dressed up in uncomfortable fancy clothes: green velvet or linen dresses that get chocolate ice cream on them, and starched lace collars that scratch your neck, and long slippery satin sashes that come untied and trip you up in games so that everybody laughs at you, or else the ends fall in the toilet. And they keep on telling you to act polite and don't get your pretty dress dirty or make too much noise or quarrel or fight and always shake hands with your hostess when you arrive and leave and say Many-happy-returns-of-the-day and Thank-you-for-a-very-nice-time.

Then *they* go and have a party, and they all put on kids' play clothes—shorts and sundresses and T-shirts and sandals—or even go barefoot the way Honey and Anna are now. They play kids' games and don't even stick to the rules. They tell lies, like saying they will watch a play that took you hours to fix up, and then leaving right in the middle of it. They shout and get dirty and are rude to each other. And the longer the party goes on, the worse they get. They were okay for a while yesterday, up until Lolly's father and Lennie started fighting about who got to let off the fireworks, but they have been getting worse ever since.

At dinner tonight they were all mad at each other the way big kids about Lennie's age get sometimes. Not yelling or fighting, but sort of laughing and saying mean things, only they didn't always say them to anybody special the way younger kids would have. Instead they made jokes about bunches of people with names like "most men today" and "the idle rich." It was as if you were real mad at somebody and you had a big handful of mud, but you were too old to throw it at him, so instead you threw it at the wall right next to him. Splat! it went and maybe some of the mud would get on him, but you would just smile and act as if you didn't know anything about that and it wasn't your fault.

Also it was kind of as if they had chosen up teams while she and Lolly weren't looking, and their mothers and Anna were on the opposite team from their fathers and Lennie, instead of each family being on its own team the way it ordinarily naturally is. When Anna served seconds of mashed potatoes Honey said Bill couldn't have any, because he was too fat already. And she tried to move the dish away, but Bill grabbed it back. "I'm not fat," he said. "I'm just a little out of condition; I could use some exercise."

That sure was the truth, Honey said, he hadn't moved a muscle all weekend. Then she and Lolly's mother and Anna started making jokes and remarks about how most men today are no use and you can't count on them for anything. They went off to hear baseball games and left women and girls to do all the hard jobs, and you would never see them picking vegetables in the hot sun or dirtying their hands with the breakfast or lunch or dinner dishes.

Then Bill and Lolly's father started throwing their mud and saying how middle-class women were so spoilt nowadays that they were completely lazy and useless. They were America's new idle rich who had beautiful houses full of every modern appliance to live in and maids to do their housework and nothing to do all day but go shopping, and husbands working their behinds off to pay the bills they ran up. Only Bill said "damn asses" instead of behinds. If Mary Ann said that she would have to go straight to her room, which just shows you how unfair grown-ups are.

The fight kept getting worse and worse. Pretty soon nobody was listening to each other and everybody was yelling at once. Lennie was yelling about how women were too dumb to be allowed into baseball games anyhow, and Honey was picking on Bill again for bringing his office work to Anna's house, and even Lolly's father stopped laughing and started swearing. "Dammit," he said. "Dammit, this is supposed to be a vacation."

Then Lolly's mother said "Well, it's no vacation for me," and she started sort of gasping and crying again like this afternoon at the play.

It was getting really awful, but then Anna stopped it. She tinged on her glass with her fork for silence and said it was very hot, and practically everyone, including her, had started squabbling just like the children at Eastwind School did sometimes on very hot days. So she thought they should have a recess. They should all go outside and play some game and cool off, the way the kids did at school, and then they could come back in and have dessert. And Anna said Lolly could choose the game, because she was the only one who hadn't been quarreling. Mary Ann hadn't been quarreling either really, except she did tell Lennie "Shut up yourself!" a couple of times.

"Pussy wants a corner!" Anna calls, and Mary Ann changes with Lolly's father, but he doesn't run fast enough and Anna gets to the tree first and shouts "You're It! Slowpoke!" Which is perfectly true because Mr. Zimmern could have got there easy if he had really tried, only he was laughing too much.

What made the fight at dinner worse was that everything both teams said was sort of true. For instance it was true that Bill and Mr. Zimmern and Lennie had just sat around this vacation while Honey and Mrs. Zimmern and Anna and Mary Ann and Lolly made beds and cooked and set the table and cleared the table and did the dishes and picked peas and carrots and lettuce and black raspberries. But it was true too that at home Honey and Mary Ann never did any housework except on Thursday and every other Sunday when it was Precious Joy's day off. Then Mary Ann had to set the table and clear the table and Honey had to cook which she liked okay and wash the dishes which she hated, and Mary Ann had to dry them which she hated even worse. Lots of times one of them broke something, and yelled at herself or the other one, so that Thursday evening was always the worst part of the week.

Precious Joy didn't yell when she was washing up; she sang hymns. Mary Ann asked her once if she didn't get sick of doing so many dishes, but Precious Joy said No. "The Good Lord put me into this world to toil and labor," she said, "and Ah bless his name." She talked like that a lot ever since she got religion.

When she first came to work for Mary Ann's family Precious Joy was named Bessie, and sometimes when he forgot Bill still called her that, but she always corrected him. "My name is Precious Joy now, Mr. Hubbard sir," she said, and sometimes she said "I've been washed in the blood of the Lamb," which sounded ucky, but it didn't mean the real blood of a real lamb like what comes off lamb chops onto the butcher's crackly yellowish paper.

Bill explained to Mary Ann that what Bessie was washed in to change her into Precious Joy was just the plain Hudson River, along with a lot of other people who wanted to join a special church run by a man named Father Divine, and not even with soap—he just sort of ducked them. Some families got mad when their maids and cooks and gardeners joined Father Divine's church, but Bill said it was none of their business. And Honey didn't mind either. "Ah've not got a single word to say against Father Divine," she told one of Mama-Lou's friends down South. "Before Bessie got religion Ah didn't know from one Thursday night to the next if she was going to come home drunk, or beaten up again by that no-good husband of hers, or maybe she wouldn't turn up at all till some time the next day, looking so low-down and miserable it practically broke your heart. Bill was after me the whole time to fire her, but Ah just couldn't do it. But ever since she found Father Divine she's been a real treasure."

Religion is sort of like gin or whiskey. It makes people feel happy and want to sing, the way some grown-ups did when Bill and Honey had a big party, and woke her up. Sometimes if they drank too much they stopped singing and shouted, and they got tipsy and tipped over and fell down. "Praise the Lord!" Precious Joy shouted sometimes in the basement when she was scrubbing clothes on the washboard or running the washing machine, but she never fell down.

Religion is a kind of medicine, too. "The opiate of the masses," Bill said once when he was talking about Precious Joy to Mr. Parker across the street. *Opiate* meant a drug, like aspirin, that made you feel better even when you really weren't, he explained afterwards. For instance when she had flu and Dr. Buchman gave her medicine that stopped her head and her throat from hurting so much, but really inside she was still sick and full of flu germs like hundreds of invisible spotty bugs, and that's why she couldn't go to school.

The masses is everybody in America who isn't as comfortably off as their family, especially maids and gardeners and people who work in factories and The Unemployed. Bill explained that singing hymns and going to Father Divine's church made Precious Joy feel happier than she really was. Which is a confusing idea, because how could you feel happier than you felt? It made you forget your sorrows, Bill said. But that was confusing too. How could hymns make Precious Joy forget that Harvey had beaten her up and knocked out two of her teeth and left for Chicago with all her money, and that she didn't have any family of her own and had to work for Mary Ann's family?

"Pussy wants a corner!" Lolly's mother calls, because she is It now. Everybody changes this time, even Lennie, and things get mixed up because it's an odd number, and so dark out you can hardly see anything. People are sort of staggering around the yard and Lolly's father and Honey start running in the same direction and bang into each other.

"Why don't you look where you're going, you big dope?" Honey shouts.

"Pardon me, Lady Jane," Mr. Zimmern says in a fake-polite voice, and he bumps into Honey again and both of them fall down in the grass and roll around laughing and acting silly.

"I guess we're cooled off now," Anna says. "Let's all go in and have some coconut cake and iced tea."

So they do.

"Come on, out here," Dan stage-whispered, holding the front door open as Honey descended the stairs.

"Ah'm not—" Honey began in a pettish, chilly voice.

"Come on, damn it." He grasped her by one, then both bare arms.

"—interested. Ooh! Leave go! I'll scream." But Honey did not scream, or even raise her voice enough to be heard in the dining room, and though she resisted, it was ineffectively.

"Help," she mewed, as Dan eased the screen door quietly shut behind them and pulled her out onto the darkened lawn. "Leave go of me." She scratched at his arm with her sharp varnished nails.

Swearing under his breath, Dan released her. They stood, close but not touching, dense shadows under the tall diffuse shadows of the trees. The rapid creaking of crickets, tuned to a pitch of impatience by the hot night, surrounded them.

"What's the matter with you, baby?" Dan asked. "And where the hell were you this afternoon?"

"Where was Ah?" In the darkness, Honey almost spat. "Ah never heard of such a question. Where were you?"

"Waiting for you."

"You were not," Honey said in a petulant, indignant whisper. "You stood me up, and Ah don't appreciate being stood up."

"Excuse me, beautiful. *You* stood *me* up." Dan smiled angrily, invisibly. "I waited till almost four."

"Oh, for the Lord's sake. Well, Ah was there at three." Honey gave a little cross laugh.

"Come on." He brushed her pale curls, as dark now in the moonless night as his own, with one hand. "I've never known you to be on time anywhere."

"Ah was on time today." She swayed slightly nearer, so that the silky fabric of her dress brushed against Dan's shirt. "Honestly. And Ah had to walk out on the girls' play, too. It made me feel real mean, doing that."

"Sorry." Dan gathered Honey toward him with one arm, feeling with the other for her face, then lowering his own face to it. Heat and moisture passed between them, but not affection.

"I told you I didn't know how fast I could get away from Lennie and Bill," Dan said presently, not adding that he had found it impossible to go directly from an amicable conversation with the latter to an assignation with his wife. "I said for you to wait." He sighed. "If you'd just do what I tell you, baby, we wouldn't have any trouble."

In the dark, in his arms, Honey stiffened like a cat that senses an enemy.

"Let's go round by the barn," Dan went on insinuatingly, pressing her to him. "Beautiful stars out tonight. I'll show you the Milky Way."

"Not now." Honey did not relax. "They'll be after us in a moment."

"All right. When? How about later tonight, after everybody's gone to bed? Can you get out then?" The frantic chirping of crickets continued; Honey said nothing. "Come on, beautiful." He rubbed his face, rough with a day's growth of beard, against hers, gently but insistently sandpapering it. "Am I going to see you?"

"Maybe." Honey turned her head so that he was sandpapering her hair. "If you're nice."

"I am nice," he said impatiently.

"If you're real polite." She giggled and moved against him, standing on tiptoe.

"I'm very polite." Dan, provoked in more ways than one, dropped his hand from her waist and pinched her rump, vulnerable beneath the thin silky summer dress.

"Ow!"

"What's the matter?" he asked, mock-concerned.

"You—"

"Did a mosquito bite you?"

"God darn you." She struggled out of his grasp.

"Lots of big mosquitoes out here." He laughed. "Relax, baby, I'll protect you."

"Honey! Hey, Honey!" A loud voice, Bill's, calling from the house.

"Don't answer," Dan whispered.

"Honey! Are you out there?"

"Leave go of me," Honey whispered furiously. "Ah've got to go back. Otherwise he'll turn the whole blasted place upside down."

"Honey!"

"Ah'm coming."

"About tonight—" Dan reached out a hand to detain

her, but missed. He stepped forward, waving both arms in the dark; but she was gone. "Oh, fuck it."

"**. . . these** new laws?"

"Well, historically speaking . . ."

Lolly's iced tea in the tall glass is sweet,wet,brown,with a pale wet slice of lemon and a dark green wet mint leaf floating and sinking in it, and two lumps of melting ice, grainy with sugar.

"What no one in this country realizes is that Germany . . ."

". . . national inferiority complex."

The lemon cake is giant-sized, its colors inside-out from a real lemon: the brightest part at the center, with a fluffy pale-yellow rind sprinkled with white sugary shreds of coconut. Coconut shreds on Lolly's plate among the flat pink flowers, and on the shiny dark tabletop. A trail of them all the way to the edge, and more down on the floor. Long and short bits, dot and dash. A message, a code, spelling? THIS WAY TO THE GIANT LEMON COCONUT CAKE. A message for?

"Moosy Leeny is a different proposition. Moosy Leeny represents . . ."

Moose, no, mouse. A coconut message for a mouse, so that after everyone has gone to bed it can creep quietly out of its hole and find its, her, way to the midnight banquet. A beautiful lady mouse named Elinore, no, what? Leena. She has pale pearl-gray fur so soft, as soft as moss, and long silky whisky whiskers, and her ears are pink inside like the tiny shells on the beach in Florida, and her tail is gray and furry too, not rubbery like most mouse's tails.

"Hitler's Brown Shirts . . ."

". . . fanatical obedience to their leader."

All the other mice who live in Anna's house have ordinary tails and are ordinary brown, and they adore their beautiful Princess Leena and follow her wherever she leads them with fanatical obedience and every other kind of obedience.

"If I lived in Germany now I'd . . ."

". . . second cousins, in Strasbourg, and Dan wondered if they . . ."

She is the only mouse who knows how to read the secret coconut messages, and she wears a collar of gray pearls around her neck and—

"So Dan wrote to them again, but they never . . ."

—a silver crown set with pearls and moonstones that shine in the dark so her followers can see to follow her.

". . . said there was no one by that name living there. The whole family had disappeared. They had a little girl, a few years younger than Lolly, named Danielle after Dan's grandfather, he'd never met her but he always sent—

". . . doesn't even know if they're alive."

It is too noisy here, she can't think mice. All the dining room is filling up with noise and words, loud frightened worried ones that don't melt away in the air the way most words do, but bounce and crowd. Like the balloons of words in comic strips, nudging and pushing, floating round Mr. Hubbard and Anna and Mummy-Celia and Lennie, piled on the floor and table and chairs.

". . . threatening calls . . ."

". . . attacked in the street . . ."

If Danny were here he'd make them stop. —Stop talking that way, everybody, he'd say, you're frightening Lolly. But he isn't; they don't. They just keep blowing up more and more balloons till all the extra space in the dining room is filled and the frightened words and letters are squeezed and jumbled together.

". . . no better than murderers."

". . . completely insane . . ."

She gets down from her chair and moves round toward Mary Ann. "Hey," she says. But Mary Ann doesn't hear; she is leaning along the table blowing up balloons too.

"So why didn't he go and. . . . Yes, but I don't get it. You mean they could have killed . . ."

Lolly slides sideways through the words into the hall, and along to the front door. It is quieter there. The lamp on the table like a white milky tulip; it flicks its tongue and spreads quiet watery light and shadow up the wall in a flower pattern. Night-bugs are buzzing and bumping the screen door, and one firefly flashing its green light. Flash-lights for mice, for the mice that live in

". . . might be dangerous."

Voices from the dining room, she can still hear them. Upstairs. No. It's too dark there; and too scary dark out-side. But Anna's sitting room is quiet, and not really dark, only softly dim, because of the flower shining in from the hall.

Mice with firefly flashlights, one for each mouse, and two for Princess Leena, special royal bluey-green ones.

Lolly climbs onto the window seat between the heavy velvet curtains, one of her favorite secret places at Anna's house, where if you lean back on the squishy cushions nobody can see you from inside or outside.

The flashlight-flies light the mice's way round inside the thick walls of Anna's house where they live, in the secret space between the bricks and the wallpaper. There is a whole city built there, with houses and stairs and tunnels and storerooms, she will tell Mary Ann about it later, and a secret mousehole entrance into every room, so that when everyone's asleep—

"Honey! Hey, Honey!" Mary Ann's father shouts sudden loud in the hall.

The mouse watchmen who are specially large smart strong mice stand by the holes and shine their flashlight-flies and poke out their heads and whiskers and look around to see who's coming.

"Honey! Are you out there?" The screen door boings open, and Mr. Hubbard shouts through it, scaring the mice. "Honey!"

"Ah'm coming." Mary Ann's mother's voice, far out in the dark, high and cross. Coming nearer. "What's the matter?"

"Oh, there you are. I wondered where you were, that's all."

"For Jesus' sake." She is outside on the doorstep now. "Ah thought something real terrible had happened, the way you were hooting at me."

"I was not hooting," Mary Ann's father says.

"You were hooting like a hoot owl," Mary Ann's mother says. "Ah'm sick and tired of it."

Yes, an owl. With his round eyes glasses, and his orangy-gray feathers sticking out both sides. Flapping one brown wing to push the door further open so more bugs and Mary Ann's mother can come in and they do but she doesn't.

"Ah'm sick and tired of your following me around the whole time like a little kid," she says. "It's getting so Ah can't step outside for one minute to look at the stars before you start going off your rocker."

The owl flaps both wings and hops outside, letting the screen door squawk and bang shut behind him. Off your rocker means crazy, completely insane. Like Uncle's old high-backed rocking chair with the straw seat: if you pushed too hard it fell over sideways and lay on the library floor looking strange and awful and no use to anybody like Uncle after his stroke and you couldn't sit on his its lap anymore. And Nurse Williams said he wasn't really Lolly's Uncle at all, he was her Greatuncle and getting on so what could you expect, and Auntie Helen wasn't her real aunt like Aunt Rose in New York.

"So you were looking at the stars," the owl says in a strange sneery voice.

"Yes, Ah was."

"And where was Dan?"

"Ah haven't the faintest idea where Dan was." Mary Ann's mother laughs the way people laugh at craziness, fast and high.

"I thought he might have followed you."

"And why on earth should he do that?"

"Because he's been hanging around you all weekend."

"Oh, for the love of Pete. He was just being sociable. He knows how to behave on a visit; how to relax and have a good time and make everybody feel comfortable," Mary Ann's mother says in a tight uncomfortable voice. "Not like some people."

"Yeah, he can put on fancy manners," the owl says.

"There's nothing wrong with good manners," Mary Ann's mother says. "Anyhow, Ah thought you liked Dan. You certainly were sticking up for everything he said at supper."

"Oh sure, I admit he's got some interesting ideas. But there's something phony about him, if you ask me."

"Who asked you?"

"Trying to pass himself off as a red-hot socialist," the crazy owl goes on in a steady radio voice, as if somebody, not Mary Ann's mother, had really asked him. "But I don't believe it for a moment. He's just a parlor pink; I know the type. And he's a real loud-mouth."

"What do you mean, a loud-mouth?"

"I mean the way he talks about women. You should have heard him this afternoon, you wouldn't think he was so darn polite."

"What did he say about women this afternoon?" Mary Ann's mother asks.

"Oh, nothing special. You know the way some men talk when their wives aren't around."

Mary Ann's mother does not say if she knows this.

"About his first wife, mostly, and, uh, a couple of other women."

"Oh, did he really?" Mary Ann's mother says in her bird's voice, fluttery and high.

"Listen, Dan's a real skirt-chaser. He's the kind of guy who's always trying to get into some girl's panties."

"Ah don't want to hear talk like that," the bird squeaks, sharp-soft. "Ah think you're positively vulgar."

"I want to take care of you, that's all," the owl hoots.

"Ah can take care of mahself, thanks," Mary Ann's mother says, opening the screen door.

Creak; boing. Slam. Mary Ann's mother and father go back down the hall through the wavery light, not looking into the sitting room. Mary Ann's mother's face hard, shut, the way Mummy-Celia's face shuts too when something is vulgar. Something you aren't supposed to see, to hear, to talk about. Dirty men spitting on the gray New York street as they walk by. Or Nurse Williams at Greatuncle's house talking about her tapeworm and asking how much did the dining-room curtains cost. Celia's face shuts and she doesn't see the spit or hear Nurse Williams. Doesn't answer her. The red message on the wall in the railroad station that she doesn't see that Lolly won't see won't remember won't.

Vulgar dirty words. Things suddenly are called a different name that makes them change invisibly and be smeared with invisible dirt. Greatuncle lying in bed, his mouth hanging open that was always shut so tight when he was Uncle. *Piss* instead of *wee-wee*, you mustn't say that, and you mustn't say *urine* either except at Dr. Buchman's. Or other times the word holds still and the thing changes behind it and some ordinary safe word is wrong and awful. Even nice pretty words like *parlor*, Greatuncle's best sitting room, and *pink*, a pretty color or a flower in the garden, suddenly they slide together and mean something disgusting, something Mr. Hubbard can't stand, what? Even special holy Bible words can slide together wrong. *Ass*, the ox and the ass in the manger on Christmas Eve; it sounds holier than if you said the cow and the donkey in the barn. Then without any warning or noise it changes and means your behind so you mustn't say it and you mustn't say *behind* either or *bottom* for that part of you except to very safe people like your parents or Mary Ann or Anna, whispering or in very safe places where nobody else can hear. It's better not to talk about that part of you ever at all, especially to strangers, especially to strange men who might be, she won't think about it.

The worst most dangerous thing of all is talking about panties, or letting them show, worse even than being naked. The story the fat man with the red bow tie told at Mary Ann's picnic. There was a little girl once, he told, and on her way home from school she met a fellow, and he said to her, "Little girl, if you'll stand on your head I'll give you a nickel." So she did, and he did. But when her mother heard about it she was very angry and said, "Don't you ever do that again. He only wanted to see your panties." So the next day when she got home her mother asked her, "Did you meet that nasty man that wanted to see your panties?" And the little girl said, "Yes, and he gave me another nickel. But I fooled him: I didn't wear any." Everybody laughed, except Mummy-Celia, whose face shut like a cupboard door.

Because you must never never let any strange man or boy see your panties. It is a terrible magic that can turn even good safe ones into monsters. Like fairy tales where the handsome prince is changed into a bear or a hungry ravening gray wolf, and he has to have his head chopped off before he can change back. And you can never tell which ones will be bears. They always seem nice and friendly, Auntie Helen said, just like, she won't think about that. Then the terrible spell comes over them and they have to chase skirts, and you can only chase a skirt if somebody is wearing it; otherwise it would just lie there. Like bulls and cows that didn't pay attention to red cloth unless you ran or waved it, they just went on peacefully lying down in the long grass chewing their dinner twice the way cows do, and talking to other cows. Because there was no red skirt to chase, or panties.

Everything sliding, names and things and people, slippery and hissing. *Asss. Pisss.* Words aren't safe and solid any-more, they slide apart into other words, like the game they played once in school, How Many Words Can You Make Out of, but Lolly was sick then and she had to go lie down. *Panties,* that are safe named and clean and folded in the bottom drawer, suddenly falls apart: into *aunties,* a word for aunts that aren't real aunts; into *pant, ants, pants,* words that are safe by themselves, but they can come together and make you sick. Like the pickles and hot dogs and chocolate macaroons at Aunt Rose's house. ("What's the matter with Lolly, Lennie? Why is she wriggling so?" "Aw, she's got ants in her pants.")

No words are safe. Nothing is safe and nobody. Everyone everywhere is vulgar horrible disgusting. She wants to vomit she mustn't *vomit* she must *throw up* she mustn't throw up. Throw. Up.

But it isn't so, isn't so. Because what insane owls and people say doesn't count. They slide words together and say crazy wrong things, that they are Napoleon and that the cow jumped over the moon. They talk talk to themselves like the lady with the baby carriage and no baby in front of Wanamaker's. They say words that don't mean anything, like some man somewhere trying to get into a little girl's panties. Which couldn't happen because he wouldn't fit. It's only craziness, sliding words about some man somewhere, far away, she won't think about it. She will wait for Mary Ann to come, and she will think about? Mice.

July 6

It is hot in the sun between the big rosebushes and the wall of Anna's house. Even the wind is hot, as if somebody was blowing it with Honey's new hair-dryer. It is awful early for it to be so hot; not even time to leave for the picnic that her mother and Lolly's mother and Anna are fixing in the kitchen.

She and Lolly started to help them, but then Anna said they were eating more egg salad than they were putting into the sandwiches, and why didn't they go outside and play croquet for a while? But Mary Ann said no it was too hot, and anyhow they wanted to do some real work, not just play games. So Anna said well if they liked they could go and catch some of the Japanese beetles that were eating up her rosebushes, and she would pay them ten cents a Mason jar.

So they did. Only Lolly quit after they brought the first jar full of bugs inside, buzzing and shining greeny-brown, and she saw Anna ladle boiling hot water into it from the big kettle on the stove, and all the beetles wiggled their legs and died. Lolly screamed Oh and said it was horrible even if they did eat roses, and she wasn't going to catch any more. So Anna sent her out to the garden for lettuce instead.

Mary Ann kept on catching beetles. If she could fill

another jar all by herself she would get ten cents more, plus five is fifteen, a week's allowance. It isn't hard work either like weeding or raking leaves, but almost sort of fun. Anna's roses aren't as prickly as the ones Bill brings home in green tissue paper from New York City when it is Honey's birthday or Mother's Day or she is mad at him. They're bigger and floppier, with more leaves, and they look like they were made of cotton instead of silk or satin.

The Japanese beetles are all over the rosebushes, sitting on the leaves and buds and exploring inside the flowers. They never see you coming the way flies do; you can just pinch them between your thumb and fingers and they can't get away. They feel light and dry and wiggly. And then you drop them into the jar, and they are too dumb to fly out again except by mistake.

"Ugh, those ugly old Japanese beetles, Ah can't stand to look at them," Honey screamed out when they brought the first jarful into the kitchen. But really they aren't ugly; they are kind of pretty, with shiny polished backs that change in the light from green to brown like the taffeta cushions on Mama-Lou's bed down South. They have little black stick legs, and tiny papery unfolding wings that aren't much use, because they can't fly very well, or very fast.

The beetles aren't old either; probably they are mostly very young, since bugs don't live too long. But they do look Japanese—like the MADE IN JAPAN tin tea-sets and wind-up mice and paper and bamboo fans from the ten-cent store, that never live very long either: usually they get broken in a couple of weeks. Probably there is a factory in Japan making these beetles too, hundreds and millions of them, to send to America and all over the world. They aren't real live squishy bugs that can feel hurt, they just have little machines inside them that stop going when you pour boiling water over them the way a wind-up mouse would. So there isn't any reason to feel sorry for them.

Holding the buzzing jar of toy beetles, Mary Ann moves alongside Anna's house toward the next rosebush, underneath the kitchen window. It's too high for her to see anything inside except the kitchen ceiling and part of a cupboard, but she can hear Honey and Anna and Lolly's mother talking while they make the picnic lunch.

At first it's pretty boring. Lolly's mother's voice says do they think that's enough carrot sticks for eight people and Anna's voice says "Oh yes, certainly," and Honey's voice says she is going to put some extra ice in the thermos because it looks as if it is going to be a mighty hot day. And Mary Ann can hear her jabbing at a block of ice with the ice pick, because Anna doesn't have a real refrigerator, only a wooden box with bluish bubbly blocks of ice dripping and melting in it on one side and the food dripping on the other.

Then they complain about the world for a while. How it seems as if everything is going wrong now, so many men still out of work, and businesses and stores closing, and even the weather. It certainly never used to be so hot when they were little girls, and look at those dreadful dust storms out West and now these ugly old Japanese beetles everywhere, what in heaven's name is the matter with this country?

"We've been greedy," Anna says. "We've taken too much out of the land all these years, and now Nature is having her revenge." And Lolly's mother and Honey say "Yes. I'm afraid so," and "That sure seems like it is true."

Mary Ann has heard a lot about Nature. She is a kind of very powerful invisible fairy godmother who is in charge of everything that happens in the world that's not because of people or machines. Nature makes trees get yellow and red in October, and turns eggs into chickens and tadpoles into frogs and all kinds of stuff like that. She decides beforehand which children will be strong and which ones will be smart. ("Nature gave you a good brain, and it's up to you to use it.") If you are sick she can make you well. ("It's just a feverish cold, Nature will take care of it in a couple of days.")

Ads on the radio announced that their cereal was full of Nature's goodness, or kept you regular in Nature's own way, which meant that if you ate nasty soggy All-Bran for breakfast every day you wouldn't ever get constipated and have to take mineral oil or Ex-Lax, which was probably a lie like most ads. Science books told how Nature gave some animals fur coats to protect them against the winter, and made coal out of fern trees that grew millions of years ago. Sometimes they called her Mother Nature, especially in stories for little kids, but that might be just to make them feel safer.

Because Nature has a scary side. She has laws you have to obey and a balance that can be upset, like if somebody was walking along a wall and you pushed them. If you broke her laws or made her lose her balance and fall off, naturally she got mad and then everything went wrong and there were droughts and floods and tornadoes and Japanese beetles, and people got sick or hurt or even killed. But it was their own fault and they should have known better. She is a huge invisible lady like North Wind in the book, with long long streaming gray hair and floaty gray clothes and bare feet walking along a high invisible wall over the world and she looks sort of like Anna if Anna suddenly grew as tall as Eastwind School.

Everybody believes in Mother Nature. She is stronger

and more important than God or Jesus. Only some people believe in them, and then mostly only on Sundays, except for Precious Joy.

Precious Joy believes in Jesus who was a man in a white nightgown who lived a long time ago at the righthand end of the Mediterranean Sea and liked little children. There is a colored picture of Jesus in their dentist's waiting-room looking a lot like Dr. Preston the dentist, only with much longer hair. He is smiling and patting some kids that are standing round him, and underneath it says "Suffer little children to come unto Me." For a long time Mary Ann thought it *was* Dr. Preston, in his white coat, and he had put it up to show that he was a really nice dentist and suffering little kids ought to come unto him when they had a toothache. Even after she found out that Jesus wasn't Dr. Preston she still had the idea that he was a dentist sort of stuck in her mind.

Grandma Hubbard and Mama-Lou believe mostly in God who is an old man with a beard. He is everywhere at once watching everything and he likes people to be telling him all the time how swell he is. That is what churches are about mostly, when Mary Ann goes to one down South with Mama-Lou or in Maine with Grandma Hubbard. Mama-Lou's church is fancy, with colored glass windows and candles and lace tableclothes and organ music, and Grandma Hubbard's is plain and serious like a school auditorium, but the same things go on in them: people in their best clothes singing or reciting about how wonderful God is. Also they asked God to forgive them for trespassing on other people's property, and to please stop the Depression and cure Grandma Hubbard's arthritis.

But God didn't stop the Depression or the arthritis. They just got worse all the time, while he sat up in the sky and watched people to see if they were being good. If they weren't he felt very very sad, Mama-Lou said, and angry. But he couldn't do much about it till after you were dead and probably not then, or else Bill and Honey and Grandpa Hubbard and Anna and Lolly's mother and father would believe in him. Instead they are agnostics, which means they think God probably doesn't exist but they are too polite to say so to people who believe he does.

"You know what I think?" Anna's voice says from inside the kitchen. "I think that if women were in charge of this world there wouldn't *be* any wars or depressions. Could you pass me the wax paper, please?"

"Yes, I believe that too," Lolly's mother's voice says.

"Well, Ah don't know," Honey's voice says. "Ah do think sometimes Ah could make as good a job of running Bill's office as he does; but lordy, Ah wouldn't want all that aggravation. Ah'm just too lazy." She giggled. "Ah think most women are kind of lazy."

"Speak for yourself," Anna says in her teacher voice.

"Oh, not you, Anna." Honey giggles again. "But the rest of us."

Something funny is going on, Mary Ann thinks, moving around the bush with her hand over the top of the jar and beetles bumping against it because it's almost full now. Why should Honey say women are lazy when they are all making sandwiches and Mary Ann is catching beetles and Lolly is in the garden picking lettuce? It's as if she suddenly doesn't want to be on a team of ladies and girls anymore, or else she is sick of sandwiches and wants to be allowed to stop.

She can't tell for sure, because they have all started in about the picnic again and if they should peel the hard-boiled eggs. First they decided not to peel them and then they decided to because it will be easier for the children, which means Mary Ann and Lolly. Then they went on about the children which was more interesting.

"Ah'm real glad for my Mary Ann to have made a friend like Lolly," Honey says. "She's so good-tempered, and she's got such pretty ladylike ways."

"Oh, thank you," Lolly's mother says.

Mary Ann puts two joined-together bugs into the jar. She has heard before about Lolly's ladylike ways. That just means that she always said Please and Thank you and never contradicted anybody, because either she wasn't listening anyhow or she was scared to.

"The way she got right up and started to clear the table this morning, the moment you asked her, sweet as sugar candy," Honey goes on. "Ah just wish mah baby had her disposition."

"Yes," Lolly's mother says. "Well I'm awfully glad that they've made friends too, because . . ." Mary Ann waits to hear what is nice about her, but Mrs. Zimmern's voice just fades away the same as Lolly's does sometimes. "You know it's lonely for her out where we live, and I'm afraid she hasn't had much . . . I used to be awfully concerned about it, because she isn't very . . . Well, I do still worry some-times, she's so impractical and dreamy. Dan's always say-ing, 'How is she ever going to get along in the world?'"

"Ah wouldn't fret about that," Honey's voice says. "Your Lolly will never have to lift a finger long as there's some man around. Not like mah poor ugly duckling. Ah really can't imagine what's going to become of her."

●   ●   ●

Mary Ann stops picking beetles off the rosebush and stands still, looking at the brick wall of Anna's house and the green vines ruffling on it in the hot breeze.

"Oh, now, I don't think she's exactly . . ." Lolly's mother's voice fades away as usual.

Ugly duckling?

"I wouldn't worry about Mary Ann," Anna's voice says. "She's going to do all right. She may not be pretty-pretty, but she's got brains, and a will of her own."

"Oh, she's smart sure enough, Ah realize that. Ah guess she'll always be able to support herself. But we all know there's more to life than making a living." Honey laughs, and so do all the voices in the kitchen. Even Anna's voice.

The ugly duckling grew up into a beautiful swan. But they weren't talking like that would ever happen to her.

"Ah don't mean Ah think every woman has to be married," Honey says. "But she ought to have the option, you know what Ah mean? For instance, Ah bet you could have got married a dozen times over if you wanted, am Ah right, Anna?"

Mary Ann doesn't listen to whether Anna thinks Honey is right. She feels as if she had just fallen out of a swing, sort of dizzy and bumped, but really she is still standing in the same place holding the same jar of Japanese beetles. Over her head is the same rosebush and the same kitchen windowsill with paint peeling off it; and inside they are still laughing and talking, because they don't care.
Ugly.

She lifts her hand off the top of the jar.

"Go ahead, beetles," she says. "Eat up the roses all you want."

A few beetles fly out, sort of by accident, but the rest just stay there. So she turns the jar upside down, and they fall onto the ground in a buzzing surprised heap, and start slowly flying and crawling away.

"Go on, eat up all Anna's and everybody's flowers," Mary Ann says. "And all their tomatoes and their lettuce and their corn and their grass and their trees. Go *on*." She shakes the jar, because some of the stupid beetles are still stuck inside. "Shoo!"

She sets the empty jar on the ground next to some beetles who are still crawling around all stupid and mixed up. Then she gets down on her hands and knees and creeps through the rosebushes out onto the lawn, and stands up, and walks round the house and in the front door and up the stairs.

Ugly?

She opens the door to her parents' room where Bill is sitting writing with his shirt-sleeves rolled up and different colored pencils stuck over his ears.

"Yes, what is it?" he says in a cross voice, not looking up.

She opens her mouth and makes a noise. "Uh," it comes out.

"Oh, Mary Ann." Bill's voice gets even crosser. "I've asked you already this weekend not to disturb me when I'm working. You should be able to remember that. Now, please." He turns his head completely away and writes something with a blue pencil, as if Mary Ann had already gone out of the room. So she does.

Across the hall Lolly's parents' room is empty, and there is a big mirror above the chest of drawers. It is too high up to see anything except a needlepoint sampler on the wall, so Mary Ann pushes a chair over and climbs on it and looks into the glass, which is all green and spotty.

What does it mean to be ugly? She never notices what people look like much, unless it is really strange, for instance giants and midgets, or the very fat lady on Rye Beach, or men in New York City with black coats and long long beards like dwarfs.

She doesn't have a beard, and she isn't especially short or especially tall. Up until this year everybody was always complaining that she was too thin—underweight for her height-and-age group on the colored chart in Dr. Buchman's office. Miss Lily Viola, who sewed her flower-girl dress for Cousin Betty-Lou's wedding down South, told Honey that Mary Ann looked skimpy, as if God didn't have enough material and had to cut her out of the end of the bolt. And in Maine Grandpa Hubbard said "Your Mary Ann looks like a real Depression baby. You ought to feed her up more." That made Honey mad, because she already did feed Mary Ann as much as she could, and was always trying to get her to drink more milk and have extra helpings of things she didn't want.

But lately they have stopped complaining, so either Mary Ann's weight has finally caught up with her height the way Dr. Buchman said it would, or else they have given up because they figured it wouldn't make any real difference, and even if she got fatter she would still never be pretty.

Pretty is little girls drinking Coca-Cola or taking baths with Ivory Soap in ads, with peaches-and-cream complexions like Honey's instead of freckles. Or like dolls, or dumb Shirley Temple. Or pictures of Honey when she was a little girl, all round and soft and curly and smiley. But in the mirror everything about Mary Ann is thin and straight: her arms and her nose and her mouth and her hair in two greeny-orange braids. Her face is all covered with brown spotty freckles, and she looks sort of mean and miserable.

Probably everybody in the world always knew that she was ugly; only she didn't know it. Probably she had been ugly ever since she was born, like the song Lolly's father sang sometimes: "You must have been a beautiful baby, 'cause baby, look at you now." Only the opposite.

And she will go on being ugly for years and years. Or maybe her whole life. She will always be skinny and skimpy, a stick figure like little kids draw, with thin beetle arms and legs, and a circle head with two straight lines inside for the nose and mouth.

She ought to have little dot eyes too, but she doesn't. "Well, she's inherited one thing from you at least, Honey," people said sometimes. "Those big gray cat's eyes." Mary Ann never minded that, she liked cats; especially Lolly's Irene who is Persian and very quiet and polite and as soft as cotton candy to hold whenever she lets you which isn't often.

But some cats are ugly, like the wild ones that live in the woods near Lolly's house. They came to her back door mewing sometimes because they wanted to visit Irene or because they were hungry. "Just skin and bone, the poor thing," Lolly's mother would say, and she would feed the cat one good meal on the back porch and then Lolly and Mary Ann would help her put it in a cardboard box and drive it to the pound in Tarrytown so it could be adopted by a nice family.

Only one afternoon Lennie was there visiting and he laughed at them and said only a real sucker would believe an ugly skinny old cat like that would ever get adopted. Nobody would want it, he said, so after a couple of days the pound men would shut it in a box and kill it with poison gas. Lennie always says mean things like that, and usually they turn out to be lies, but not always.

If you were pretty and soft and curly, when you grew up lots of different men loved you and wanted to marry you. That happened to Honey. "Ah could have had mah pick of all the eligible fellows in Greensboro, and Ah chose you," she said to Bill sometimes. Lolly is pretty. "Pretty as a picture," Precious Joy said. Men would be lifting things for her all the time the way Honey said, and asking her to please marry them.

But nobody would want to marry Mary Ann; and so Theodora and Edward and Anna and Arthur will never be born.

Ugly.

Suppose they existed, she could ask God or Jesus or Mother Nature to make her pretty. It is worth trying, at least.

Mary Ann squinches her eyes shut. "O Lord or Lady," she says out loud to the ceiling, "make me pretty, please. If it is Thy will," she adds, because that's what Grandma Hubbard always says when she prays. Then she starts to count to a hundred, to give them time.

". . . ninety-eight, ninety-nine, one hundred. Ready or not." Mary Ann opens her eyes.

Either They don't exist, or They don't care, any of them. Of course if They did exist and care They would probably have done something about it years ago.

Mary Ann looks at her face reflected in the big spotty mirror behind a candlestick with a red candle in it and its mirror twin. Red is her favorite color, only her mother will never let her get a red dress or sweater or hat or anything because it would "clash" with her hair, which is a sort of orange color but called "red," why? It's stupid to call orange hair red.

Everything is stupid, and unfair; and when she gets grown up she is going to have lots of bright red clothes even if they clash as loud as the cymbals in the school orchestra and make her look even uglier than she is already, so there. Mary Ann kicks the front of the chest of drawers as hard as she can, and hurts her foot so bad she starts crying.

At the lowest point of the shallow valley a line of trees and bushes marked where a creek wound through the fields in long relaxed curves, between banks of clay and shoals of sandy gravel on which weeds flowered among the debris of last spring's floods. Now, in July, the water ran low and lazy, hardly a foot deep except where a drop of ground or a wider curve had created a natural swimming hole.

Beside the largest of these, under a huge spreading willow, Anna and her house guests sat and lay on the grass among the remains of a picnic lunch. It was very hot, and a thick heaviness to the air made even speech an effort. For nearly five minutes no one had said anything.

"Okay, boys and girls." Dan broke the silence. "Got to get into that water before I pass out." He yawned and raised himself on one elbow. "It's almost an hour since we ate."

"Thirty-five minutes." Anna smiled.

"All right. If I start to drown you can all rescue me." He sat up slowly, stood, and began undoing his shirt.

As if this were a signal, six of the other people scattered on the grass began to rise and remove their outer clothing. Only Lennie Zimmern, seated apart from the rest on the fallen trunk of another willow, reading a book, did not move.

"Aren't you coming swimming with us, Lennie?" Celia called, folding the skirt of her seersucker playsuit and hanging it over a honeysuckle bush.

"Nah." Lennie turned away, resting his elbows on his knees and his face on his fists to block out further interruption. Celia stood gazing at him for a moment; then she sighed and continued undressing, revealing a small but well-rounded, even voluptuous figure in a modest brown-and-white bathing suit. She pulled a bathing cap printed with a pattern of tight-waved white rubber hair over her tight-waved brown hair, and fastened the strap under her chin.

The rest of the party were also undressing, with varying effect. Lolly and Mary Ann, already barefoot and with only sundresses over their bathing suits, were the first to splash into the clear cool water: Lolly ahead, sinking smoothly; then Mary Ann, skinnier and more awkward, with sharp pale elbows and freckled protruding shoulderblades, testing the unfamiliar bottom with each step and then, with a piping cry, plunging in full-length.

On the bank Dan, in a new and brief pair of bright red trunks, smiled at the children, then cast a sideways glance of condescension, almost pity, at the equally large but relatively pale and soft body of Bill Hubbard. Then he strode to the edge of the pool and dove in, filling the air with spray.

"Any rocks in there?" Bill called, edging toward the brink in an old-fashioned black wool bathing suit which covered his chest like an undershirt and his legs almost to the knees.

"None that I know of."

"Mm." Bill hesitated, peering into the water—hazy

now with churned-up silt. He raised his pale, freckled arms as if to dive, then lowered them, and splashed sideways down the bank toward Lolly and Mary Ann.

"Come on, Mummy, it's so nice!" Lolly called.

"I'm coming." Celia waded through the shallows, then spread her arms and sank like a bird settling on water, giving a low, birdlike cry of pleasure. "Oh. Lovely."

Under the willow tree Anna, already undressed and with a white beach towel hung over one shoulder, paused to loosen the heavy roll of chestnut hair at the nape of her neck and secure it again to the crown of her head. As she stood there with her arms raised, surrounded by silvery gray and green descending foliage, she resembled a Greek or Roman statue—a stony Juno or Diana such as might appear in some myrtle-bordered clearing of a private park, or at the end of an avenue of trees in a public garden. Hers too was a figure pocked and roughened by time and weather, but classically proportioned, with broad hips and shoulders, strong rounded arms, long columnar legs, and the high firm breasts and flat stomach of a woman who has never borne children. Then she lowered her arms, smiled, and the illusion vanished. She dropped her towel and dived in, sinking for a long minute and then reappearing with a splash among her guests on the far side of the pool.

"Hi." Dan gave Anna a grin of admiration; Bill glanced toward but not at her, focusing instead on the group of mulberry bushes behind which his wife had retired to change her clothes. Faint fluttering movements were visible between the leaves; then finally Honey appeared, fetchingly attired in a red-white-and-blue polka-dot bathing suit with a ruffled décolletage and skirt.

"Come on in, Kitten, the water's fine!" he cried.

"Isn't it awful cold?" She tripped nearer.

"No, just right!" Dan shouted.

"Ah don't know if Ah should believe you." Honey put one small high-arched foot out toward the creek, dimpling the surface with her varnished toes, then snatched it back. "Oooh! You liar! It's perfectly freezing. Ah'm not going in there." She sat down on the bank, displaying her costume and figure to good advantage.

"Come on, sissy!" Dan called, plunging across the pool toward her. "It's nice and warm, once you get used to it. Just put one of those pretty little feet in again. . . . Now the other one."

Slowly, with much squealing, giggling, and coaxing, Honey was persuaded to dangle her feet in the creek, then to stand, then to wade forward a step at a time. But when the ground dropped away and the water washed above her knees she gave a theatrical shriek and clutched Dan with both hands.

"Eow! Ah felt a crab, right there under mah foot."

"Aw, you did not. Let me see." Dan bent and felt round in the now opaque water. "There's nothing here. Just a stick. You stepped on this old stick, that's all. Look." He held up a wet piece of wood fringed with weed, then tossed it aside onto the far bank. "Come on, scaredy-cat."

"It was a crab." Honey pouted charmingly. "A big mean old crab." She tossed her fluffy curls. "Anyways, Ah'm getting cold. Ah'm going back."

"Oh, come on, not yet." Dan laughed. "You've got to go in once, at least." He grasped Honey's upper arms, drawing her toward the deepest part of the pool.

"Ah don't want to." Honey giggled. "Let me go, Dan. Really." She pulled back, at first playfully and then, as she lost ground, with more determination. "Ah mean it!"

"Aw, come on."

"No. Quit it!" Honey's voice rose to a scream. Thirty feet downstream Bill, who was explaining the geological stratifications of the bank to Anna and the girls, paused in his discourse.

"Hey, now!" he called, starting to splash his way upstream. "Hold on there."

Neither Honey nor Dan seemed to hear him.

"No, no! Let go of me, you big old bully."

"Not till you've gone in." Dan relaxed his pull for a moment to roar a laugh; then he gave a sudden yank that upset Honey's balance and plunged her, shrieking, beneath the surface of the pool.

"Awoogl . . ."

Before the ripples made by her disappearance could break on shore, or Bill cover half the intervening distance, Honey rose again, but transformed—no longer a pretty kittenish blonde, but a half-drowned cat in clown costume, dripping, choking, spitting, with her polka-dot ruffles muddy and drenched, and her hair in wet dark strings over her face, down which wet dark strings of mascara were running.

"Hey, look at you!" Dan broke into a roar of laughter. The clown swiveled her head blindly toward his voice, took one unsteady step in the same direction, and attempted to slap him in the face, but missed as he ducked.

"Are you all right, dear?" Bill cried, puffing and shedding water.

"What do you think?" she spluttered, looking for a moment as if she might try to hit him also. Instead she turned her back on both men and splashed toward shore.

"Hey, Honey—" Dan called, following, trying without success to contain his amusement.

She stopped knee-deep. "You wait," she spat over her bare shoulder. "Ah'll fix you for this. You see if Ah don't."

"Listen, I'm sorry—"

"Why don't you just—" Bill began.

Honey splashed on. "Why don't you just both go to hell?" she asked. She scrambled onto the shore, snatched up the nearest towel, and vanished around the mulberry bushes.

Water. Slippery jello cool. Parting to slide round Lolly's arm, through her spread fingers; rejoining. Sliding along Mummy-Celia's bare pale-brown back, and Anna's larger back divided with bathing-suit straps into four pieces of freckled cinnamon toast. Backs going away up the creek toward where the other grown-ups are shouting and splashing, angry voices, she doesn't want to know what they say.

Water slipping and smoothing Lolly's skin like a green cool jello snake. Turning, wriggling, smoothing its own long ribbon skin of brown sand and gray gravel and chocolate clay, the snakeskin-striped creek bed that (Mary Ann's father says) has lain here in the lap of the valley for hundreds of years, thousands of years.

She lies down in the creek and is the green transparent snake, she hisses soft over the gravel, dips her long head and blows a string of bubbles, flicks her long long watery tail. She feels herself swimming away down down the valley, speckled by sun and shaded by willow trees dancing. Tall dancers with gray skirts and green waving arms, dancing slow in the wind, bending and stroking her back with their leafy fingers . . .

"Lolly!" Mary Ann's voice calls, thin, jangly.

The snake stops swimming, raises its head.

"I'm bored. Let's do something."

"Okay."

"So what do you want to do?" Mary Ann's face is pinched up white and sour. Behind it a bird flies across the creek, into the sun and out again, flicker flutter, lands on a bush by the bank.

"We could make something out of clay," Lolly says.

"What clay? I don't see any clay."

"There." Lolly points below the still-shaking green bush and the bird. "All that's clay."

"I don't see—" Mary Ann splashes across the creek and pats the bank, first the sandy upper part where white roots of grass poke out and wiggle surprised in the air, then lower down "There isn't any—You mean this brown stuff?"

Lolly nods.

"Okay. Let's dig out a whole lot and take it over there, on those flat rocks, and make some dishes."

"Okay."

Lolly stands in the sliding water and digs at the bank, first with her hands, oozy squeezy, then with a wet stick, until a big lump of it comes away with a sucking sigh. "Don't cry, clay," she whispers. "I'm going to make you into lovely chocolate dishes." Holding it together in both hands, dripping bits that melt like fudge into the water, she wades back across the creek after Mary Ann.

"Here," Mary Ann says. "You can have that rock, and I'll have this one."

Lolly sits on her rock and begins turning and throwing her fudgy lump of clay against its warm flat slate surface to get the water and air bubbles out, the way Marnie taught them in art class. Thunk, squish, turn. It's not like Marnie's gray polite clay out of the crock, wrapped carefully in clay-soaked burlap; it is wet and coarse with sand, but a nicer color. Milk chocolate. Thunk. Squish.

"This is pretty dumb no-good clay," says Mary Ann,

who is already rolling hers out. "It won't do anything right. It just falls apart into a big ugly ugliness."

"You have to pound it to get the water out. Like this." Thunk-thunk.

Mary Ann doesn't say All right. Doesn't pound her clay. She just sits, looking at Lolly in a mean way Lolly never saw before.

"That's a stupid ugly bathing suit," she says suddenly, jabbing Lolly with sharp ice-pick eyes. "Pink is the stupidest ugliest color in the whole world, especially dumb baby pink with rabbits all over it."

Lolly stops looking at Mary Ann and tries not to think about her. Whatever is wrong she can't do anything about, and if she doesn't say anything it might go away. She pulls a bit of her clay off and begins rolling it into a tiny brown ball. Pretty soon she hears a plop-thunk sound; not quite safe yet, too fast and loud to be safe, but better than nothing. She doesn't look up, only at the dollhouse-size teacup she is making, with a tiny curly handle.

Plop-thunk. Plop-thunk. She looks up. Mary Ann is working too, her head bent; safe. Lolly divides her clay and rolls it out. Another teacup. One, two, three chocolate-brown saucers. A darling tiny sugar bowl, with a lid. There will be enough clay for a whole dolls' tea-set, no, a fairy tea-set, and Anna will bake it for them very very carefully in her big kitchen stove, and they will have a party for all the fairies that live in her garden, Rose, and Hollyhock, and Sweet William.

"YOUR DISHES ARE TOO SMALL," a thin mean voice says from right on top of Lolly where Mary Ann suddenly is standing. "Much too small. Nobody can eat out of dishes that small, not even dolls."

"Fairies can," Lolly whispers, not looking up. "See, this is the cream-pitcher. We can have a fairy tea party."

"There aren't any fairies," the thin voice says, and a hand caked with scaly dried clay pinches up the cream-pitcher. "I don't want to . . . you always . . . same stupid . . . dumb . . . ugly . . ." Lolly doesn't hear all the words, only a loud sharp noise jabbing and jabbing at her. The scaly hand drops the cream-pitcher back on the rock and squashes it flat, and then it starts pinching and squashing the teacups.

"Oh, don't!" She looks up, she can't help it, and Mary Ann's eyes make holes in her face. Then they blink shut. Mary Ann turns and shrinks. She is going away, has gone away.

There are two saucers left whole and one teacup lying on its side without a handle. Lolly starts to roll a tiny snake of clay to fix it; but crying begins inside her, and she has to stop.

Now only Dan and Anna were still in the creek. Its golden-green water, flowing stronger as the channel narrowed, had carried them nearly fifty feet downstream from the swimming hole. There a giant uprooted sycamore lying across the stream had gathered enough fallen leaves and other floating debris to form a kind of natural dam. Anna sat on the white, stripped trunk, her legs in the water, her freckled face, neck, and arms freckled again with sun and shadow.

"Something I'd like to talk to you about," she said.

"Oh, no." Dan, facing her, sank out of sight with a splash.

"Seriously," she added as he resurfaced, his hair and mustache dripping.

"Yes, ma'am." He clasped his hands before his wet curly chest.

"About Bill. The way you've been teasing him today." Anna fell easily into her usual manner with Dan, that of a schoolmistress with a favorite pupil. Though this manner suggested intimacy, it also prevented it. Certain topics were by mutual consent always avoided; their common past, for instance, had never been mentioned.

"Me, teasing him?" Dan opened his mouth and eyes in a parody of innocent surprise.

"Yes, you. For instance, imitating the way he swims."

"You mean?" Dan parted the warm air in a clumsy mock breaststroke, puffing and blowing. "I thought I was pretty good. Everybody laughed. Bill was hooting like crazy himself."

"Well, of course. He had to, or he'd have looked an awfully poor sport. But I know he didn't like it. He's not the kind of man who can take a joke."

"Then it's time he learnt."

"No, Dan. I want you to leave him alone." In spite of herself, Anna smiled. Like many persons who hold themselves to a difficult standard of conduct, she read murder mysteries for pleasure (preferring those of Hammett and Chandler) and enjoyed the company of sinners.

"Naughty Danny mustn't make fun of poor little Billy, or hurt his poor little feelings. Or Miss Anna's nice house party for the class will be all spoilt." Dan grinned attractively and swung the edge of his hand along the surface of the pool, sending up a fan of water that did not quite miss Anna. "Okay. For you. I'll try to be good the rest of the weekend. Only it's a pity; he's such a perfect straight man."

"I want you to leave him alone," Anna repeated, discommoded by this parody of their usual mode of discourse. "And not just this weekend. Until he's on the board, at least. You know our budget's in bad shape, and now that Larry Arnold's leaving we've absolutely got to find someone else who's good at figures, and at the same time isn't a complete reactionary. I think Bill would be ideal. I'm sure he'll agree to do it, too, if nothing goes wrong. And then I don't see why he shouldn't be elected treasurer at the September meeting. Louis wants him, and I know Nan will vote any way you tell her to, and even Midge— Are you listening?"

"Yeah, I'm listening." Dan had moved out of the center of the pool and was jogging in rippling knee-deep shallows like an impatient runner, gazing toward the far bank, along which Lennie was picking his way. "That kid weighs on my mind," he said. "Why the hell wouldn't he go in swimming? And he gave us a real funny look just now, did you notice?"

"No."

"All you care about is that damned school."

"I care about it, yes."

"You used to care about some other things." Though Dan said this casually, the effect was as if he had ripped the bright summer scene of sky, trees, and flowery river bank apart like a painted canvas backdrop.

"That was a hundred years ago." Anna, frowning into the crowded, untidy dark space behind the backdrop, imitated his casual tone with evident strain.

"Not quite so long." He spoke slowly, deliberately, his curiosity, and more, aroused by the uncharacteristic waver in her voice.

"Fifteen at least. Ancient history." She laughed shortly and unconvincingly, and slid off the tree trunk into the deep water, as if to escape the pressure of his stare.

"You should have stuck with me." Though Dan continued to look at her, he said this in an offhand manner, as if it were a matter of no importance that had often been discussed between them. "Then you wouldn't have to worry about whether Eastwind's going to make it through the next year. You could have been a lady of leisure."

"God forbid." Anna had regained control, and spoke with good-natured emphasis. "And what would have happened to the school? Anyhow, the point is," she went on, wrenching the subject back, "I don't want you quarreling with Bill Hubbard. He may not swim very well, or have your sense of humor, but he's a decent, intelligent man. And just as liberal politically as you are. I think you'd like him if you got to know him."

"Maybe. He doesn't seem to take to me very much." Dan played with a handful of water as if it were a ball.

"No, not now." Anna smiled across the pool at him with the relief of someone who has successfully repaired a damaged object. "But you can make him like you very easily; you know you can. You can make anyone like you." Though she meant only to flatter and convince, this last sentence sounded accusing.

Dan tossed his ball of water from one hand to the other. "You want me to get chummy with Bill Hubbard so we can run Eastwind together for you," he said. "Is that why you asked them up here this weekend?"

"Well. Yes, partly. I wanted to see what he was like, too; and of course I knew Lolly would be pleased to have Mary Ann—"

"All for the sake of Eastwind School," Dan interrupted. Under his mustache, he flashed a movie-bandit's smile. "And I thought it was for my sake—because you know how I love to have pretty women around."

Anna was silent a moment, compressing her lips. "And that's another thing," she then said, resuming her affectionately scolding manner with effort. "I wish you'd pay a little less attention to Honey. I know it's hard for you not to flirt with whoever's handy, and I admit she's giving you every encouragement. But it's sending Bill round the bend."

"Oh, yeah?"

"He told me so himself."

"He did, did he?" Dan turned and looked back up the creek. Bill could be seen sitting between Honey and Celia on the bank by the swimming hole, with his straw city hat set square on his head to protect it from the sun.

"Not in so many words. But you know he's terribly in love with her. Obsessed, really. You must have noticed how he watches her the whole time."

"Yeah, I've noticed it. The poor sap." Dan shook his head. "She's got him coming and going."

"Well, then." Anna smiled, concluding her argument. "Why not ease up? It isn't as if Honey meant anything to you."

"Says who?" Dan glanced sideways at Anna, watching her face, which registered first surprise, then doubt, finally something more complex than disapproval.

"Of course, if you're serious—" she said in a very different, very distant voice.

"Oh, Anna." Dan sighed. "Of course I'm not. Honey's a lot of fun, and you've got to admit she's cute. But she's a damn sight too pleased with herself. Trouble is, she's been spoiled by her husband. Did you see her face when I ducked her?"

"I saw it," Anna said.

"Was she surprised, huh?" Noticing that Celia and Honey were looking in his direction, Dan grinned and waved at them. They waved back.

"That's right," he said, laughing. "A dame like that ought to be ducked every day, just to keep her in line."

Though Anna rather liked naughtiness, she despised

bullying; she did not laugh, or even smile. "I thought it was mean," she said. "When Honey came out of the creek, all muddy and choking on the water, I felt really sorry for her. She's so small, she looked like a miserable angry little girl."

"Honey can take care of herself," Dan said, turning back to Anna. "Don't let her fool you with those curls and that Southern baby talk. She's probably tougher than any of us." He kicked at the flowing water. "She's also a bit of a gold digger."

"You're quite wrong," Anna declared. "I don't know Honey very well, but I do know she's been awfully generous to Eastwind. She worked for weeks organizing that tiresome White Elephant Sale last month, and gave us so many things for it. I'm sure she's not what you call a gold digger."

"The hell she's not." Dan splashed down into the water again to cool off. "You should see her at lunch in a restaurant. It's all lobster salad and peach melba and 'Ooh, Ah'd just love to try one of those champagne cocktails, they look so delicious and bubbly.'" He waved his arm in imitation of someone grabbing at passing drinks. "Your Mrs. Hubbard's got expensive tastes. She can shovel it out the back door a lot faster than her husband can bring it in the front."

"You've taken her to lunch." Long experience of listening to children enabled Anna to say this without expressing any opinion whatsoever.

"Yeah, a couple of times. Not that I got anything much out of it." He laughed. "She's a real professional—flirt. I know a better word for that, but I wouldn't want to shock you."

Anna did not ask to hear this word. "Well," she said rather stiffly. "If you feel that way, why are you giving her such a rush?"

"Because it's fun," Dan said. "Besides, you never know.

I might be able to persuade her to go further than she plans to."

"But you're driving Bill Hubbard crazy." Anna reverted to her original point. "If you must have a flirtation with somebody, why not some pretty girl at your office? I'm sure there's lots who'd enjoy it." She suggested this in the good-natured, slightly impatient manner in which she might have advised a small child found digging up the Eastwind flowerbeds that he would have more fun in the sandbox.

"I'm tired of the girls at the agency," Dan said. "They're always boring in the long run. And they make so Goddamned much fuss. They sulk, and they cry, and they call up the house with phony messages and send Celia into a fit."

"Yes." Anna frowned and raised both arms to her piled-up hair, which was beginning to loosen and slide. "Celia says she always gets upset whenever your office calls."

"Sure she does. She was one of the girls at the agency herself." Dan sighed.

"Engaged to a nice boy back home, wasn't she?"

"That's right." He grinned, stirring the water with his arm.

"She was just about to be married to him, the way I heard it, down in Baltimore or somewhere." Anna, searching through her hair for pins, did not smile. "And then you turned up and carried her off."

"Philadelphia. Yeah." He smiled reminiscently.

"And now you're making her miserable." Anna finally allowed her opinions to show in her voice.

Dan's habitual open expression shut. He dug at the bed of the creek with his heel, churning up sand and mud; the clear broth of water pouring toward Anna thickened to a turbulent pea soup. "So what am I supposed to do?"

Anna smiled now, as if pleased to be asked. "Well, you could try not chasing after anyone, for a start."

"Oh, Anna. You know me better than that." He gave her a slow, thoughtful look. "Why, I think you're jealous."

"Don't be silly." She spoke through a mouth clenched on hairpins.

"No, you didn't believe in jealousy, did you?" Dan said with a hard smile. "That was convenient for you."

"All right," Anna said. "If you want to talk about it, let's talk about it. Let's talk about it this once, and then forget it." Her voice shook in a way that had never been heard at Eastwind. "All right, what do you want to say?"

"Me? Nothing." Dan imitated an ingenuous tone again, not as smoothly as before. "I thought we covered about everything when you left me."

"What do you mean? I did not leave you."

"Excuse me; you certainly did," he said, striking the surface of the pea soup with one fist as if it were solid. "The first and last time in my life I ever let a dame do that to me."

"That's ridiculous," Anna declared, working to secure her heavy damp rolls of hair; she had reverted slightly to her schoolmistress manner. "I took a job an hour and a half away by train. I could have been in New York every week from Friday afternoon to Monday morning; well, I was, till I moved out to—"

"So what?" Dan smashed the water with his fist. "You didn't really expect me to wait for somebody to come home weekends."

"Why not? Plenty of women do."

"Yeah, well, I'm not a woman," Dan said. As he stood there, waist-deep in the cloudy water, to all appearances naked, this was more than evident.

"So what?" Anna replied. Under the hot pale summer sky, they faced each other with the same stubborn, hurt expressions they had worn on a rainy winter night in a Greenwich village apartment fifteen and a half years earlier.

"And I'm not dumb, either," Dan added. "I know when I'm being shown the door."

"It wasn't that way—" Anna paused.

"I know it didn't mean anything to you," Dan went on, looking down into the soup and stirring it about. "It was just, what did you call it, an episode."

"That's not—" Anna began with force, and again, with even greater force, stopped herself. "Let's not talk about it anymore," she said, twisting her hair into a knot. "It's so many years ago, it doesn't do any good—"

"You never cared for men very much anyhow, did you?" Dan went on, ignoring this. "Except in bed. What you really like is children," he added, walking about in the water. "And that damned school of yours."

Anna did not speak, but stood holding up her heavy knot of chestnut hair, staring not at Dan but past him, as if silently reciting a long and passionate refutation of these old charges.

"Yeah." Dan stopped sloshing about in the creek, and gave her a long, penetrating look. "Okay; let's forget it," he said.

"Yes," Anna agreed, taking a long breath.

"I'll tell you what," he went on in a completely different tone, jokingly confidential. "I'll make a deal with you."

"A deal?" She blinked.

"Yeah. I'll lay off Honey. And I'll be real nice to Bill, so he'll want to come onto the board, and balance Eastwind's accounts for free, and vote just the way we like at all our meetings."

"That's grand." Anna gave a sigh of released tension. "Thank you." She smiled at Dan in as friendly and impersonal a way as she could manage. "And what would you like me to do for you?"

"Oh, something much much easier." Dan smiled. "You'll even like it. You always did." He set his hand on Anna's hip. At once she moved back, feeling for the tree behind her. Her long hair, released, tumbled untidily over her face and shoulders.

"Danny, really," she exclaimed in the voice of a teacher teased past her limit. "Damn it, you've made me drop all my hairpins. Be serious for a moment. If you and Bill—"

"I am serious." Dan waded forward, pressing Anna back against the fallen sycamore and its matted cargo of leaves, twigs, and grass.

"Dan, for Christ's sake. Everyone can see us." She gave him an angry shove. He resisted just as strongly; then, with a half-laugh, stepped back.

"That's better," she said, breathing a little hard.

"Hell, it would be so easy for us." Dan waded nearer again, lowering his voice. "Now that I'm president of the board I've got an excuse to come over to Eastwind any evening I want. Or up to your place, the way Larry did all the time. I used to wonder if—"

"Of course not," Anna interrupted in her most schoolmistressy tone. She splashed herself, throwing up a screen of bright drops like chips of ice.

"If you say so, ma'am. But you've got to remember, I know you pretty well." He reached beneath the cloudy green water and touched Anna gently, insinuatingly.

"Leave me alone." She struck his arm down. "What's the matter with you? If you're really serious, you should be ashamed of yourself. You know I'm Celia's friend."

"If you're really Celia's friend, you should be ashamed of yourself," he retorted, mocking her intonation. "You know she's in an hysterical state half the time now because she thinks I'm going to fall for some other broad and run off with her. What a laugh." Dan did not laugh. "I'd have to be crazy to pull that Young Lochinvar act again. Anyhow, I can't afford it; I'm supporting two families already. You should see my bills."

"Celia loves you very much," Anna said. "Too much, maybe. I think—"

"Yeah, she loves me all right," Dan interrupted, kicking the water. "You ought to try sometime being loved the way Celia loves me. I don't know how much longer I can take it. Just the way she looks at me whenever I leave the house, or even the room, all sad and hurt and suspicious, it's enough to drive a guy up the walls."

"I think too much love is bad for you." Anna continued with her idea. "Like sugar. Celia needs something else to occupy her mind. If she were to come back to work at the library, I think—"

"She doesn't need anything to occupy her mind. She reads more damn books than *Publisher's Weekly*. And it's not as if I'm, you know, neglecting her. The truth is she's getting all worn out keeping up with my sex drive. Once a week would be plenty for Celia." He looked across at Anna as she stood firm in the sliding water, with her dampened dark-red hair falling over her face and bare shoulders. "That's why I figure it's your bounden duty as her friend, and mine, to take up the burden."

"You're impossible." Anna's tone was balanced precariously between disapproval and amusement.

"Yeah, I know." He laughed. "So how about it, Miss Anna? Are you going to take advantage of this unique absolutely-free satisfaction-guaranteed offer?"

Smiling now, relieved by the lightness of his manner, Anna shook her head. "Sorry. I'm not interested."

"Tell that to the Marines." Dan flung a handful of water at her. "Look at you. Right now."

Above the smooth, again translucent surface of the creek, Anna's breasts had risen to hard points, clearly outlined beneath the wool of her bathing suit.

"That's nothing, the cold water—" she stammered, crossing her arms over her chest. "You just mind your own affairs." She waded sideways, then dived shallowly into the pool past Dan. Her long hair floated up behind her in the current and streamed outward like some kind of exotic red-brown pondweed.

"But that's what I'm doing," Dan cried after her. "I'm just minding—"

"I can't hear you," Anna called back. She turned onto her side and began to swim upstream toward the others.

Mary Ann keeps walking upstream away from the stupid picnic, shoving at the ugly weeds and bushes that get in her path, stamping and squashing them. The woods are thicker here, full of flies and midges and ugly tent caterpillars building their sticky white nests in the bushes, and the creek is all ucky with mud and dead tree trunks. Her head aches and her tummy aches and she feels hot and dizzy and ugly and sour and terrible. She doesn't care where she is going or if she ever gets back.

And nobody else does either. All day the grown-ups have been getting dumber and younger, like yesterday only more so. They already didn't notice Lolly crying or Lennie being rude about the ham sandwiches and eating all the extra cookies out of the basket so nobody else could have seconds, because they were too busy swimming and splashing each other. So just to make them notice something Mary Ann started kicking everybody's towels that were lying on the bank right at the edge, and she kicked them until they fell into the creek splosh splosh.

When the grown-ups saw all the wet muddy towels floating and sinking in the water they noticed. "Mary Ann Hubbard, did you do that?" Bill shouted, and Honey shouted, "Mary Ann, that's the limit! Ah wish Ah'd left you back home." Which was a dumb thing to say because if Mary Ann had been left back home she probably would have done something much much worse. But Honey was always wishing dumb things like that. Of course they never came true, like most wishes.

—Once upon a time there was a princess who had a wish-box, Mary Ann tells herself, smashing the plants along the path. —But she didn't use it much, she just kept it in her closet, because she already had everything she wanted. But one day her mother the queen was looking for something in the closet, and she saw the wish-box. And she took it out so she could wish for something, but she couldn't think what, because she had so much stuff already, and a new Buick roadster and a hundred new dresses from Lord and Taylor. So she just carried the box back to her own room till she could decide what to want next. She forgot what the fairy godmother told them about how they should always be very very careful not to leave the wish-box lying around where it could hear them. In case of wishing for things they didn't really want, by mistake.

—So that afternoon it was very hot, like today. So the queen was thirsty and she ordered her maid to bring her a strawberry soda with peach ice cream, uck, because it was her very favorite. But the maid didn't come fast enough. So she got aggravated and said, "Oh I just wish strawberry soda syrup and peach ice cream came out of the bathroom faucets instead of stupid old water." So then of course they did.

—"Oh that's lovely," the queen said, and she filled up her toothbrush glass. But then after it was full she tried to turn the faucet off. And it wouldn't turn off, and it wouldn't. And strawberry-and-peach-ice-cream soda came out and came out and ran over the basin and onto the bathroom floor and out into the bedroom all over the rug and out into the hall. And it ran and ran and ran, and pretty soon the whole castle was getting full of soda and ice cream. It came up over the queen's feet and up over her ankles.

—And the king came home, wading through the ucky sticky soda, and he shouted, "Did you do that? For Jesus God's sake turn it off!" But he couldn't either and the strawberry soda syrup and the peach ice cream kept right on coming. It came up over their knees and up over their bottoms and up over their tummies. They got scared and tried to run away out of the castle but everything was so ucky and slippery they slipped and fell down. And so the strawberry soda and peach ice cream got in their hair and in their faces. And it got in their ears and in their eyes and in their noses and mouths. They tried to get up but they couldn't, it was too slippery. And the queen was screaming "Stop, stop! I'm drowning!"

—So they drowned and were dead. And a little thin voice came out of the hole in the top of the wish-box, and it said, "Nyah, nyah. You asked for it."

Ow! Her leg. Something mean is grabbing at Mary Ann's leg with sharp claws. She looks down and it is the long green arm of a big pricker bush, reaching out into the path on purpose to hurt her, with little hard things on it that will be blackberries next month, but she won't come here next month or to Anna's ever again, so there.

It is bleeding, her leg, spotted red with shiny drops. Mary Ann turns round and starts to run wobbly back along the path, through the heat and the squashed weeds and the flies, till she comes out into the grassy wide place with trees and her mother and father and Lolly's mother down by the water.

"I'm hurt!" she shouts. "A mean bush hurt me."

"Come here, baby," Honey calls. "Let's see . . . Oh, that's just a little bramble scratch, darling. It's not even bleeding."

"It is so." Mary Ann looks, but all the bright drops are dried up or rubbed off, and there is nothing but a red scratch line. "It was bleeding," she says. "It hurts."

"Let me kiss it and make it well," Honey says, like she used to when Mary Ann was a little baby girl. She kisses the leg. "There. All better now." She yawns and lies down again and shuts her eyes. "Why don't you go play with Lolly?" she says with her eyes shut.

"I don't want to. I want to go back to the house," Mary Ann says in a quite loud voice; but nobody answers her.

"My head hurts," she says, louder.

Nobody answers.

"My head hurts, and my tummy hurts," she says, very loud, kicking the grass near Honey's leg. "I don't like it here. It's too hot. I want to go back to the house." A thick shaky feeling begins inside her, a feeling she knows, sort of like having to go to the bathroom only further up, that means she is going to lose her temper and yell and scream like when the Parkers' dumb baby sat down in her Easter basket and broke all the eggs.

"Mary Ann, please. Don't bother your mother," Bill says.

"I don't care," Mary Ann says, kicking the grass and Honey. "I want to go home."

"That's enough of that," Honey says, sitting up again. "You stop that now, this instant."

Mary Ann tries to stop kicking, to stop the temper getting loose, but it is no good. "I want to go home!" she hears herself scream. "I hate this damn ugly place! I hate everybody here!" And even when she sees Lolly's mother turning round to watch in a surprised frightened way, and Anna and Lolly's father wading back up the creek looking at her, she can't stop.

Dark and angry. Everything everybody at Anna's house has turned dark and angry; even Anna. "For goodness' sake, Lolly, would you stay out of the way till supper's ready," she says.

And Danny says, "Go and play something, Princess, don't bother Daddy."

And Mummy-Celia says, "Not now, darling, I'm so tired."

And Mary Ann says, "There aren't any fairies."

Even the air has turned bad. It is blowing in hard gray puffs with the sun gone away and clouds scooting up the sky heavy black and blue from behind lumpy dark hills. And the trees in front of the house are holding up their arms whispering bad things to each other.

Lolly leans against one of them, moving round, feeling the warm zigzag cardboard bark against her face. Suddenly something big and heavy bangs her, knocks her down.

"Owh!"

Her knee scrapes the dirt, her side. Before she can move, again, from behind the tree, the same heavy thing rushes forward and hits her, not so hard this time, and rushes back.

It is a big black rubber donut hanging from a rope. It is the tire swing, an old truck tire, with Lennie sitting inside it kicking his feet.

"Why doncha ever look where you're going, dumbo?" Lennie says, stopping it with his feet in the dust. "Now I suppose you're going to run crying to Mommy and say Lennie hurt you." He makes a mean face. "Boo hoo hoo," he says, though she isn't really crying. "Go on, run to Mommy and Daddy."

But she doesn't. She doesn't tell on Lennie much anymore, it only makes everything worse, with shouting and arguing and lying.

"You dumb kid, you think Daddy's so wonderful, don't you?" Lennie says. "You should have seen what I saw this afternoon. Him and Miss King—" He stops, looking at Lolly, staring at her.

"Hey, listen, I'm sorry," he says in a different voice from ever before. "I didn't bang into you on purpose." Lolly doesn't say anything. "I mean I didn't even see you. I was reading." He holds up a book. On its cover is a picture of a tall handsome man in fancy party clothes, with shiny black hair and two thin black lines of mustache on his lip, carrying a lady in a nightgown. "Are you hurt?"

Lolly folds her knee up to look. It is scraped red and rubbed with dirt, and stings in a kind of distant nice way.

"Lessee." Lennie pokes his head through the tire, swinging nearer. "Aw, that's nothing," he says in his ordinary voice. "Just a bruise."

She looks at her knee, red now. Tomorrow it will be puffy black and blue, like the clouds. Or maybe purple. Then green and yellow; then pink again. Like a sunset, if sunset hurt the sky. Suppose it does. Blood red, a bruise, then purple green yellow, every night.

"This is some great book," Lennie is saying. "You really

ought to read this book, only you're too little. You'd be scared."

"I like scary books . . . What's it about?"

"Dracula. Aahgg!" Lennie's face in the black circle of tire turns into a snarl with teeth; he claws the air with his brown thin hands.

She starts back; a squeaky scream comes out of her, then a kind of giggle. "Where'd you get it? Can I read it after you?"

"You better not. It'll give you nightmares. It's about a vampire. You know what a vampire is?" Lolly nods. "I bet you don't."

"I do too. Our class saw one in the Bronx Zoo. They're a kind of little bat that lives in South America, and they have big ears and eyes and soft gray fur and wings all folded up. Some people are scared of them, but Terry says they really just chase bugs and things. They're only about so big." She holds her hands apart.

"Dracula's not a bat, stupid," he says, kicking the dirt with his sneakers. "He's a man, and he chases people; women mostly. He smiles at you and grabs you and hugs you in his arms and sucks out your blood." Lennie smiles horribly. "Especially little dumb girls."

"Lolly!" A voice calling somewhere.

"He does not," she says faintly.

"He does so." Lennie scuffs the ground; the tire begins to turn, winding up its rope. "Who's reading this book, me or you?"

"He couldn't come here."

"Lolly! Lennie!"

"Sure he could." Lennie pushes the tire round again. "He can fly anywhere the wind can blow. And he's coming to the Catskill Mountains tonight, because he's hungry for BLOOD!" He shouts it loud sudden

"I don't believe you," Lolly says, but she can see Dracula already, a man with big furry wings like a bat, flying up the valley toward Anna's house.

"Yeah? Just wait and see. He's coming here, and he'll be watching this house like a lynx."

"What's a lynx?"

"It's a kind of wildcat. It watches people." Lennie puts a finger below each eye, pulls the skin down, and snarls. Then he lifts his feet so that the rope starts to unwind, the tire to spin round. "Aaggh!" he cries, changing the wildcat face to a Dracula face as he whirls past. "Aaggh!"

"Lennie! Lolly! Oh, there you are, children. Didn't you hear me calling? Come on in now; supper's ready."

Though it was dark now in the mountains, the thick heat continued, filling the air. Occasionally, in the distance, there was an electrical stuttering of thunder. Restless gusts of wind swept the yard, and rearranged the chaff on the barn floor. They lifted, bounced, and dropped the clusters of colored balloons that Anna, mounted on a kitchen chair, was fastening to the crossbeams of the barn in preparation for her party. She wore a long flowered skirt, hoop earrings, many strings of beads, and a cowboy hat fastened under her chin which gave her a South American air.

"Here you are, ma'am. That's the lot." Dan strode into the barn with two more kitchen chairs. He also wore a party hat—a shiny black topper. "Where do you want them?"

"Oh, anywhere. Over there, maybe?" Anna pointed toward a long table which had been improvised out of planks and sawhorses.

As Dan arranged the chairs, another puff of wind seemed to blow Honey into the barn. Though she was dressed and made up carefully, her total appearance was still comic, even clownish. She was carrying a china chamber pot brimming with salted pretzels, and wore a pink crepe-paper hat with a silver cockade, from beneath which her hair stuck out in pale untidy wisps; her ducking that afternoon had washed out all its set.

"Ooh, Dan!" she cried, picking her way across the uneven floor on her high-heeled red sandals. "What a good-looking shirt! Wherever did you find it?"

Dan looked up from the stack of phonograph records he was sorting by the light of a kerosene lamp. His face was tight with the wariness of someone who fears he is being mocked, for Honey had not addressed a civil word to him since the picnic. "Altman's," he said shortly; then, his suspicion easing a little, "But it's nothing to your dress."

"Aw, this old rag?" Honey glanced down at a strikingly cut red silk frock, tight over the hips and falling in a series of flounces below. "Ah've had it for centuries." She giggled. "Honestly, though, Dan. You look so handsome tonight. Doesn't he, Anna?"

"Dan always looks handsome," Anna said rather flatly; stepping down from her chair. Dan, bending over the old wind-up Victrola, allowed himself a half-smile.

"But specially tonight," Honey persisted. "Except—" (she narrowed her cat's eyes)"—except for his hair. It's awful long; and kind of out of control, you know?"

"Really?" Dan put the records down and felt his shiny dark head. "Getting time for a haircut, I guess."

"It looks all right to me," Anna said, climbing onto the chair with another cluster of colored balloons.

"Aw, no. It's much too long. Specially in back." Honey circled him. "Ooh, it's awful raggedy there. Ah know what,

Dan. Ah'll give you a little trim before the rest of Anna's company comes."

"Well, I—" Dan grinned uneasily.

"Ah'm a real good barber. Aren't I, Hubby?" She appealed to Bill, who had just come in lugging a galvanized tin pail full of ice and beer bottles.

"What? Yeah, that's right." Bill took a bottle of beer from the pail. "She always cuts my hair for me. What there is of it." He laughed.

"Well—" Dan laughed also.

"Ah'll run right now and get the scissors from mah workbox. Ah won't be a minute."

"Honey, wait—" Bill began.

"What's the matter?" Celia asked, coming into the barn as Honey ran out. She wore a rather formal beige lace dress and carried another lamp, the upward-striking light of which illuminated her face oddly and made her yellow crepe-paper hat seem to float above her brown hair.

"I'm going to have a haircut." Dan grinned.

"I don't see the need," Anna remarked. She took the lamp from Celia and hung it on a post, where it cast wavering wedges of light and spokes of shadow up into the rafters.

"Anna prefers the shaggy bohemian type," Dan said. "The Larry Arnold type." Anna's face tightened, but she made no comment. "Hey, we ought to have some haircut music. There must be something good here." He shuffled the black discs.

"Darling, I don't think . . ." Celia began, and became inaudible. No one asked her what she did not think, or even seemed to have heard her. "Can I help?" she added a moment later; hardly louder, but Anna, Bill, and Dan all replied:

"Yes, could you hand me that ball of string?"

"No, but how about a beer?"

"Sure, love. Help me look through these records. I can't read the labels too well in this light."

Celia handed up the string, received the beer, and began reading the titles of records aloud. " 'Banks of the Wabash.' 'Marching through Georgia.' "

"Nah."

" 'Stars and Stripes Forever.' 'O Sole Mio' . . ."

"Trying to find us some barbershop quartets," Dan called out to Honey as she tripped back into the barn.

"Ooh, swell. What have you got?"

" 'Listen to the Mocking Bird,' " Celia read out in a colorless voice. " 'Memories.' 'When You and I Were Young.' "

"Nah, those are all too sad." Dan held another disc to the light. "Here. This'll be perfect." He fitted it on the turntable and wound the handle.

There was a whisper, a hum, a series of scratchy chords, and then the voices of men in close harmony issued from the fluted horn, joined on the chorus by Dan's rich, slightly off-key baritone:

> *Daisy, Daisy,*
> *Give me your answer, do.*
> *I'm half crazy,*
> *All for the love of you.*

"Okay, Miss Honey, go ahead. Do your worst." He sat down on one of the kitchen chairs he had carried from the house.

Giggling, Honey draped a white beach towel round his shoulders and tucked it in. "There. Now this is mine, but Ah swear it's clean." She flourished a pink celluloid comb before Dan's eyes, then began to make delicate flitting passes through his oiled curls. "Oh my, you've got such beautiful thick hair. But it sure does need a trim." She transferred the comb to her other hand and took up a pair of small shiny scissors, snapping the blades in the air.

"Take it easy," Dan said, flinching.

"Ah'll be real careful. Don't you worry." Honey began to circle him, cooing, petting, combing, snipping.

"Ah've always had a natural gift for hair, 'specially men's hair," she said. "Eddie Rose, who runs the barbershop down home, told me I could have had a job with him any time I wanted if I was a boy. Did Ah ever tell you about the haircut he gave Frank Fergusson?" She looked over at Bill, who was leaning against the haymow opening another beer.

"Yup, you did."

"Never mind him, baby," Dan said. "You tell us." He raised one hand to feel his hair, then lowered it and sat back, reassured. An expression of enjoyment appeared upon his face, contrasting with the expressions of Bill and Celia.

"Well," Honey said. "Frank Fergusson was this no-good guy down home that Eddie Rose's kid sister Evalyn got mixed up with, though she should have known better. He came to town right after the war out of nowhere and opened up a jewelry store, and started running after the local girls. He was a hefty tall fellow, Big Frank they called him. Good-looking in a beefy way, with a red complexion and thick wavy golden-brown hair that he was real fond of. About thirty-five he was then, Ah guess.

"Now you know any man that age that says he's never got married because he never saw a girl he could care for, either there's something real peculiar about him, or else he's lying. No girl with sense would trust him as far as she could throw him. But Evalyn Rose, Eddie's sister, didn't have all that much sense. When Big Frank asked her to the pictures she thought her prince had come, and pretty soon she had her silver and china patterns all picked out, and names for her first baby. And from what Ah heard, the way they carried on she was just plain lucky there wasn't any baby.

"Then one afternoon Evalyn got home from her job in the dry goods store and her mother showed her the newspaper. It said right on the society page that Big Frank was engaged to marry this other girl, with her picture and all.

"Poor old Evalyn's feathers really fell off when she saw that paper. She didn't have enough sense to shut up and pretend she knew about it all along and didn't care. She ran around telling all her friends, and she went into Frank's jewelry store and started crying and carrying on, but of course it didn't help any. All that happened was everybody in town got to hear she'd been jilted. And you know how some people are, 'specially men. Mean. They would come into the barbershop and pass remarks about Frank and Eddie's sister, and ask Eddie how her trousseau was getting on. And Eddie had to stand there and take it. He couldn't tell the customers to shut up or get out, because he didn't own the place back then like he does now.

"Well, finally one day Frank Fergusson himself walked into the shop and sat right down in Eddie's chair, just like he used to do every week before that paper came out. 'Give me a shampoo and trim,' he said. 'No hard feelings?' 'No,' Eddie said. And he put the sheet round Big Frank and he cut his hair, and he washed it, and he put on some kind of fancy lotion to cover up where the golden-brown was going grey, and make it smell like flowers. And all the time he was boiling up inside like a pot of hominy grits.

"But what could he do? Eddie's a real short plump little man, and he's only got one foot. He lost the other in the war, in some accident in an army camp. Never even got overseas. But he's real patriotic; now that it's his he's got the barbershop all decorated with flags and photos and war souvenirs that other fellows in his outfit brought back from France.

"And of course Frank Fergusson was a great big tough guy, always bulging out his muscles and inviting people to hit him in the stomach to see how hard it was. He could have licked Eddie Rose with one hand tied.

"Well, the next thing that happened was it got to be June, and Big Frank was about to be married. And that gave Eddie Rose an idea. When Frank came in to get prettied up the day before the wedding, Eddie said Sorry, he was just leaving, had to go out of town; but if Frank would come back early the next morning he would open the barbershop for him special. So just a couple of hours before he was due at the church Frank Fergusson walked in and sat down in Eddie's chair, a little hung over from his bachelor dinner the night before, but real smug and full of himself. 'Give me the deluxe treatment,' he said. 'Ah'm marrying the only good-looking girl in this hick town.'

"Well, Frank Fergusson was a big man and a strong man and a handsome man, and he had two feet. He'd only got one disability: he was color blind. When he went out driving in his open-top Ford, he couldn't tell Stop from Go, except one was above the other. He lay back in the barber chair and shut his eyes, and Eddie Rose limped around him, trimming his hair. And wetting it. And soaping it. And rinsing it. And combing the special lotion through it, and blowing on it with a hair dryer, till it was as shiny as a racehorse's rear end. Only it wasn't golden-brown any more. It was real bright grass-green.

" 'How's that?' Eddie Rose asked, whisking away the sheet. 'Not bad,' Big Frank said. And he grinned and simpered at himself in the barbershop mirror like a girl in love, and put on his new hat and went off to his wedding . . . Never lived it down, either. Had to leave Greensboro with his new wife just to get away from the kidding!"

"Uh-huh, there's more than one way to cook a goose," Honey added, as the laughter subsided. "Now, that looks better." She smoothed Dan's hair and stood back, admiring her work. "Just one second more. Hold real still."

She bent over Dan, placing one hand caressingly against his cheek, and with a flash of the little scissors cut off one side of his thick mustache. "Oooh, mah goodness!" She sprang back. "Look what Ah did!"

There were exclamations from Celia and Anna; a loud guffaw from Bill. Dan fought his arms free of the towel and felt his lip.

"What the— Goddamn it! My mustache. You cut off my mustache!"

"You moved. Ah told you to keep still." A bubbling sound rose in Honey's throat, and burst out as a loud giggle.

"I did not move. You little bitch." He rose threateningly. Honey skipped away. Dan, still dragging the towel, pursued her, his lopsided face grim.

"Ooh, help!" Giggling, Honey took shelter behind her husband, who was still laughing loudly. "My, you do look funny!" she cried, peeking round his arm. Another burst of giggles. "Ah warned you."

"You goddamn mean, sneaky—" Dan faltered, seeming to realize that he was the focus of general mirth; even Celia's face bore a frightened smile. Holding one hand to his face as if to cover a wound, he ran from the barn.

In the dark closeness of the attic Mary Ann turns over in bed, shoving Theodore Ilgenfritz out of the way. Everything about her is hot and uncomfortable. The pillow is lumpy and the mattress is full of buttons and bulges, and she has sunburn on her shoulders and mosquito bites on her legs that itch and itch, and her tummy hurts from too much potato salad and gingerbread with whipped cream. She wants it to be tomorrow so she can feel okay again. "I don't want to talk to you," she said to Lolly after Anna tucked them in and went away down the stairs with her flashlight. "I just want to sleep."

Only now she can't. It is too hot and stuffy, and there is a mosquito whining around waiting to land on her and bite her, or maybe two mosquitoes, and outside there is a loud stupid noise of dance music coming from the barn where the grown-ups are having their party. They moved it out there so the noise wouldn't bother Lennie who is downstairs reading, or keep the children awake, but it does anyhow. And besides cars kept stopping and starting and people kept coming in and out of the house and banging the screen doors and shouting things and laughing in the dumb loud way they always do at parties.

Now that she is safe in bed Mary Ann feels sort of better than before, but not really okay like after an ordinary okay day. Too many bad stupid things had got into this day: she had thrown away a whole jar of Japanese beetles worth ten cents, and been mean to Lolly for no reason, and yelled and kicked and screamed at the picnic like a spoiled brat only child, and everybody had seen it, even Anna.

The only good thing is that now Mary Ann knows that

she and Anna are specially secretly connected, because their names are alike and they both have red hair and sudden bad tempers.

It was just something some people were born with, Anna said, especially red-haired people, that they had to learn to manage, like learning to live on top of a volcano. Sometimes it was much harder. Mary Ann was lucky because her temper was like a volcano that didn't erupt very often. Only every once in a while when things got really awful and unfair then she sort of went all kerflooey like the washing machine the time Precious Joy's apron strings got stuck in it. Then the washing machine started making a horrible grinding growling noise that you could hear all over the house, and banging against the basement sink and kicking the cement floor. Precious Joy was afraid to touch it to turn it off. A whole mess of devils was in it, she said; and by the time Honey got there and pulled out the plug they had chewed up a load of laundry.

Anna said she used to lose her temper every few weeks when she was little. Once when her father shut her up in the back pantry to learn better manners she kicked a hole in the door. You could still see where it had been mended with a different kind of board, because Mary Ann looked. But now whenever Anna's temper wanted to explode she went out and chopped wood, or if there wasn't any wood around she went into another room fast and walked up and down alone counting backward from 100 to 1. Forwards didn't work, because that was too easy. And after you won you gave yourself a reward, like a chocolate bar you had been saving up or a ticket to the opera.

It was good to have a strong fierce temper in a way, Anna said. Once you learnt how to control it you could let it out in little bits to scare bad people and fight for important things. Like a strong fierce horse that you knew how to ride, and it could carry you into battle, instead of a weak little wobbly one that wasn't any use.

When she is grown up Mary Ann isn't going to lose her temper ever again, and her hair will be horsechestnut color instead of orange, and she will change her dumb name around to Anna Mary. Or Anna Miranda. Anna Miranda Hubbard. Miranda Anna Hubbard . . .

She wakes and turns over again, making the springs of the cot squawk. It is late now, probably practically midnight, because nobody remembered to send Mary Ann and Lolly to bed till the party was almost starting and Anna noticed them. Honey and Bill and Lolly's parents hadn't noticed because they were too busy getting everything ready. They didn't act like it was going to be a grown-up party, but one for little kids, with balloons and party favors Anna found in the cupboard. When she brought them out they didn't even wait for their company to come, they started right in blowing the whistles and uncurling the tissue-paper snails and popping the crackers open and reading the silly fortunes and trying on the paper hats and laughing and shouting. Anna could have stopped them like she did last night, but instead she sort of encouraged them. She liked children's parties better than grown-up parties, she said once, because children were nicer than grown-ups and knew how to have a good time better.

Maybe so. But grown-ups were supposed to act grown-up. When they didn't it could be lovely fun for a little while, like driving to the village store Thursday. But if they went on too long it got sort of embarrassing and awful, and even scary.

Suppose there was a sort of magic spell on Anna's house that made everybody who visited her slowly turn into children, if they weren't already. And if Honey and Bill and

Mr. and Mrs. Zimmern didn't go home soon they would get to be Lennie's age, and then Mary Ann's age; and if they still didn't leave they would get younger and younger and smaller and smaller and turn into little tiny babies, and Mary Ann and Lolly and Anna would have to look after them.

Mary Ann turns on her other side again, facing Theodore Ilgenfritz. He is awake too and even hotter than her because of his fur, so it isn't comfy to hold him or even touch him. He doesn't like it here anymore, he wants to go home.

It was past midnight; the last of Anna's party guests had driven away, the chirping of their car's engine fading into that of crickets. In the barn most of the colored balloons had deflated or been deliberately popped, and all but one oil lamp had sputtered out. The chaff on the floor was scuffed with the marks of many feet, the tin ice-bucket awash in lukewarm water.

"Don't you think it's about time for bed, darling?" Celia looked up at Dan with the pale, strained expression of someone who has not slept well for many nights.

"Hell, no. We're just getting started." Unlike his wife, Dan still wore his party hat—a tall shiny black topper, held on at a rakish angle by elastic. In the dim warm light, without his heavy mustache, he looked like a younger man: one still wide awake and determined to keep the party going in spite of his flagging middle-aged companions. "You feeling sleepy?"

"I'm exhausted," Celia admitted.

"Go ahead then, Cilly, why don't you?" He caressed her

shoulder through the beige lace. "Get yourself some rest."

"No." She shook her head slightly. "That's all right. I'll wait for you."

"Up to you, love," Dan said. He went over and fitted a record onto the turntable of the Victrola, then began to crank it up. "Come on, everybody! Let's dance."

Sketching a jazz step, he crossed the barn toward where Honey sat on the edge of the haymow, her legs displayed in a calyx of flame-red ruffles, her sulky, sleepy expression lighting into a smile as he approached. But at the last moment, as if accidentally, he danced a quarter turn and presented himself instead, with a bow, to his wife.

"May I have the honor?"

Celia, with a weary half-smile, stepped into his arms and was whirled away.

Honey's rosebud mouth tightened. She straightened her pink paper hat, surveyed the barn, and jumped down. "C'mon, Hubby," she said, standing over Bill.

"Aw, Kitten. 'M'm worn out." He spoke thickly from a collapsed position on a heap of straw.

"Don't you want to dance with me anymore?" Her voice was light, peevish, drawling.

"Love to dance with you anytime, only—"

"Come on, then." She gave him a tiny kick in the haunch with one red silk sandal.

Bill rose to his feet with difficulty, rumpled and blurry. "Love to dance with you," he repeated. He put one arm round Honey's waist and began to jog unevenly, out of step with both her and the Victrola.

"Music too fast," he announced, breaking off. "Gotta find us something a lot slowther." He shuffled toward the machine, pulling his wife with him. "Now lessee. Ah. Here we are." He lifted the playing arm as the jazz tune ended, and dropped another disc on top.

"Aw, come on!" Dan called. "Not that again."

"What's wrong with it? 'S a good song." Bill began to do a slow two-step with Honey.

"It's for the birds." Dan flapped his elbows at them, imitating a large chicken, then turned and flapped back across the barn toward the machine.

Ah! lovuuuh . . .

He moved the playing arm back; the jazz tune began again.

"Dan," Anna said warningly.

Dan turned toward her, smiling. "Better, huh? Let's go." He took the empty glass out of her hand, set it on another chair, and pulled her up.

Bill Hubbard's face, already red with sunburn, reddened further. "Goddamn nerve," he muttered, trying to unhitch himself from Honey.

"Ah, forget it." She clung on, digging her pink nails into his shoulder. "He's just tight. Let's dance."

"I can't keep up with that beat, this time night."

"You don't have to. Just take it easy. Like this." She swayed, smiling up at him.

Clumsily, Bill followed her lead. "Goddamn nerve," he repeated. "Who's he think he is, Kay Keyser?"

Across the barn, their separate shadows thrown large onto the far wall, Anna and Dan were also moving more slowly. "That better?" he asked.

"Yes. I'm still dizzy though," Anna said. "When I close my eyes the barn goes round. Too much beer." She laughed. "Listen, Dan," she added in a lower voice, leaning away to look into his face.

"Yeah."

"You've got to let Bill alone."

Dan raised his heavy eyebrows.

"I mean it. You've been riding him all evening. And Honey too. I saw that trick you played just now, pretending you were going to ask her to dance."

"Sorry, Miss Anna." Dan pulled her back toward him. "You turned down my sensational free offer; it's open season now on Hubbards." He bent nearer. "Especially after her little number tonight. You got any idea how long it's going to take to grow my mustache back?" He released Anna's hand to feel what was no longer a furry small animal nestling above his mouth, but two thin mangy caterpillars.

"It's not so bad short. Makes you look rather like, who's that movie star? Ronald Colman."

"I don't want to look like Ronald Colman. I'm no sentimental pantywaist aristocrat."

"No." She laughed a little tipsily.

"Aw, Anna," Dan whispered, resting his cheek against hers. "Why don't you reconsider? I need you. You're the only woman in the world I can't con. The only one who loves me the way I am."

Anna frowned. She turned her head and looked at him from a few inches away. "How about Celia?"

"Are you kidding?" He laughed. "She's the worst of the lot. Never satisfied."

"Oh, Dan," Anna protested, looking over his shoulder to where Celia sat on a kitchen chair in the half-conscious slumped posture of someone waiting in a clinic. "I've never heard her say a critical word to you. Or about you."

Dan held Anna away from him, signaling a walk step. "No, she's too much of a lady for that," he said. "What she does is suffer in silence. Whenever I step out of line—"

he demonstrated, stumbling suddenly sideways— "she gives me this martyred-look, as if I've just shot her full of arrows, but she's not going to say a word." He waved across the barn to his wife; she blinked and managed a sleepy, sad smile and lift of the hand. "See that?" He turned Anna round, then pulled her back toward him. "One thing about you, you'd never put on that kind of act. You're too straight. Not like most women."

"I'm not so straight," Anna said in a low, charged voice. "It's true what you said this afternoon: if I'm Celia's friend, I should be ashamed. Listening to her troubles, as if I'd never—" She hesitated and missed a step. "And then talking with you the way we do, talking about her, even— I feel as if I was caught in a bramble-bush."

"Yeah," Dan said. "Who isn't?"

"The whole thing is wrong," Anna went on. "I shouldn't have let you put Lolly into Eastwind in the first place. Or else you should have told Celia that we— But it was so long ago, I didn't think it mattered. And Lolly was so like you, I—" Anna's voice had thickened; she took a breath and controlled it. "Besides, we didn't have enough girls in that class " she said, more briskly than necessary. "We still don't, as a matter of fact." She laughed meaninglessly. "I don't want you to take Lolly out of Eastwind," she went on. "But Celia should know. You've got to tell her."

"No thanks." Dan shook his head. "That's a terrible idea," he said with conviction. "I mean, what's the point?" He did not wait for Anna's reply, but anticipated it. "Sure maybe it'd ease your conscience. And mine, if I had any." He laughed roughly. "But Celia would just feel worse than she does already. You know she would."

"Yes," Anna admitted on a painful, descending note.

"We can't get out of it that way." Dan held her close. "We're in it for keeps. Always have been. Only if we'd stayed together I wouldn't be such a bastard now."

"Oh, Dan." Anna made a strange noise, halfway between laugh and groan.

"I love you, Anna. My bad luck."

"Don't say that." She stopped dancing, pulled back. "I don't want to hear that."

"I'll say whatever I damn please," Dan retorted, and then said nothing. For several minutes they danced silently, at a formal distance.

"What have you got against love?" he asked finally.

"Everything." Anna did not smile.

"It's been pretty popular, over the years. How do you explain that?"

"It's—" Anna frowned and shook her head, trying to clear the smoky fumes of strong drink and strong feeling. "It's philosophically comforting. Like all illusions. When you're in love the world seems to make sense for a little while. All your— thoughts, and efforts, and plans have a direction. The same direction."

"Yeah, okay."

"And it beats believing in God, because you can see and know the person you worship. Or so you think. But it's like all religions. It leads to frightful crimes and excesses. Persecution, and self-destruction, and martyrdom." She took care not to look in Celia's direction, but Dan did so, and laughed.

"You've got a point," he said.

"And besides, it keeps you from doing anything else, from caring what goes on in the world, or what happens to anybody, except you and one other person."

"The opiate of the masses," he said, easing Anna closer.

"Absolutely."

"In your ideal universe, nobody will be in love with anyone or anything."

"I didn't say that." Anna shook her head. "They'll love — I don't know—" She leant back. "Freedom, and justice, and, oh—music and art, and beautiful places, and, I don't know, I've had too much beer." She gestured loosely round the barn. "Everything that's good."

"The way you love this place. Or Eastwind." Dan steered her across to the Victrola, lifted the needle, and replaced it at the start of the record.

"Yes, exactly." Anna smiled and allowed Dan to dance her away from the table.

"And there won't be any sex. Some ideal universe."

"I didn't say that either," she protested, yawning and sagging against him.

"But if there isn't any love, who will everyone sleep with in your Utopia? Partners assigned to them by the state?" Dan made a face.

"They'll sleep with their friends."

"Well, I'm all in favor of that." He smiled, lowered his voice. "That's what I want to do." She said nothing. "And. so. do. you," he whispered into her ear, a breath to each word.

Anna gave a long sigh and was silent. The jazz record blared round them. Dan held her closer, steering her away from the phonograph toward the back of the barn; their shadows on the wall diminished, darkened, merged.

"Mary Ann," Lolly's voice says suddenly in the dark, a wavery whisper. "Mary Ann? Are you asleep?"

"No, of course not," she answers, out loud. "Nobody could be asleep; it's too hot and too noisy."

"I have to go to the bathroom."

"Well, go then." Anna's bathroom isn't in her house. It is out by the barn, in a wooden shed named The Privy— short for "private," Bill explained—with old elderberry bushes all round it and flies and a smell. Inside the sunshine comes through in bright dusty strips between boards, and there is a wooden bench thing along one side with two holes in it worn shiny smooth by people's behinds. If you look down through the holes you can see their number two on top of a heap of yellow-stained white powder. That is lime, to take away the smell, Bill said, but it doesn't really. The last two nights Mary Ann and Lolly went to The Privy together just before bedtime. But tonight Mary Ann was feeling ornery and went alone; and then when Anna asked them, Lolly said she didn't have to go. So of course now she does.

"Mary Ann."

"Yeah."

"Would you come with me?"

"I don't have to. I went already." Mary Ann turns her hot lumpy pillow over again.

"Please."

"What for?"

There is a silence full of night noises and stupid grown-up music. Finally Lolly says in a thin voice, "I'm scared."

"What of?" Mary Ann remembers what the big kids at Eastwind said when younger ones didn't want to go to the bathroom before a school trip. "Afraid you might fall in?" she asks in a big-kid voice.

"I'm afraid of Dracula." Lolly sits up in bed, a blurry whispering shape in her nightgown. "He's like a bat, only he's a man too, and he flies around at night and swoops down on you and sucks out your blood. One of them . . . One of him's out there now."

"Says who?"

"Lennie."

"Aw, pooh. Lennie is a meanie and a liar. You know he's always telling you dumb stuff like that. For instance about those alligators in Florida that lived in the drains under the hotel, and he said they were going to come up the drain-pipes and get into the bathtub with you. Just 'cause he was jealous of you for going to Miami Beach and he couldn't."

"I know," Lolly says. But she doesn't get up.

Nyah nyah, fraidy-cat, Mary Ann thinks. Pretty as a picture. Go ahead, wet the bed, see if I care. But then she thinks, Oh well. Besides, if Lolly does wet her bed the whole attic will smell awful.

"Okay," she says. "I'll go with you."

Downstairs Anna's house is empty and dark except for one lamp in the sitting room for Lennie to read by. He doesn't look up which is good because he might have said more about bats. The kitchen is very dark and full of big black shapes that are probably the stove and the icebox and the kitchen table.

Outside it is better. It's cooler there and you can see light from the barn lying on the grass between the trees. Anyhow whenever it gets spooky Mary Ann always likes it outdoors better: there is more space there and you can run if you want to. She holds onto Lolly's hand so Lolly won't be scared and they run barefoot over the cool damp grass. They pass the barn with its tall door slid wide open and balloons hanging up. Standing near the door is Anna's big phonograph that usually lives in the sitting room, shaped like a square fat lady on four bird-claw legs, with a ruffled trumpet head and her name written across her tummy: VICTROLA. She is singing noisy music and the grown-ups are dancing. Enough light comes out past them so that Mary Ann can see most of the way across the yard to the big black clump of bushes where The Privy is.

It is even blacker inside The Privy and sort of creepy, so Mary Ann doesn't shut the door all the way. She stands by it watching in case anybody or anything is coming through the bushes, while Lolly climbs up onto the wooden seat in the dark and makes the Ahh noise of somebody who has been waiting and waiting to go to the bathroom. The music keeps on playing, and then it stops, and Mary Ann can hear voices talking, low at first, and then turning louder, but too far away to tell what it is about.

Interesting things happen at grown-up parties sometimes. Once there was a man who worked in Bill's office that could make a noise with his mouth exactly like a rooster, and a noise like a train starting and going away; and another time a lady did a dance with the floor lamp pretending it was some Spanish movie star. Of course she had to unplug him first. Other times people got mad about current events and shouted and swore at each other, usually men. And once when Mary Ann went into the bathroom to get a drink of water there was a man and a lady she never saw before lying in the bathtub together with all their clothes on.

Mary Ann wasn't supposed to go to these parties except at the very beginning for people to see how much she had grown and show her their rooster noises, but sometimes when they woke her up later she would come halfway down the stairs and look through the banisters at the company, all dressed up fancy and talking louder than usual and getting tipsy, which meant that they had drunk so much beer or cocktails that if you gave them just a little push they would tip over. It sounds that way now from the barn, with laughing and shouting mixed together.

"Come on," she says to Lolly, who has found the roll of paper in the dark and is wiping herself. "Let's go see what's happening."

"**Party's over,**" Bill announced as the jazz record wound to an end, releasing his wife and embracing a post.

"Ah, no." Dan did not completely let go of Anna. "It's early yet."

"Is not. It's damn late."

"Only one-fifteen," Anna said. Within the loose arc of Dan's arm she continued swaying to a tune which had ceased to sound.

"Got work to do tomorrow," Bill said stubbornly. "Got a report to write."

"Oh, come on. Forget your job for a while. Nobody's going to starve in New York if you don't finish that report."

"What the hell do you know about it?" Bill stood upright with the help of his post. "Guy like you, never did a real day's work in his life."

"Oh, yeah?" Dan laughed good-naturedly. "Listen, pal, I was breaking my back loading trucks on Seventh Avenue ten hours a day when you were jerking off behind the woodshed. Excuse me, ladies." Honey giggled; Anna frowned vaguely; Celia, half-asleep, registered nothing.

"Guys like you," continued Bill, oblivious. "Guys like you got nothing to do all day but— Nothing to worry about, except convincing some poor sap that can't even keep up his mortgage payments to buy a new Buick on time. And a fur coat for his wife, and—"

"Now hold on," Dan said, less good-naturedly.

"—and a lot of other junk he doesn't need. Just to keep

this bankrupt capitalist system running little longer'

"Just a minute. I'm a socialist myself—"

"Oh yeah, sure." Bill smiled with one side of his mouth

"Sure," Dan insisted. "Listen, half the guys in my agency are socialists. We're plotting to destroy the system from within. Going to make the workers want Buicks and fur coats so much they'll revolt and overthrow their bosses. And you know what?" He grinned. "You'll be one of the first to go."

"Uh-uh." Bill shook his head several times. "You and your friends are just kidding yourselves. Elitist thinking. Phony bastards fooling people for their own good, uh-uh."

"Just who are you calling a phony bastard?" Dan said with a dangerous smile, moving nearer. But Bill, equally large and considerably drunker, was not intimidated.

"Treating the American people like children," he went on. "Like little kids that want cheap toys, and can be fooled by cheap lies."

"You make me laugh." Dan did not laugh. "It's you and your pals that treat people like kids. You take away their jobs with chicken-shit regulations and taxes, and then you make them line up and beg for handouts, and that makes you feel oh so generous." His voice and face were shaky. "My father, he used to have a store—Oh, forget it." He turned away.

"Handouts, huh?" said Bill, who had been mumbling this word to himself, oblivious of those which followed. "If I was in your business, be ashamed of what I did for a living," he said loudly to Dan's back. "Spending whole damn life making up lies—"

"That's enough of that, buddy." Dan's voice roughened abruptly; he took a step toward Bill.

Both Celia, sunk half-asleep on her chair, and Honey,

searching among the empty beer bottles on the table for a full one, raised their heads. Both looked first, with blurry concern at their husbands; then, expectantly, at Anna, who was now leaning against a post under a cluster of drooping colored balloons. She seemed to feel their gaze, for she stopped moving her head in time with the inaudible music.

"Dan," she said. "Leave it alone. We've all had one too many." But her words lacked force, and appeared to come from some distance away.

"Time for bed, Hubby." Honey took Bill's arm and began to lead him toward the door. He moved a few awkward steps, then shook her off and turned.

"Socialist," he shouted, making a gargling, unpleasant sound in his throat. "Call yourself a socialist. You're nothing but a goddamned Republican." He stumbled toward Dan. "And a goddamned skirt-chaser. You think I can't see what you're up to. See what you're up to, all right. This whole goddamn weekend, sniffing around my wife. You leave my wife alone."

"Don't you worry." Dan jerked his head in Honey's direction, smiling unkindly. "I wouldn't touch that mean little pussycat of yours now with a ten-foot pole."

"Issat so," Bill growled. "Insult my wife, issat so. You goddamn Republican playboy." He lunged forward, fists up.

"Hey. Hold on." Dan tried to ward off the heavy but ill-aimed blows. "Ow! Damn. All right, if you want to fight."

"Dan—" Celia squeaked, rising. But her husband had already struck back, more accurately.

"Awf." Bill staggered sideways. He grabbed at the table, dislodging a stack of phonograph records, and collapsed against the wall, the wind knocked out of him.

"Oh, hell," Dan said. "Sorry."

"Are you all right?" Anna, shaken out of her daze, came forward.

"Hubby!" Honey hastened toward him over the fallen and broken records. "Did he hurt you?"

"Awright," Bill muttered, not moving.

"I didn't hit him all that hard, honest. He just—" Dan laughed suddenly, "—just kind of folded up."

"You disgusting old bully," Honey mewed. She began to beat Dan on the chest and stomach with both fists. "Hitting a man when he's boozed up, doesn't even know what all he's saying—"

"Hey. Quit it!" Dan laughed more angrily, trying to fend her off.

"Honey, really!" Anna cried, strongly but too late. "Dan—"

"He didn't mean—" Celia cried. "Stop it, you're hurting him!" She seized Honey's arm.

"Leave go of me, you saphead," Honey screeched. "He deserves it." She continued her blows. Celia did not let go, but clung to Honey frantically. Then, still holding on, she froze.

"Oh, my God," she said, looking past the others out into the yard. "Lolly? Is that you?"

They are fighting in the barn, everybody at once, shouting and pushing and yelling swear words, like in movies that Mary Ann isn't allowed to see but sometimes she gets to watch pieces of them in previews.

"Let's go away," Lolly whispers. But it is too late even if they wanted to: Lolly's mother has seen them. She stops fighting and comes running into the yard.

"Lolly! Mary Ann!" she says in a strange loud frightened voice. "What are you doing out here in the middle of the night?"

"We aren't doing anything," Mary Ann says.

Next Honey is there. She squats down and puts her arms round Mary Ann. She feels sticky and warm and smells of people and face powder and beer, but she sounds all right. "What's the matter, duckie?" she says.

"Nothing," Mary Ann says, leaning against her. "We just went to the bathroom."

"Not sick, are you, baby?"

"Uh-uh." Mary Ann shakes her head. Over her mother's shoulder she can see Anna and Mr. Zimmern helping Bill stand up. When he is on his feet again, all of them come out into the yard.

"All right, what the hell's going on here?" Bill says in his tipsy voice.

"Nothing," Mary Ann says again. "Lolly had to go to the bathroom, and I came too on account of she was afraid of the spookies."

"There is no such thing as a spookie," Bill says, uneven and too loud. "Don't you know that?"

"I know that," Mary Ann says, standing away from Honey to show she isn't afraid of anything. "I wasn't scared; it was Lolly."

"What were you scared of, Princess?" Lolly's father asks.

Lolly doesn't answer; she just stands there in the yard in her nightie.

"Come on. Tell Daddy." He moves round the other grown-ups and bends down by Lolly so the light from the barn shines on him. He doesn't seem really tipsy; but he looks different somehow; he has a tall shiny hat on and there is something funny about his face.

But before she can figure out what, Lolly begins to scream, very loud like a fire engine. She pulls away from him and grabs hold of her mother and hides her face against her mother's party dress, screaming and screaming.

"What is it, Lolly darling?" her father says in a scared voice, trying to pull her away, but she hangs on so hard that the dress tears.

"She was scared of Draculas," Mary Ann explains, when Lolly stops screaming to breathe.

"What?" Lolly's father lets go of her and looks at Mary Ann.

"She was scared because Lennie told her a Dracula was flying around Anna's house tonight, waiting to eat her up."

"Draculas," Mr. Zimmern says, looking at Lolly all squnched-up against her mother but not screaming any-more. "That little creep." He stands up and starts running toward the house, dodging trees in the dark.

"Wait, Dan!" Lolly's mother calls after him. "I'm sure Lennie didn't mean to . . ."

"Dan, wait!" Anna calls too, but he doesn't wait, so she runs after him, and Mary Ann goes too, to see what will happen next.

By the time she gets to the sitting room, Mr. Zimmern has hold of Lennie by the top part of one arm and is sort of jerking him back and forth. Anna is telling him to take it easy and calm down, but he isn't.

"Where's Lolly?" he shouts, and comes to the door, dragging Lennie with him. "Celia!" he shouts into the hall-way.

Then Lolly's mother comes through the kitchen with Lolly holding onto her and sort of hiccuping. Lolly doesn't want to go into the sitting room. She hangs onto the edge of the doorway and her mother and won't even look in.

"All right," her father says, pulling Lennie round by his

arm. "Now you tell Lolly you were lying to her."

"Okay, leggo of me, willya!" Lennie shouts. But his father doesn't, he just gives him a jerk. "Okay, dammit," Lennie says. "I was only kidding. Dracula doesn't even live in America, for God's sake. He lives in Europe, everybody knows that."

"There is no Dracula. You tell her there is no Dracula," Lolly's father says, giving him another hard jerk.

"Awright, there is no Dracula. For God's sake. I was just teasing you. I didn't think you'd be dumb enough to believe me."

"There you are, dear," Mrs. Zimmern says.

"I told you so," Mary Ann says. But Lolly doesn't say anything or look at anybody.

"Okay." Lolly's father finally lets go of Lennie. "For two cents I'd knock your teeth in," he says, and he shows his own teeth in a fierce way.

"Go ahead and try," Lennie shouts. "You—" he says and stops as if he was trying to think of something awful to call his father. "You lousy adulterer," he says, whatever that is.

Mr. Zimmern doesn't like being called it, anyhow. His face sort of freezes up. There is still something wrong and different about it too; what? His mustache, Mary Ann thinks. It has suddenly got much much smaller, and makes him look like somebody else, somebody who isn't so nice.

"You shut your trap," he says, and he gives Lennie a big shove so that he sort of falls across the room. Then he lifts his arms as if he was going to hit him again.

But instead he holds his arms up and out, as if he was going to sing in a concert, and he grins his big grin and laughs. He looks at Honey and Bill who have come in now and says, "You ever hear of such a crazy thankless kid? After we were nice enough to move our party out to the barn, so he could have the whole damn house to himself, what does he go and do?"

"Excuse me for living," Lennie says in his same mean voice, only now it sounds sort of choked because he is picking himself up from the floor.

"Time for bed, girls," Anna says.

"I'll take them up," Lolly's mother says. "Come on, dear . . . Is there a flashlight?"

"I think so, somewhere. Let me look."

Excuse me for living. It was a funny thing to say, Mary Ann thinks, looking at Lennie. Excuse me is for when you burp, or get in somebody's way on the street. But it is sort of right, because Lennie is in people's way. Everybody would be having a nicer time if he wasn't at Anna's house to scare Lolly with lies and be rude about sandwiches and burn himself with fireworks; or if he never came to Lolly's on weekends to tease her and Mary Ann and kick over their cardboard play store accidentally on purpose pretending to shoot baskets by the garage. If he didn't even exist that would be just swell.

"Here's one; I'm afraid it's a bit run down."

"Go on up to bed now, Mary Ann, duckie," Honey says, stooping to kiss her good-night; and Bill kisses her too, a damp blurry kind of kiss, missing her cheek and landing in her eye.

"Okay." She yawns and starts for the stairs.

Lennie was crying, she thinks as she follows the weak rings of light sliding up from step to step. That's why his voice sounded so funny and squeezed up. And when he leaned over it wasn't just to get his book; it was because he didn't want anybody to see. Big kids like him aren't supposed to cry.

In the attic Lolly's mother sets the flashlight on end so it shines pale circles up at the ceiling. She smooths out their sheets and puffs up the pillows.

"There you are," she says. "You're not frightened anymore, are you?"

"I never was frightened," Mary Ann says, climbing into bed next to Theodore Ilgenfritz.

"And you're all right too, aren't you, dear? . . . Not scared anymore?"

"No," Lolly whispers, but Mary Ann can tell she is lying. She is still scared of Draculas and a whole lot of other things and probably she always will be.

Maybe it wouldn't be so wonderful to be as pretty as a picture if you had to be frightened of everything, even things that never existed, Mary Ann thinks, looking at the rings of light and shadow overhead like the diagram of planets in their science book. And you had to have mean old Lennie for half a brother, and you couldn't do easy fractions.

Or suppose you were somebody like Lennie, whose whole life was like a burp; that nobody wanted to have around, even your own family.

"Hey, Lolly," she says. "You can get into bed with me if you want. If you bring your pillow."

"Okay." Lolly sits up again.

"I don't know," her mother says. "Will you really be able to sleep like that?"

"Sure we will. There's lots of room." Mary Ann pushes Theodore Ilgenfritz over against the wall.

"We'll go to sleep right away if you sing us a song," Lolly promises, climbing onto the bed with her pillow.

"Well . . . All right." Lolly's mother bends over them, tucking the sheet in.

"Mrs. Zimmern?" Mary Ann says.

"Mm."

"What happened to Mr. Zimmern's mustache?"

"Oh . . . uh," Lolly's mother says. "He cut it shorter."

"What for?"

"Well . . . I guess he thought it was too hot."

"Oh."

"Don't you think it looks nice short?"

"No," Mary Ann says. "Not especially."

Lolly's mother makes a tired noise and sits down in the shadows at the end of the bed. She is quiet for a minute. Then she begins to sing, in her high sweet whispery voice:

> *Row, row, row your boat—*

That is a round really, with four parts when they sing it at Eastwind. But Mary Ann and Lolly are too sleepy now to join in, and so is Theodore Ilgenfritz.

> *—Gently down the stream.*
> *Merrily, merrily, merrily, merrily,*
> *Life is but a dream.*

July 7

The wind. It slides clouds across the flat white sky, creaks the trees, slaps the screen doors at Lolly. Bang. Bang. Sunday morning—but all empty, wrong. No Sunday papers, no Sunday breakfast with pancakes and bacon and golden pouring Log Cabin syrup in its tin house. Nobody in the kitchen making breakfast. Nobody outside on the lawn, or in the barn—only bottles and chairs and shriveled-up dead balloons and sat-on hay and broken black pieces of phonograph record

"Well, come on," Mary Ann says. "Let's wake somebody up." She goes back across the hot windy grass and into the house and climbs the stairs, and Lolly comes on, behind her. Watches her open the door to her parents' room.

Sun. A stale smell. The windows rattling with wind, papers clothes sheets blankets blown around the floor. And on the big high bed Mr. Hubbard lying with his mouth open and no clothes on. He is bright red all over in horrible blotchy patches like a disease, except for his tummy which is white and hairy orange with a thing, she can see it, an awful red gun thing, but she won't see it, won't look.

"Hey!" Mary Ann calls out. "We're hungry."

Mr. Hubbard doesn't move. But next to him, curled up around him pink bulgy soft with no clothes too, Mrs.

Hubbard opens one green-smudged eye.

"Aw, baby," she says, pulling the sheet toward her. "Ah feel like a stewed witch. Why don't you-all just go down to the kitchen and find yourselves something to eat uhhh." She closes her eye again and lies there, soft stewed pink against sick blotchy red. Bang. Rattle-bang.

Lolly's parents' room across the hall is different, dark and cool and sucked full of wind. A nice sound like slow drum music—Danny snoring. But she doesn't want to look, in case—

"Go on. Wake them up," Mary Ann says, pushing her into the room.

Lolly looks at the floor. She opens her mouth, but no sounds come out.

"Hey," Mary Ann says. "Hey, Mrs. Zimmern, please wake up. We're hungry."

Lolly peeks, and it is all right. The sheets spread over like always, and Mummy-Celia in her best tan lace night-gown. And behind her Danny's strong back, his yellow silky pajamas.

"Hello," she says.

He stops snoring, groans out of tune, turns over. And it isn't all right. It isn't him, it is someone else, with a face like, like— She won't think what. And he doesn't smile sleepy and say —Hello there, Princess; hop up and visit us. He says, "Ugh goddamnit. Go away, let Daddy sleep."

It is still him really, with his mustache trimmed shorter like Mummy-Celia said. But it isn't too, because his voice is mean, and because. She won't think about it.

"Let's try and wake up Anna," Mary Ann says, closing the room behind them.

"Okay," Lolly says. They go down the stairs.

"You do it; you've been here more times." She shoves Lolly toward the door. Anna will be behind it, asleep in her fourposter bed with the white ruffled awning and the orange and yellow sun-pattern patchwork quilt, with her old-fashioned white nightgown and her hair in a long thick mahogany-brown braid that once she let Lolly brush out, wavy to her waist and crackling with magic sparks. She will open her eyes and smile and the wind will stop.

Lolly puts her hand on the white china knob and turns it. The room and the bed are empty, tidy, smooth. Anna's turtle-shell brush and comb and the big tomato pincushion are on the chest of drawers, but Anna is gone. Bang.

"Where's Anna?" she says.

"How should I know? Maybe she vanished," Mary Ann says. "Come on, I want some breakfast."

She shuts the door and goes through the other downstairs rooms again, and Lolly after her. But Anna has been vanished away, and the house is changed, emptied. The furniture stands back against the walls not talking to each other. All the rooms have turned into dead, fake rooms, like the ones in the Metropolitan Museum, with printed labels and polished silver dishes, where nobody ever lived.

Mary Ann goes through the sitting room and out onto the terrace. The wind is on the other side of the house now, but it keeps reaching round the corners, grabbing at Lolly's hair and dress. The trees are shaking, and the bushes and the grass and everything. Empty white iron tables and chairs are standing around like skinny lost frozen sheep, waiting for Anna to come back.

"Suppose Anna did vanish," Lolly says.

"How could she vanish?" Mary Ann stops, turns.

"If she was magicked away last night. By a bad spell."

"Oh, well." Mary Ann leans on one of the frozen sheep. 'Then we'd go look for her. We'd have a, you know, a quest."

'We could ride our horses," Lolly says. "The ones from the play."

"Okay," Mary Ann says. "I dibs Falada. Let's start after we get something to eat." She turns back toward the house.

The wind reaches round the corner, angry, ruffling the vines. "What if it was really?" Lolly asks, hurrying after Mary Ann.

"What?" Mary Ann turns again.

"If there was a . . . a real evil spell."

"Don't be dumb," Mary Ann says in a different cold voice like yesterday at the picnic. The voice of a shouting person who smashes things. "There aren't any real evil spells."

Bang. Bang. The wind is trying to get into Anna's house, pulling and slamming the screen doors, shaking the windows. It is an invisible monster flying across the world, swallowing trees, clawing at the old lady vines on the wall, screaming OOOOH.

In the kitchen all the chairs are vanished and there is nothing to eat. No cookies in the big jar; no bread in the yellow rolltop-desk breadbox. There is no pot of hot steamy porridge on the stove, with cream and raisins. No pitcher of foamy milk in the icebox. Nothing in the icebox but butter on a plate and half a lemon and some bottles of beer and two dead naked chickens with blotchy gooseflesh skin like, she won't think what, and a glass bowl that has chopped shiny red jello sticking to one side.

"You want some raspberry jello?" Mary Ann says in her ordinary voice.

"Uh-uh."

But Mary Ann does, so she carries the bowl into the dining room where there still are chairs, and puts it on the long table. The wind is screeching in through a crack at the bottom of one of the windows, blowing white strips of net curtain up and out into the room like flapping awful ghosts.

"You better have some of this jello," Mary Ann says, dividing it with a spoon into two wobbly red islands. "I bet none of the grown-ups are going to get up for hours."

Lolly takes a spoon out of the silver drawer. There is an evil spell on Anna's farm now. Dracula brought it yesterday, flying up the valley with his wind. He swooped over the house and barn and creek, and shook it down like black salt, and everything began to change. When the salt fell on people they weren't like themselves anymore, they were turned into monsters and witches, shouting and hurting and fighting. Only Anna was too strong to be changed, so she was magicked away.

"Are they . . ."

"Are they what?" Mary Ann asks.

Lolly moves her mouth. "Sick," she says finally.

"Nah. They just got tipsy last night." Mary Ann spoons jello into her mouth. "Didn't your father and mother ever get tipsy before?"

Lolly shakes her head no. The Dracula wind is blowing inside her, in her stomach and legs, blowing her away, making her empty and sick. She puts her spoon down and holds onto the back of her chair.

Bang. Sounds in the hall. Not the wind; steps. Anna comes in.

"Hello, girls! What have you got there? Heavens, don't eat that old jello! Lennie and I have been down to Millers's farm and got some lovely things for Sunday breakfast. We're going to have waffles and bacon, with maple syrup from their own woods." She sets a big wicker basket down on the table. "Lolly, dear. Are you all right?"

"I feel sick." Her voice sounds thin inside her head.

"After that ancient jello, I'm not surprised." Anna

laughs and hugs Lolly toward her. "Shall I fix you some baking soda?"

Lolly shakes her head, moving it against Anna's shirt, warm from the sun, rough, blue.

"Lolly didn't eat any ancient jello," Mary Ann says "Only me."

"Would you like some baking soda?"

"I'm not sick. I'm just very hungry and very thirsty."

"I'll start breakfast now." Anna lets go of Lolly but doesn't move away. "Lennie should be back soon; he's waiting for the milk. It's from the Millers's cows, that we saw in the field before the picnic."

Yes, before the picnic. When everything was still safe. Square cows, brown and white in spots, big soft sleepy, lying in the meadow chewing grass all day, and clover and daisies. It would be nice to be a cow, peaceful. With big brown eyes and a long tail to swish, and a deep moo voice and

Bang-bang. Lennie comes into the room, tipped sideways by the shiny can he is carrying. "I milked the cow," he shouts, breathing hard. "I milked it myself."

"Why, Lennie, did you really? Good for you."

"I want to milk a cow," Mary Ann says. "Can I go down to the farm after breakfast and milk a cow?"

"Maybe you can next time you come, dear. Cows only give milk twice a day, you know; and you'll be gone by this evening's milking."

"I got nearly a quart," Lennie goes on. "That big brown cow tried to kick at me, but I made her stop. You have to talk to them soft, just like women, Mr. Miller says. You have to have strong hands like I do." He spreads out his hands.

Lolly couldn't be a cow, because she isn't a grown-up woman. Mummy-Celia and Mrs. Hubbard are cows, walking on their hands and feet in the grass, with pink naked bulgy bags of milk hanging down. Grabbed and squeezed twice a day by men's hands. Lolly won't be a cow, ever. Won't think anymore about cows. She leans closer against Anna, holding her blue shirt, rubbing it rough against her face.

"Can I help make the waffles?" Mary Ann is saying.

"Of course you can. Lolly? Do you want to help too, or would you rather go lie down for a while?" Lolly shakes her head no, rubbing it against Anna's shirt. "Come on, then. Let go of me now, dear, so I can go cook," Anna says, and jerks her shirt away, jerks herself away.

Lolly follows Anna and Mary Ann into the kitchen. It is safer there with them but not safe. The chairs have all run away into the barn where the broken music and fighting is, and there is nothing to sit on or hold onto.

Bang. Bang. The wind slaps the house the doors. He can't get in while Anna is here, but he wants to. And Anna can will go away again, anytime. Bang.

Nobody is safe anymore and nowhere is safe. Except in the castle of Princess Elinore of the White Meadows, far far away up high in the ice mountains. Where the wind never blows and the rain never falls and nobody can come. It is all blue and cool and high and far, with powdered sugar snow on the pointed castle roofs, and icicles hanging like sparkly sugar necklaces from the tall stone towers and walls. The gates are closed and the drawbridge is cranked up tight on its iron chains against the wall, and crusted shut with chunks of diamond ice, so that nobody can come in. Even if they cross the hot burning desert and the spooky dark forest, and kill all the ghost wolves and bears, and climb the steep ice mountain, they can't get in. Nobody. Ever.

Midmorning. The wind, as if weary of shaking the bedroom windows, shifted direction and began to knock on the glass with a maple branch. Tap. Tap-tap.

Bill Hubbard, alone in the room now, his naked body flung across the bed like something dropped onto it from a height, groaned, heaved, turned. Even asleep he looked uncomfortable, damaged. His old-fashioned black bathing suit had been imprinted on his torso in pasty-white negative; the rest of his skin was flaming sore sunburn red.

Tap-tap.

"Wha' is it?" He half opened red-rimmed eyes. "Justa minute." He groped for the covers; did not find them.

Tap-tap.

"Don' come in." He half rolled, half fell, over the side of the mattress and grabbed for the tangle of blankets and sheets. "Holy Jesus Christ," he muttered, his head sagging against the side of the mattress. With evident pain and effort he raised it, and his body, back onto the bed, dragging the covers with him. "Awright. Come in."

No one entered. At the window the maple tree continued to knock for admittance.

Bill opened both eyes, lifted his head, and looked round the room. "Aw, shit," he said, identifying the sound. He fell back and lay still, uttering further exclamations at intervals in a dismal half-tone.

At length, very slowly, he shoved the covers aside and sat up, supporting his head with both hands. He found his watch on the bedside table, looked at it, groaned, and strapped it round his wrist. He stood. He located the china chamberpot painted with pansies and used it; he located his underwear and put it on. He sponged his sore face with stale lukewarm water from a china basin. He found and put on his shirt, pants, socks, and shoes, pausing frequently to curse or groan. He wet his brush in the basin and passed it over what remained of his hair, plastering some of the faded orange locks to his scalp.

In front of the dressing table he stooped and regarded himself in the mirror. Behind Honey's array of bottles and jars and lipstick tubes, he beheld a comic character wearing a skullcap of damp pale freckled scalp which shaded into a long sad red countenance, the nose scabbed and peeling, the eyes puffed and bleary. "Goddamn asshole," Bill remarked to this image.

He opened the door. Across the sunlit hall, in the other front bedroom, a woman bending over a half-packed suitcase glanced up.

"Uh, good morning," he said dully.

"Good morning," Celia replied with no greater enthusiasm. Like Bill, she looked emotionally and physically dilapidated. Her hair was badly brushed, her eyes sunken and stained from lack of sleep, and the subtle lines and tints of her face blurred by ill-applied makeup. "I hope it's a good morning . . . I mean . . ." She smiled helplessly.

"Goddamn awful morning," Bill said. "Everybody else up already, huh?"

"Yes. Some of them hours ago." Celia folded a sweater, placed it in the suitcase, looked at it, and took it out again. "They've all had breakfast and gone to get the Sunday papers. I just wasn't equal to it . . . The packing . . . It's so hard to decide what . . . with the weather so changeable . . ."

"Yeah." Bill advanced and leaned against the doorway. "Listen, Celia, I kind of remember, last night—" He blinked. "Seems like I recall getting into some kind of fight with Dan, am I right?"

She nodded.

"I was rude to him, huh?" She nodded again. "And then did I try to sock him? Maybe I dreamt that."

Celia shook her head.

"Christ. I hoped it was a dream." Bill rested his head against the door jamb, holding it steady with one hand. "Yeah. I remember hitting him." He groaned. "I could shoot myself. I haven't been that drunk in twenty years. Twenty-five years."

Celia ceased moving clothes about in the suitcase and looked up at Bill as he stood there, untidy, red, and peeling. "How do you feel now?" she asked.

"Terrible." He tried to smile, without success. "How the hell could I have behaved so badly?"

"It wasn't only you," she said, laying more clothes on the bed. "We all behaved very badly. Shouting and fighting."

"Not you," Bill said with conviction.

"Yes, me too."

"Aw, come on. What were you fighting about?"

"Well." Celia flushed, swallowed. "When Dan knocked you down, Honey got upset and started hitting and scratching him, and I was afraid she'd hurt him, so I tried to stop her. It was dreadful."

"God damn." Bill shook his head, registering this information. "I missed that. Honey started beating up on Dan because she thought he'd hurt me?"

"That's right."

"What do you know." Suddenly, apparently to his own surprise, Bill broke out in a loud guffaw. "Sorry, I didn't mean— I was thinking about Honey; I guess I don't give her enough credit."

"Enough credit?" Celia repeated.

"Yeah. For caring about me, I mean."

"But of course she cares about you."

"I guess so." Bill grinned. "Only I have trouble believing it sometimes. She was such a beautiful girl, you know, Celia. She had so damn many men after her; I never thought I had a hope in hell. But she married me, so I figure she must have loved me, God knows why."

"She must have loved you," Celia repeated rather than asserted.

"That's right. You know, I give Honey kind of a hard time," he said, more to himself than to her. "I'm so damn jealous. All this weekend, for example, I've been jealous of your husband. And she doesn't even like him. . . . I mean of course he's a nice guy, and I'm sure Honey likes him fine, but you know what I mean. I can't think straight this morning. My head's killing me."

"I know what you mean," Celia said in a shaky voice.

"Hitting him like that, what do you know? And after she'd already cut off his mustache." He suppressed another unexpected loud laugh. "Was he furious!"

"Yes, he was." Celia replied as if to a question.

"It was a silly kid's trick, I admit that." Bill nodded agreement with his own remark. "All the same, I don't see why he made so much fuss about it. Who gives a hoot how long a guy's mustache is?"

"People do care about . . ." Her voice faded. "Honey was awfully cross yesterday . . . when Dan . . ."

"Yeah, but it's different for her," Bill explained. "Dan ruined her whole getup. That's one thing no woman can forgive."

"I don't know . . . I think it depends on the woman."

"Maybe." He frowned. "I guess Anna's furious with the lot of us."

"I don't think so. . . . She didn't say anything about it."

"No? That was decent of her. She's a remarkable

woman, you know that?" Bill nodded again in agreement with himself. "Remarkable."

"Mm, yes," Celia murmured, folding a skirt. "It's easy to be decent," she added abruptly. "If you don't care about anybody too much."

Bill ceased nodding and focused on Celia. "What?" he said.

"I mean, Anna doesn't really know . . . She's like a child who hasn't ever . . . I realize that sounds funny." Celia's voice wavered. "I mean, I think she's probably never been in love in her whole life, not really . . . So everything seems simple to her, the way it does to Lolly and Mary Ann. That's probably why she gets on with them so well . . . children, I mean."

"You might be right," Bill said, staring at Celia.

She met his eyes briefly, then looked down and away. They stood, listening to the wind beat against the side of the house. Then Celia gave a little sigh and lifted a beige lace dress from the pile on the bed. The skirt had been ripped from the bodice in the previous night's brawl and now hung loose at one side.

"You never can tell about women," Bill pronounced. "Who would have thought two ladies like you and Honey would start scrapping that way?"

Celia flinched visibly. "It wasn't very ladylike. No." She laid her dress back on the bed and stood looking at it, her head bent. "It was disgraceful."

"Aw, no, I didn't mean—" Bill said, moving further into the room. "Hell, it's just, uh, you know; it's the pioneer spirit. Defending your man against the Red Indians . . . And I damn well look like a Red Indian today," he added, staring into the speckled mirror over the chest of drawers.

"You really got a sunburn yesterday," Celia said.

"Yeah."

"That s a shame. Sne smiled nervously, but with sympathy.

"My own damn fault." Bill shrugged, then concentrated his gaze on the far wall. "I called Dan a Republican playboy," he said.

Celia nodded, tightening her mouth. She eased the lace dress off its hanger, carried it across the room to the wastebasket, hesitated, then dropped it in.

"Hell, I didn't mean— I was so goddamn soused, I didn't know what I was saying. I'll apologize soon as he gets back."

"I don't think you need to. Dan wasn't very polite to you either."

"All the same. A Republican playboy." He shook his head slowly.

"I don't think *that*"—she put the slightest emphasis on the word—"really bothered him so much."

"Oh?" Bill stared at her a moment. "What really bothered him?"

Celia rolled up a pair of silk stockings and fitted them into a side pocket. "What you said about his job, I suppose," she murmured finally.

"What did I say about Dan's job?"

"Well . . . That writing advertising was . . . That it wasn't really honest, and he ought to be ashamed of it."

"Oh, Jesus." He groaned and sat down heavily on the tufted bedspread. "I don't remember that."

"Of course he is ashamed." Celia continued to roll stockings. "He wanted to be a real writer, but he couldn't make a success of it."

"Jesus," Bill repeated, not listening.

"He did have some of his work printed, but they didn't pay him much. Not enough for the things he wanted."

"Things he wanted," Bill repeated, in the manner of

one trying to reenter a conversation.

"Yes. Dan wants . . . He wants everything he sees that's pretty or shiny or new. And then after he's got it, he doesn't want it anymore." Celia's head was lowered again, her face hidden; but her voice shook noticeably. "He's that way with . . . people too." She gave a choking gasp and sat down on the far end of the bedspread.

"Uh, I. Hey, don't," Bill said, glancing round the room and toward the hall as if seeking escape. "Listen, I know what you mean. I mean I used to think that kind of thing about Honey, but it wasn't so." Celia was now weeping into the open suitcase. "I mean I know Dan cares a lot about you," Bill said desperately. "He— Why, you remember how he kissed your hand at supper, last night, and said—"

"Oh, yes," Celia interrupted, sobbing. "I know he says it. Dan's always telling everybody how much he loves me, and Lolly, and Lennie, and his mother, and his awful sister, and thousands of people." She looked up, sore-eyed, her face streaked with water-soluble makeup. "He doesn't love a soul on this earth except himself," she said with conviction.

"Celia. Oh hell." Bill gave a glance toward the hall; then shifted nearer along the side of the bed.

"I'm sorry. I don't want to make a fuss," Celia gasped. "I'll stop now." She stood up. "I know I'm just being silly," she sobbed, retreating across the room. "Don't pay any attention to me. Go away."

Bill looked at Celia's back, outlined against a window full of shaking branches and rushing clouds. Making a sound that was half a murmur of sympathy, half a groan of effort, he rose from the bed, circumnavigated the suitcase, and put an arm across this back.

"Hey, Celia," he said. "Please. Don't go on like that."

He patted her brown-and-white seersucker shoulder several times. "Get ahold of yourself now."

"I'm sorry . . . Didn't mean . . ." Celia's weeping began to slacken. "Such a silly fuss."

"Here, have a handkerchief." Bill pulled a wrinkled one from his pocket with his free hand. "It's clean."

"Thank you." Celia mopped her eyes and nose. "I'm all right now. I just didn't sleep much last night; that's all it is." She swallowed another sob. "I don't sleep very well anyhow, and when I have a night like that . . ."

"Sure," Bill said. He dropped his arm and moved aside. "I understand. I get insomnia sometimes."

"You do?" Celia turned to stare at him. Her face, now wiped almost free of paint, looked young, pale, pretty, weary.

"Yeah, sort of. You know. I get to lying awake, worrying about things."

"I know . . . Dreadful ideas going round and round one's head, and one can't stop them. And then it's so dark, especially out here in the country."

"Yeah."

"And one lies there, and the clock ticks, but it doesn't move, it seems to be frozen."

"You're damn right." Bill laughed.

"And one's trying not to turn over, or move too much and disturb . . . the other person. And one's angry with them at the same time, because they're asleep." Celia laughed too, a little. "Dan almost never has insomnia, you know."

"Neither does Honey. And she can fall asleep anywhere; like a dog or a cat. On trains, out in the country under a tree, any damn place."

"I'd give anything to sleep like that," Celia said. "Just to be able to lie down and close my eyes and forget everything, for hours and hours. Or days and days. Or months . . . years." She sighed. "Anything. If it wasn't for Lolly, I sometimes think I'd . . . You know." She met Bill's stare for a second, then laughed lightly and looked away out the window toward the hills. "Of course I don't mean that." Another little laugh.

"God, I hope not."

"Mm . . . Well . . ." Celia took a step back, increasing the already conventional distance between herself and Bill. "Thank you for being so nice to me."

"That's okay," Bill said.

"And you won't say anything about . . . this conversation," she added in a scarcely audible monotone. "Please? Not even to Honey . . . I shouldn't have . . ."

"All right, sure." Bill smiled, embarrassed.

"Thank you. Oh. Here's your handkerchief." She held it out, smeared now with powder and lipstick. "Oh, heavens. Look at the mess I've made. I'm so sorry."

"That's okay," he repeated, then guffawed suddenly. "If Honey was to see that, she'd think I'd been running around on her. You'd better keep it."

"Oh, I couldn't do that! Your good linen handkerchief." She smoothed the cloth, held it out again. "Besides, it's got your initials, look." She smiled faintly. "If Dan was to find it, he'd think I knew you better than I ought to."

"That's right." Bill laughed again, differently. For a moment, both of them were silent, contemplating this possibility. Then both, as if by agreement, took another step back, so that now almost the whole width of the bedroom was between them.

"Well, guess I better get some breakfast; or maybe I mean lunch," Bill remarked. "See you later."

"See you later," Celia echoed. She looked after him as he left the room, then slowly resumed her packing. She rolled another pair of stockings. Then she rose abruptly, crossed the room, and removed the beige lace dress from the wastebasket. She stared at it for a long moment, then folded it carefully and laid it in the suitcase.

Late afternoon. At the edge of the dirt road, beside a clump of lilac bushes, a 1930 Franklin was backed onto the grass next to Anna's old station wagon. Two women and a little girl in summer dresses stood beside the car; a man's feet, in brown perforated shoes and tan socks, protruded from beneath it.

"Goddarn . . . can't figure out . . ." Bill Hubbard muttered. With a caterpillarlike motion, he humped his long body over the ground, cleared the running-board, and stood up, looking even worse than he had that morning. His gabardine pants and white shirt were stained with dust and grass; his face grease-streaked, his nose inflamed and peeling. "Can't figure it out," he repeated.

"There's a pretty good garage in Cowskill," Anna said, not for the first time. "He's not usually open on Sundays, but we could drive over and see."

"No thanks." Not for the first time, Bill bent over the open hood of the Franklin, a wrench in his hand.

"Are you fixing it?" Mary Ann asked, climbing onto the running-board beside him.

"Not yet." Bill leaned in further. "I haven't found out what's wrong yet."

"Well, Ah don't see the point of us all standing round here bothering Hubby," Honey announced. "We might as well go sit down somewhere." She reached through the open window of the car and retrieved her red handbag.

"I don't want to sit down," Mary Ann said. "I'm not bothering you, am I?"

"You're not bothering me." Bill's voice was muffled by the hood.

Accompanied by Anna, Honey picked her way across the lawn on her high-heeled sandals, and sat on the broad doorstep, in view but not in earshot of the Franklin.

"Ah just knew something like this would happen to that old jalopy," she said. "Now even if Bill does get it going we'll be right in the middle of the most miserable traffic the whole way home."

. "If you like you can certainly stay over till tomorrow," Anna offered, sitting beside her. "There's nearly a whole roast chicken left, and plenty of vegetables in the garden. I'd be happy to have you."

"You would not either," Honey said. "Ah know perfectly well you're just about dying for us all to leave so you can get some peace and quiet. 'Specially after last night."

"I'll have enough peace and quiet the rest of this summer." Anna smiled and smoothed the skirt of her striped caftan over her knees.

"Anyhow, Bill would never agree to miss a day's work." Honey slid nearer along the worn marble, and lowered her voice. "Anna."

"Mm?"

"Do you think Mary Ann was real upset about us all carrying on like that last night?"

"I don't think so, no. I expect she was surprised. But so were we." Anna sighed.

"Ah talked to the girls about it after lunch. Ah explained how people can act real silly if they drink too much alcohol. Ah've told Mary Ann about that already, had to, the way some of our friends booze it up. Ah said Dan and Bill couldn't agree on what records to play on the Victrola, and so they started fighting. Well, it's the truth in a way." She pouted. "And it's the kind of thing kids fight about, so Ah figured they'd understand." Honey looked across the lawn at Bill bent over the engine of the Franklin, and Mary Ann standing tiptoe on the front bumper watching him. She smiled, then sighed. "Mary Ann sure asked a lot of questions. She wanted to know if beer was stronger than gin, and what kind of music were they playing, and why didn't you make them take turns like you do at school, and I don't know what all. Ah was a little uneasy, 'cause Lolly didn't ask any questions. She didn't even seem to be listening to me much."

"I'd be more uneasy about Lolly, then," Anna remarked.

"Maybe so. Well, anyways, Ah expect they'll forget the whole thing soon. After all, they're only children." She giggled. "It sure was something, wasn't it, the way Bill lit into Dan for insulting me? Ah never saw anything like it since the time at the church social when mah Uncle Dick overheard these two boys passing comical remarks about Aunt Jennie's weight, and comparing her to a dressed-up hippopotamus. He must have been over sixty then, but he went after them with his cane, and did they skedaddle!" Honey rummaged in her handbag and brought out a flat gold compact. She snapped it open, dusted off the mirror, and began patting powder onto her tilted nose and the bluish, sagging skin beneath her wide gray eyes. Gradually a floury pink film appeared on her face, and an injured, cross expression.

"Ah just don't know," she complained, snapping the compact shut. "After a night like last one, it's getting so Ah can't stand to look at mahself."

"I guess we're all a little the worse for wear today," said Anna, of whom this was not especially true. She smiled at

Mary Ann, who was now crossing the lawn toward them. "Yes, dear, what is it?"

"Bill says, can he borrow a pair of pliers?"

"Of course he can. You know where the tools are, in the pantry." She moved aside so that Mary Ann could get by.

"It used to be Ah could dance till dawn and look fresh as a tea rose next day," Honey said with feeling as the screen door slammed behind her daughter. "Ah wouldn't even feel sleepy. Mah beaus just couldn't get over it." She smiled and hugged herself. "Yes, we certainly had some times. Ah was the cutest thing in Greensboro, if Ah do say so mahself. Ah was having the most fun you ever can imagine, right through the war. And after the boys came home it was even better." She was silent for a moment, looking up at the trees, and the fast-moving clouds making soapy patterns behind them. "And then, all of a sudden, Ah was twenty-six years old, and most of the girls Ah grew up with were married and having babies, 'cept for the natural-born spinsters. Geezus. It's just plain awful growing old." Her accented sharpened to a hillbilly twang. "Ah don't know why it is, but after a while most everybody turns so dull and proper, and everything that used to be fun gets kind of real stupid and boring. Ah think when Ah get to be forty Ah'm just going to shoot mahself."

Anna laughed.

"Ah am, honestly."

"No, you're not."

"How are you so sure?" Honey asked, half sulky, half giggling.

"Because you're not the type," Anna said. "Besides, you're forty already."

Honey looked peeved; then she giggled again. "Okay then; when Ah'm fifty." Anna shook her head.

"Well, maybe not," Honey admitted. "Ah suppose

Mary Ann told you I was forty." Anna did not deny this. "She's a great one for facts and figures. Just like her daddy." Honey gazed across the lawn at Bill.

"There's certain advantages to being older, you know," Anna said presently.

"Ah wish you'd tell me some." Honey crossed her silky legs.

"It's—well, a lot freer. I've always thought most of life was like walking through thick woods; say those woods down there." She pointed past the road and fields to a heavily green stand of trees at the bottom of the valley along the creek. "They're always overgrown and brambly. Very damp and marshy in places, too, awfully hard to make your way through. Well, it's like that, all crowded and confused: so many intense sensations and emotions, and so many people around you, so close."

"Ah know what you mean." Honey's voice had lost its usual lazy, drawling intonation. "All of them touching you, grabbing at you, wanting something."

"Yes. Well, so you keep on walking through those woods most of your life. You get all hot and sweaty and scratched and bitten, and you step on things. You hurt yourself, and other people, not out of meanness or spite usually, but because you're frightened, or you need something. And the trees are so thick you can't ever see very far ahead, or behind you, or sideways. So you lose control, and do stupid things." Anna looked toward the barn, frowning as if she saw something ugly there. Then she took a long breath and turned back.

"That's how it is," she said. "But then, finally, just when you're getting exhausted, the trees and bushes and briers start to be farther apart, and you begin to come out into open country, where you can move around easier, and breathe more freely, and see for miles and miles in every direction. You can see the sky, and the clouds, and the hills, and the dry grass blowing."

"Mm." Honey followed Anna's gaze out across the valley to where the fields rose in yellowing waves. "Ah don't know," she said. "It sounds kind of lonely to me. Kind of sad and empty."

"Yes; it is, sometimes."

"Don't you mind that?" She turned and looked full at Anna.

"No." Anna's faint, tight smile faded, then slowly reformed. "Well, sometimes. Sometimes I think I want to go back. But not very often. I've seen enough of what it's like down in the woods."

"Yeah," Honey said after a pause. "But it's not always so damn easy to get out, even if you want to. If there's people that need— Well, Ah mean, when somebody loves you—"

"I hate the word 'love,'" Anna said with force. "It's like a kind of nasty sweet syrup people spread on things to disguise their real taste. . . . I knew a man once who used it every other sentence. It was his excuse for everything he did. For instance he used to snore very loudly, and thrash about in his sleep, and take up the whole bed. He said it was because he loved me so much he could relax completely; and if I really loved him too I wouldn't mind."

"Uh-huh," Honey said. "Did you find the pliers, ducky?" she asked Mary Ann, who had just come out of the house behind them. "That's good. Now you go see if you can hurry your daddy up some."

"Bill snores," she added, giggling a little. "Ah don't know, you kind of get used to it."

"I never did: it kept me awake for hours. Or when it didn't, it gave me bad dreams. . . . I would dream that I was standing on the top floor of some big house; or sometimes it would be an office building or a school or a museum. I would be on the highest landing, and down below there was a big baggy hairy monster climbing up the stairs toward me, step by step, snorting 'Love! . . . Love!' I used to scream out loud in my sleep, and my friend would wake up, and put his arms around me and hold me and comfort me."

"That must have helped some," Honey said.

"No. Because he was the monster. The noise it made was his snoring."

"Yeah. Ah see what you mean. Ah've felt kind of like that sometimes. Still—" She turned from Anna toward the road, where an irregular clunking noise now came from the Franklin.

"Listen to that," she remarked. "Ah just don't know why mah hubby didn't get rid of that old car years ago. This isn't the first time it's acted up, let me tell you. But he's so darn pigheaded, he's just got to hang onto it." She smiled almost fondly.

"Some people prefer old things to new ones," Anna remarked.

"Ah guess so."

"Probably just as well."

Honey turned and gave Anna a sharp look; then she laughed. "Bill would never trade me in for a brand-new model the way some men do, if that's what you mean. And not just 'cause he promised in church. He—" She broke off. Across the lawn, the automobile had begun to produce a mechanical gargling noise, followed by a louder, steadier hum. Mary Ann jumped down from the bumper and raced toward them.

"We fixed it, we fixed it!" she cried shrilly.

"Yeah, we're okay now," Bill said, following his daughter. "The ground wire was loose, that's all it was." He grinned with satisfaction and wiped his brow with the back of his hand—leaving, nevertheless, a broad smear of grease. "We can get going soon as I wash up."

"Looks like we're getting into some traffic," Mary Ann's father says as he swings The Franklin round the turn onto the Parkway, and the orange sun comes in through the side window instead of the rear one. It hurts Mary Ann's eyes, so she slides off the back seat onto the floor and puts her head down to rest it. And sees, stuck between the floor-mat and the seat, something little and lumpy and light brown. It is the hen from her farm set, the one she thought was lost for good. That poor dumb hen has been all the way to Anna's house without ever getting out of the car or seeing anything. Mary Ann picks her up and holds her on the windowsill so she can look out, but of course all there is to see now is other cars.

"Still," Mary Ann's father's voice says, "we've made pretty good time so far."

"Aw well," Mary Ann's mother's voice says. It doesn't sound cross, even though she hates traffic. "We'll get home, long as this car holds out." She yawns a little yawn.

"Course it'll hold out," Bill says. "There wasn't anything really wrong with it, just the wire on the ignition coil. Probably shook loose yesterday, when we were driving over those washboard roads by the creek."

Honey doesn't say anything. She doesn't know what an ignition coil is, or most anything else about cars, and she doesn't want to know, she says sometimes when Mary Ann or Bill try to explain it to her.

Bill understands cars, specially The Franklin, but he is wrong now. It wasn't the washboard roads. The Franklin had loosened his wire on purpose because he didn't want to go home to Larchmont yet. He wanted to stay longer at Anna's house, resting on the long soft grass by the lilac bushes, looking at the valley and mountains with his round white headlight eyes and talking to Anna's wise old station wagon who has been all across America to Texas and Mexico and back and seen Indians and alligators and the Chicago World's Fair.

"I think I'm going to tell Anna I can sit on the Eastwind board," Bill's voice says, as he speeds up to pass another car.

"Really?" Honey's voice says in a lazy surprised way. "Ah thought you weren't going to, 'cause of Dan Zimmern's being on it."

Mary Ann wants to ask what board, and why Anna wants Bill to sit on a board at Eastwind, and what Lolly's father has to do with it, but she decides to wait till later. If she says anything now they'll remember she is there and know she is listening.

"Yeah, well. I decided I ought to help her out," Bill says. "She really needs another liberal to balance the board now, with Larry Arnold gone." He cleared out his throat. "And Dan's not such a bad fellow. I figure I can get along with him."

Mary Ann imagines the board. It is like an extra-big seesaw, in the middle of the playground, with her father and Lolly's father sitting at opposite ends and a sort of engine connected to the middle. They pump it up and down and make a special kind of electricity to run Eastwind School with. But course it wouldn't be like that; it would turn out to be some invisible grown-up thing.

"He spoke to me just before they left, when you were with the girls," Bill says.

"Oh, really?"

"Said he was sorry for the way he behaved to me last night."

"Oh, really," Mary Ann's mother says again, but in a different voice. "How about the way he behaved to me? Did he mention that?"

"Well, kind of. He said he was sorry about everything. Said he knew he'd gone too far."

"Huh," Honey says.

"I admire a man who's big enough to admit it when he's wrong."

Mary Ann's mother doesn't say anything to that, probably because she has heard it lots of times before. Bill thinks that if you say you are sorry it makes up for whatever you did, and so do Grandma and Grandpa Hubbard. Saying you're sorry sort of erases it out, they think, and in a way makes you gooder than you were before. Whenever Mary Ann does something bad Bill always tries to get her to apologize, even if it takes days and days like the time Bobby McCarty broke her Gyro-Art machine. He couldn't get it to make the patterns, because he was too little and too dumb, so he threw it on the floor and bent one of the metal pieces with holes the pencil was supposed to go through, so she lost her temper and hit him. Bobby would probably have forgotten all about it by next time, except the grown-ups came in then from looking at the garden and saw them. Bobby's mother who is a very silly lady ran over and grabbed onto him and of course he started crying because he is only six years old. And Bill grabbed Mary Ann and pushed her in front of Bobby and Mrs. McCarty and said to tell them she was sorry she hit Bobby. But she wouldn't, because she didn't want to and it was a lie. "You want me to tell a lie," she screamed.

Honey tries to get Mary Ann to say she is sorry too, sometimes, but just out of politeness. When somebody has been mean or unfair to her she doesn't care much whether they apologize or not. She wants them to make it up to her, for instance by giving her flowers, or candy, or making her special pecan pie if it was Precious Joy, or if it was Mary Ann and there aren't any flowers in the garden she could help sort the laundry or draw Honey a picture. Soon as they do something like that it is all right again. If they don't, either pretty soon Honey will do something just as mean right back to them, or else, mostly, she will just forget about it.

"Ah wouldn't want to be on any darn board with Dan Zimmern," Mary Ann's mother says. "He's a big old bully."

"I thought you liked him," Bill says.

"Are you kidding?" Honey asks, lazy.

"You were pretty chummy with him this weekend."

"Ah was not," she says, sitting up and patting her hair. "What do you mean, chummy?"

"I mean whispering with him all the time, and driving off to the store with him, and going out to look at the stars with him," Bill says in the sore voice he always uses to complain that Honey is paying too much attention to other people, usually company, but sometimes just Mary Ann or Grandma Lou or fat old Mrs. Henry next door.

"Ah told you twice already Ah did not go to look at the stars with Dan Zimmern," Honey says, spitting like Lolly's cat Irene. "What is this, the FBI? You want me to take a lie-detector test?" Then suddenly she giggles, as if she could see herself sitting in a police station like pictures in the paper, with wires going from her arm to a kind of barometer thing that made marks on a piece of graph paper when she told a lie, and a lot of big policemen standing around watching.

No matter how angry Honey gets she can't stay that way for long even if she wants, because something about it always starts to seem funny to her. Mary Ann can stay angry for days if she really tries, and Bill can stay angry for months, like at the Gulf station man in New Rochelle who pretended to put a brand-new battery in The Franklin and didn't really. But of course Bill is older than Mary Ann and has more practice.

"It's not funny," he says now, in an almost-angry voice "It bothers me when I see you getting so friendly with somebody like Dan Zimmern, even though I know you don't mean anything by it. Because I know what he's got on his mind."

"Well, Ah bet he's got something else on his mind now, after the haircut Ah gave him," Honey says, and she giggles very loud for some reason.

"Yeah. Maybe now," Bill says, and he laughs just as loud.

"Anyways, Ah honestly never was much interested in getting friendly with Dan, thank you," Honey says in a voice like when Lolly's mother or some other lady tried to pass her more cake at tea that she knew would make her put on weight but sometimes in the end she took it anyhow because it looked so delicious. "He's too darn stuck on himself to suit me. He thinks he's God's gift to women.

And the way he treats his wife is plumb disgraceful."

"Yeah, he's got her coming and going. When he says 'frog,' she jumps."

Mary Ann has never heard Lolly's father say "frog," but it's true that Lolly's mother sometimes sort of jumps when he speaks, as if she was scared of him. Which is peculiar because Lolly's father isn't at all scary. Mary Ann has never even seen him get cross at anybody except Lennie. Even last night in the barn when all the grown-ups were tipsy and people were hitting Lolly's father and shouting at him, he didn't act angry; he just laughed. And he isn't a bully either like Honey said.

The only wrong thing about Lolly's father is that before he was married to her mother he was married to another lady and had another child, mean Lennie, and lived in a different house. Then he decided he didn't want them any more, and he got himself new ones, the same as he got a new De Soto every year. It was sort of as if he used up families the way he used up cars, only slower of course. He didn't take good enough care of them, like Clementine, thumping on her gas pedal and ruining her motor, and scratching her paint by driving too near the stone wall by his garage.

That could be why Lennie is so skinny with spots all over his face, and why Lolly's mother looks kind of worn out most of the time, even though she is younger than most mothers. Only once in a while she looks brand-new. For instance once when Mary Ann was spending the night at Lolly's and Mrs. Zimmern got all dressed up fancy to go to a party in New York City, in a floaty silk dress the color of canned salmon and long sparkly earrings. All of a sudden she was like the picture in their hall of the beautiful lady with the lacy hat and dress and ropes of pearls, that Mary

Ann always thought before was somebody else she hadn't ever met.

". . . making her run upstairs and unpack that whole darn suitcase to find his other sweater, and then changing his mind so she had to run back in and pack it again. Ah don't know why Celia stands for that kind of thing."

"Mm," Bill says, frowning. "She loves him, I guess."

"Yeah, Ah guess she does, the poor dope. She's got it bad."

Grown-ups and their magazines and newspapers talked about love as if it was a disease, like mumps and chicken pox, only it lasted longer. You didn't catch it from other people but from an invisible baby who shot arrows at you with germs of love on them, like the poison arrows of cannibal tribes. When one of these arrows hit you the germs got into you and you had to be in love with the next person you saw.

Love made you sicker than chicken pox or even mumps. It was no wonder Anna hated it as much as nasty medicine disguised with syrup. It made people scream and cry, the way Lolly's mother was crying the other afternoon at the play of "The Goose Girl." "I love him so much it's killing me," she screamed, right out in the front yard, just because Lolly's father was somewhere else when she wanted him, like a little baby. Grown-ups aren't supposed to cry ever, unless they are hurt very bad, and even then they usually just shouted and cursed like the time Bill shut the garage door on his thumb. Or if something real awful happens. When Daddy-Jack died, Honey said once to company, Mama-Lou cried for two days without stopping and tore out her hair by handfuls. But Lolly's father wasn't dead or even away on a trip. He was only down in the general store listening to a baseball game on the radio, for goodness' sake.

Love made people hurt themselves, and other people too. Like when Mary Ann went out on the breakwater in Maine, and Grandma Hubbard spanked her with the tortoise-shell hairbrush. "I'm doing this because I love you, Mary Ann. It hurts me just as much as it does you," she said. Mary Ann thought that was a big lie, because nobody was hitting Grandma Hubbard with a hairbrush.

But then it was over and she stood up and saw Grandma Hubbard's face, and she was crying. "Oh, child," she cried and snuffled. "I thought you were drowned." And her face was all red and collapsed, the way Bill's face had been when he wouldn't let Honey go up in the airplane at the county fair, and she got so mad at him. She had never flown in a plane, and it only cost two dollars. "Ah'm going up, and don't you try to stop me," she said. But Bill did stop her. He shouted and grabbed her arm and dragged her away from the ticket booth in front of everybody. "No, you haven't got a right to risk your life if you damn please," he said later back in the car, "because I couldn't stand it, I love you too much."

The disease of love can make you act mean and even crazy. It is like, as near as she can understand it, as if you were very very hungry, practically starving, but there was only one single food in the whole wide world you could eat. For instance raspberry jello, and you could only even eat raspberry jello if this single person fed it to you spoonful by spoonful, like a baby in a highchair. So naturally you would be hungry most of the time, and you would do practically anything to keep that person around and get them to feed you their jello. If you were stronger than them you would shout at them and hang onto them, and if you were weaker you would run up and down stairs to get their sweaters and give them all your allowance and toys and do anything they wanted, just to get a couple of spoonfuls once in a while.

Some people did much much worse things after they got hit with the poison arrows. In the *Journal American* that came to Lolly's house it told how because of fights about love people shot and killed each other with guns and stabbed each other with knives and pushed each other into lakes and fed each other rat poison. Or sometimes they killed whoever it was that some person loved instead of them, out of jealousy. Because usually if you caught the bad disease of love you got jealousy too, the same way as when you have a bad cold you usually get a sore throat which hurts even worse. Like with their old dog Woozle. He was in love with Honey, so he used to growl at everybody else who came to the house. He really wanted to bite them, but he didn't dare try, because he knew that if he did Bill or Honey or Precious Joy would hit him with a rolled-up newspaper.

"Ah wouldn't take that from any man," Honey says. "But Celia didn't even open her mouth. She just about worships the ground he walks on."

"I don't know," Bill says. "I don't think it's quite like that. But she cares for him, all right." He laughs as if he was choking on something. "I wish sometimes you cared about me that way."

"Aw, Hubby," Honey says. "Ah like you better than any man Ah've ever seen in mah life."

"That's not saying much," Bill says, and he laughs again the same way.

It is true that Honey doesn't like men as much as she does ladies and children. She is nice to them while they are there, but as soon as they go away she makes fun of them and says how poor and dumb and old they are. "What else can you expect from a man?" she says, the exact same way she used to say "What else can you expect from a mutt?" whenever Woozle growled at somebody he knew perfectly well or chewed up something like Precious Joy's hat with the shiny wooden cherries on it.

Honey didn't love Woozle or even like him much, because he was so homely. He was part Welsh terrier and part dachshund and looked like a long unhappy fuzzy sausage with floppy ears, and if you picked him up he dripped on you. Whenever cars went by the house he barked at them, and if he was outside he ran after them, and Mary Ann ran after him to make him stop. It was dangerous for Woozle to chase cars because his legs were too short to run very fast. Nobody in the house liked Woozle much except for Mary Ann who was sorry for him. The only reason he lived with them was that Sliver got out and caught puppies by mistake. People adopted the other two even though they were mutts, but nobody wanted Woozle.

Lolly said Woozle was an enchanted prince who had had an evil spell put on him, and some day he would be disenchanted back into his true prince shape. But instead he got hit by a truck and died; and nobody cared really except Mary Ann, and after a while even she didn't care, which sort of made it worse.

Of course there aren't any enchanted princes really, or invisible arrows. It is just a story, like Jesus or the Easter Bunny. Nobody has to be sick with love if they don't want to.

When Mary Ann is grown up she isn't going to love anybody. She will live all by herself in a big house with a barn and an apple orchard and a creek to swim in and lots of company, and nobody will be able to stop her from doing whatever she wants to. She won't get anybody's sweaters and if she feels like going up in a plane she just will. She will go on planes and boats and trains all round the world, and see every country there is and ride on camels and elephants and polar bears and hippopotamuses and kangaroos.

The Franklin is slowing down, so Mary Ann stands up and looks out. The sun is bigger and redder, swollen up like a balloon that is going to pop as soon as it hits the sharp tops of the pine trees. They aren't anywhere near home, they are still on the highway in a long untidy parade of cars headed back to the city from vacation, breathing out gas and oil smells, moving ahead and stopping and moving ahead, with her father driving and her mother leaning back against the seat with her hair untidy and her eyes shut.

Mary Ann doesn't feel tired, but she lies down anyhow with Teddy so that the red balloon sun won't hurt their eyes. Now all she can see out the window is trees and thick pinkish sky with lumps of whipped-cream cloud, and the black tops of other cars with other families in them going home together, stopping and starting. Stopping and starting.

—Once upon a time there was a dog named Woozle who could fly, only he didn't know it. All he had to do was wag his tail once and then bark twice and then wag his tail three times. He was really an enchanted prince from a country east of the sun and west of the moon, only he didn't know that either. When he was born a wicked fairy flew in the hospital window and turned him into a funny-looking puppy. "Ugh, how homely he is!" his mother the queen and his father the king said, and they didn't want him anymore. There was one good fairy left at the party, and she couldn't undo the bad spell, but she made a good

.pell so that Woozle could fly. But they still didn't like him. "Who wants a funny-looking dog flying round the .astle bothering everybody?" his father the king said. So the good fairy carried him far away and found him a nice family to live with.

—So he lived in Larchmont and was a puppy, and then he grew up and was a dog. Then one day he was running along Weaver Street chasing cars and by accident he wagged his tail once and barked twice and wagged his tail three times. Suddenly big red and orange shining butterfly wings came out of his back and he was flying in the air. He flew over Weaver Street and round and around all over Larchmont. The good fairy saw him flying, and sent a wind to blow him away east of the sun and west of the moon. And she made a spell to leave something that looked like a run-over dog on Weaver Street, so Woozle's family wouldn't just think he had run away because they didn't like him very much, and look and look for him everywhere and feel bad.

—So Woozle flew on with the wind further and further until he was flying over the country where he was born, but he didn't know that. He flew over the city and over the castle where his real family lived, and he looked down and he saw— he saw—

—He saw his mother the queen and his father the king in the courtyard, drowning in strawberry soda and peach ice cream from the wish-box, and he heard them screaming and screaming. He didn't know who they were, but he felt sorry for them; so he flew down and held out his front paws, and the king and queen each grabbed onto one of them, and he lifted them up out of the ice-cream soda and flew away to a high hill.

—"Oh thank you, thank you," said the queen and king. And they told him what had happened. So Woozle flew back to the castle and flew through all the rooms full of messy ice cream till he found the wish-box in the queen's room. "I wish— I wish everything that's wrong in this castle was all right again," he said.

—And suddenly whoosh the strawberry soda and peach ice cream were gone; and he was turned back into a prince; and they all lived happily ever after.

About the Author

ALISON LURIE lives in Ithaca, New York, and teaches at Cornell University. She has written five other novels, the most recent of which is *The War Between the Tates*, and has three grown sons.

OUTSTANDING NONFICTION

MIDNIGHT EXPRESS 04302 $2.25
by Billy Hayes with William Hoffer
   True story of life in a Turkish prison. The basis for the motion picture.

PEOPLE WHO LIVE IN SOLAR HOUSES
by Chester and Martha Davis 04441 $2.25
   The owners and occupants of 32 solar houses give you a clear look at what may be your home of the future.

THE BATTLE FOR JERUSALEM 04326 $2.50
by General Mordechai Gur
   Military history by the Israeli chief of staff and field commander of the battle.

THE THIRTEENTH TRIBE 04242 $2.25
by Arthur Koestler
   An account of the Khazar people and their conversion to Judaism.

ALL TIME BESTSELLERS
FROM POPULAR LIBRARY

THE BEST PEOPLE—Helen Van Slyke	08456	$2.25
A BRIDGE TOO FAR—Cornelius Ryan	08373	$2.50
DEATH OF AN EXPERT WITNESS —P. D. James	04301	$1.95
THE ICE AGE—Margaret Drabble	04300	$2.25
SISTERS AND STRANGERS —Helen Van Slyke	04445	$2.50
TO KILL A MOCKINGBIRD—Harper Lee	08376	$1.95
THE UNORIGINAL SINNER AND THE ICE-CREAM GOD—John G. Powers	04287	$1.95
YOUR SINS AND MINE—Taylor Caldwell	00331	$1.75

JOHN D. MACDONALD

"The king of the adventure novel" John D. MacDonald is one of the world's most popular authors of mystery and suspense. Here he is at his bestselling best.

CONDOMINIUM	23525	$2.25
ALL THESE CONDEMNED	14239	$1.50
APRIL EVIL	14128	$1.75
BALLROOM OF THE SKIES	14143	$1.75
THE BEACH GIRLS	14081	$1.75
THE BRASS CUPCAKE	14141	$1.75
A BULLET FOR CINDERELLA	14106	$1.75
CANCEL ALL OUR VOWS	13764	$1.75
CLEMMIE	14015	$1.75
CONTRARY PLEASURE	14104	$1.75
THE CROSSROADS	14033	$1.75
DEADLOW TIDE	14166	$1.75
DEADLY WELCOME	13682	$1.50
DEATH TRAP	13557	$1.50
THE DECEIVERS	14016	$1.75
THE DROWNERS	13582	$1.75
THE EMPTY TRAP	14185	$1.75
THE END OF THE NIGHT	14192	$1.75
THE LAST ONE LEFT	13958	$1.95